Prologue

The man on the television. With the dark brown eyes and the bright white smile. The man who had a tall, slim figure and wore a salt and pepper mane with pride. He put on his grey suit jacket and looked in the mirror once more, priming his hair for the show before walking onto his stage. He waved to the crowd and took a theatrical bow before sitting behind the large, black metal desk with a screen displaying *The Evening Show with Harold Evans*, another play on late night television. Harold asked the audience to quiet down as he sat back in his chair.

"Hello everyone and welcome to The Evening Show!" he shouted to the adoring crowd.

They cheered for him and applauded once more. Harold raised his hand, a sign they knew meant he wanted them to sit down once again.

"Well, we have quite the show for you today," he continued, "We're starting off the show a bit differently. As you may know, many people from the last couple of generations have had a fascination with video games. I won't lie to all of you, I was guilty of playing games regularly when I should've been doing my homework in college."

He gave them a charismatic grin and a television host chuckle as the crowd laughed at his comment.

"But seriously, a new company known as Alpha Softworks has been developing a new game for the public, and their CEO has been kind enough to come in and let us ask him a few questions about it. So, without further ado, Mr. Marcus Achar!"

Meanwhile, while Evans introduced the episode, Marcus stood in a dressing room, straightening the tie that matched his black suit. The crew gave him a light dusting of stage makeup before he shooed them away. His phone rang and Marcus checked the caller ID. The letters "JW" lit up on the screen. He immediately answered the call.

"Yes sir," Marcus said quietly as he held the device to his ear. He heard the tired voice of an overworked man reply with, "Keep me on the line and do exactly as I say."

"Yes sir," Marcus said once more. He reached into the pocket of his jacket with his free hand, retrieving a small wireless earpiece that was nearly invisible to the naked eye. He slipped it in his ear and pressed a small spot in the bottom left corner of the phone's touchscreen.

"You know what this means to us Achar, don't fail," the voice said.

"I won't sir," he replied.

Marcus ran his hands over his hair, shiny and coated with too much hair gel. He put on a freshly faked smile for the mirror. The same he would use on the crowd. The same one he used when he met with the man in his ear.

He heard Harold shout his name and the applause from the crowd. With the smile still plastered across his pale face, he strode toward the bright red armchair next to the desk and shook Harold's hand before he sat down.

"Now, Mr. Achar," Harold began.

"Please Harold, we're all friends here, aren't we folks?" Marcus said addressing the audience, whose members cheered enthusiastically. "Please, just Marcus will do."

"Well then Marcus, let's discuss Alpha Softworks, which the name alone is a bit to unpack. Why Alpha Softworks?"

Marcus repeated the words he was given by the man in his ear, "It's quite simple really. We plan to be at the top of the industry, ready to crush any who seek to stand in our way or to topple us."

"And I suppose your new release is meant to do that?"

"Precisely. It is the first that Alpha has ever released and we are confident that it will take the community by storm."

"Why is that?"

"Because my team and I have developed a virtual reality system that is unlike any other. One that only has one game."

"Only one? And you really think that will sell?"

"Of course."

"And why's that?"

"Because it only needs one game."

"Why?"

"You'll just have to play and find out."

"Well, to tell you the truth, virtual reality isn't really my thing, but I have two children who I'm sure would love it if it's as exceptional as you say it is."

"It's not just exceptional, it's magnificent. Unlike anything this world has ever seen."

The Beginning...I Think

I was riding on a dingy, yellow bus heading to my new school in the middle of my last semester of my senior year. Stupid decision to change schools then, if you ask me. Sure, I was almost done, but it is hard when you have lost everything. Still, Jared said I had to go, so I was stuck doing it anyway.

The rundown vehicle pulled over at the curb. A couple dozen students around my age jumped from their seats and hurried out, nearly trampling each other to reach the spring air. A blur of clothing painted black, white, and every color in between. When only the stragglers remained, I stood and slung my backpack over one shoulder. It was hard to believe that a few days before I was sitting in a children's shelter, waiting for the day I would turn eighteen. Praying and pleading for it. Instead, I was adopted by a rich southern man that lived in the middle of nowhere, Arkansas. I was not a fan of his either at the time, but it also was not really my choice.

I soon discovered the chaos had not disappeared once it went outside. It just merged with the complete disarray marching along the sidewalk. It traveled up the large concrete stairs at the middle of the front of the school. At each side were large metal buildings, or rather frames for buildings, filled with large glass windows and concrete. Along the front of the two buildings, the concrete patches were covered with decorative bricks. Inside the windows were white floors and white brick walls with sets of metal stairs.

I hurried up the concrete steps to avoid being flattened by the herd of wild teens from the next bus. At the top there was a courtyard, which was empty aside from small pockets of students chatting, reading, or doing the day's homework that they still had not finished. Beyond that was another building, much larger than the first two, made of the same materials with glass highlighting classrooms on the three floors. The two buildings on either side of me both had doors at the top of the steps, to the left was an arena, to the right was a cafeteria. The herd funneled into the glass doors to the cafeteria, so I followed suit.

No sense in getting yelled at by a coach on the first day, I thought to myself.

My eyes skimmed along the long cafeteria tables until I found an empty one and sat down. Once I was settled, I took my phone out of my pocket and scrolled through my playlist for a different song, settling on a rock hit from the eighties. At the first chorus, I was yanked out of my seat by the collar and thrown onto the tile floor. My phone skidded off to the side, along with my headphones.

Note to self, get Bluetooth.

I looked up at my attacker. He was a tall, muscular boy with tanned skin and sleek, blond hair. He had a short, patchy beard that looked like he had just started growing it in, or maybe he just did not know how to shave. He wore a pair of denim shorts with black cleats and a green shirt with the words "Deer

Hills High" across his chest. In his right hand he held a dark green duffle bag with the mascot logo. A white-tailed deer charging toward the letters "DHH".

Despite that, all I could think was, *What kind of moron wears cleats indoors?* I thought about the days my mom took me to soccer practice as a kid. She drilled the fact that hard floors tear up cleats into my head from day one so we would not have to buy them as often.

The Blond Bozo glared down at me, and I then noticed his two friends. To his left stood another tall, muscular boy, and to his right a much shorter, skinnier girl sneered at me. Both of the lackeys had short dark hair. The girl was covered in freckles, which were much more attractive than the brown haired boy's face full of acne.

"This is my table. I suggest you go somewhere else," Bozo growled.

I stood and dusted the dirt off of my jacket. I made a spectacle of turning my head toward the table, then back to him before saying, "Are you sure? I don't see a name on it."

He clenched his jaw and drew back his fist. I side stepped him before the punch landed on my face. My arms rose into a defensive position as he turned and stepped closer. I ducked under another swing, but he lunged at me by the time I rose up again. We landed in a heap on the floor before he sat on my chest and slammed his fist into my jaw. His friends cheered for him. A crowd started forming around us. I struggled against his weight to escape, keeping my hands up to defend against him. After a few more blows, he started to slow down and I struck his nose, then jabbed his throat. He jerked away from me instinctively and held his neck, gasping to regain control of his breathing. I stood and tried to get out, but the crowd stopped me from running, many members eager to see the fight continue. As the blond boy rose, his eyes burned like a wildfire.

"I'm gonna kill you," he rasped.

He gritted his teeth and charged, shoving me backwards. The students watching scurried out of the way, not breaking the barrier, but changing the shape to stay away from his rage. He grabbed me by my hair and yanked hard. I grabbed the hand and pushed it against my head before using my free hand to punch his elbow and bash his stomach with my knee with one swift motion. As he jumped back, I released his hand and stepped away.

"Are you done?" I asked, feeling just a bit over-confident.

Before I could react, he swung hard and hit my temple. I fell to the floor again before slowly rising to my hands and knees. One of the cleats planted itself on my back and pushed me down, the studs digging into my skin. I felt dizzy from the damage to my temple and struggled to recover.

"That's enough Damien!" someone shouted.

Another boy around our age shoved past the crowd and pushed the blond off of me. The new boy was slightly taller than the assailant, with black hair, light skin, and angry green eyes.

He blocked Bozo with his arms crossed, a steely gaze to match his set jaw.

"What did Coach tell you about pulling crap like this?" the new boy asked, a hint of twang in his voice.

The blond sneered, "What's it to you? Ain't none of your business."

"Actually D, it is."

"How's that?"

"Because Anderson said, and I quote, 'Damien Nash if you keep this up you can just go ahead and walk your ass off my field and off my team.' And I don't want to have to find a new linebacker just to fill your spot for the off season."

"Guess you'll just have to keep your mouth shut, huh?" Damien taunted.

The other boy cocked his head to the side and asked, "Want to test that theory?"

Damien's cruel smile reshaped itself into a snarl. He huffed and marched off, his two friends in tow as they got in the breakfast line.

The new boy shook his head, then turned to the audience. He raised his hands and shouted, "Go on now! Nothin' to see here!"

The crowd dispersed, a few students grumbling about how the fight was a letdown. The boy turned to me and held his hand out. I took it and he pulled me off the ground.

"Thanks," I said as I picked up my phone, checking the screen for cracks.

He smiled a little and said, "No problem."

I looked him over a little more. He wore a black band T-shirt with a crowned triangle and three purple letters in the center, which I assumed were the initials for a band name. His tennis shoes were as dark as his hair, and his jeans were only bright enough to show that they were blue. I could see a silver chain around his neck, which was attached to a set of military dog tags.

"I'm guessing you're new around here?" he asked.

"What gave it away?" I replied.

He chuckled and said, "The fact that you sat

here of all places. Damien's a hot head, in case you couldn't tell. And on top of that he considers it criminal to sit at his table if you're not his friend or on the football team. So, either you're new, or just really stupid."

"Gee, thanks for the vote of confidence."

"Well, in all fairness, I said 'or,'" he said before grinning and holding his hand out to me again, "Name's Melvin."

I shook it, "Logan."

"Nice to meet you, Logan."

I smiled, then the bell rang, or more accurately the intercoms made a ringing sound. I reached into my jacket pocket and pulled out my schedule, then the map Jared printed off and gave to me before I left that morning. Melvin chuckled again when he saw it. I raised an eyebrow.

"What's so funny?" I asked.

"Trust me man, that map won't do you any good. All the floors look the same, but different, if you know what I mean."

"No, I don't," I said, more confused than before.

He held his hand out, "Let me see your schedule."

Hesitantly, I set the paper in his hand and he unfolded it, his eyes skimming over the lines to find the room numbers.

"Come on, I'll show you where your class is," he said, starting forward without looking up or waiting for me. I grabbed my bag off of the floor and scrambled to follow him. As we walked, he handed me the schedule and held the glass door open for me.

"You're just Mr. Helpful, aren't you?" I joked.

He shrugged and said, "I try."

We walked across the courtyard toward the next set of stairs into the back building.

"So, where ya from?" he asked as we started up.

"Well, I was born in New York, but I've moved around a lot since. I lived in Colorado for about five years, but that's the longest I've stayed anywhere."

"Do your parents move a lot for work?"

"Yeah, they did," I paused before continuing with, "but I think I'm sticking around for at least a little while."

"Cool."

I opened the door and held it for him to walk inside.

"Wouldn't hold that door very long," he warned, "You'll be stuck there all morning if you do."

I looked back and saw hundreds of other students funneling out of the cafeteria or running up the first set of steps and quickly went through the doorway. Melvin led me down the hall to the right and up a set of stairs to the second floor, then a left and another right. In the middle of that hall, he pointed and said, "There ya go man. My class is a few rooms down. If you need help finding your next one, just let me know."

"Seriously Melvin, thanks."

"Happy to help. Besides, it keeps me from sitting and being bored before class."

He waved and walked three doors down to a room on the other side of the hall. I walked into my own classroom. I sat down at a desk in the back, put my earbuds in my pocket and sat back waiting for my new World History class to end.

After the first class, I made my way to the second one, with Melvin's help. He hurried down the halls and up to the third floor. I walked inside to Statistics as the bell rang. The desks were in a weird triangular shape with the corners rounded off, which were arranged in groups of four throughout the room. Sadly, none of the groups were empty, just a few scattered seats within some of them.

"Can I help you?" someone asked.

I turned and saw who I assumed was my teacher. She was a short, muscular woman wearing a green polo with the school's mascot in the corner, along with a set of jeans and green tennis shoes. She had brown hair and thick glasses on her face.

"Uh, yeah. I'm Logan, I think my class is here."

She walked to her desk and looked at her computer, which I assumed had the class roster.

"Logan Wood?" she asked.

I nodded.

"Gotcha right here, take a seat anywhere you like."

I turned and looked for the empty chairs, noticing one right next to me and sat down cautiously. In the group, there was a boy sitting to my right, and at the other two desks were girls.

The girl to my left said, "You can relax. We don't bite." She smiled when she said it, as if trying to let me know she was just joking.

"Alright, but if I leave this room with teeth marks, I'm blaming you," I replied, giving her a small smile in return. She was skinny with amber skin, dark wavy hair, and her eyes were a familiar shade of green. She wore a navy blue jacket over a grey T-shirt with jeans.

"Wow, what a comeback," the boy said sarcastically, smiling as well.

"As if you could do any better Diego," the second girl said, rolling her eyes as she spoke.

She and Diego both had dark brown hair and eyes to match with sandy complexions. The boy had on a black polo, slacks, and a pair of dress shoes, while she wore a loose fitting shirt and shorts with sandals.

I reached into my backpack and grabbed my notebook while the three of them teased each other. The teacher, Mrs. Carey, started teaching the lesson. I scribbled notes about probability distributions and such. Considering I had not been in the class the whole year until then, I needed all the notes I could get. She explained definitions for things like qualitative random variables and wrote the equation for Probability Mass Function. I wrote so quickly my hand started to cramp. Then she stopped about thirty minutes later.

"Alright guys, go ahead and try some of these practice problems on your own for a few minutes," Mrs. Carey said.

She walked back to her desk to grab a stack of papers and began passing them out. Then Diego spoke again.

"Ash stop!" he whined.

I raised an eyebrow as he continued to say this. The girls laughed a little, and the one next to me looked at him and replied, "You stop Diego."

"Okay," he said, then looked back at Mrs. Carey as she asked if anyone had any questions, acting as if nothing had happened.

It happened again about ten minutes later as I finished the practice problems. After noting that I was still obviously confused, the girl across from me turned and said, "Don't mind them. They've been friends for years, so this is just some weird thing they do."

"It's not that weird," the boy said.

She raised an eyebrow at him.

"Okay, fine, it is weird," he said grinning.

She turned back to me and said, "I'm Natalie."

The boy clapped my shoulder and said, "And I'm Diego. She's my sister," he said, pointing at Natalie.

"Step-sister," she corrected.

"Dang, why are you always getting so technical?" he asked.

"Maybe I like being technical."

"So, you're a robot now too?" he asked. He turned to look at me and the other girl, eyes wide, "Guys, my sister's a cyborg! Isn't that awesome?"

Her eyes narrowed, but she couldn't stop the small smile from forming as she replied with, "Shut up."

The other girl rolled her eyes. She was smiling too.

"You'll get used to it pretty soon, it's fun to watch them do this. Even better to bring it up to bug them later," she assured me, "my name's Ashley, but most people just call me Ash."

"Logan," I said.

The obnoxious intercom bell rang again and everyone stood as if on command.

"Enjoy your lunch guys, we'll go over the problems and I'll give you your homework after," Mrs. Carey said.

Everyone grabbed either lunch bags or their wallets from their backpacks, or nothing at all, before hurrying out the door.

I checked my pocket, unsure if I had left my own wallet there, before leaving after them.

As I made my way back to the cafeteria, I was careful to avoid the table where Damien was sitting, just in case he still wanted to brawl. I stepped into the herd of hungry students that crowded a doorway inside. The opening led to the real lunch lines, with different options depending on which way you chose. I looked over the crowd to see hamburgers with fries in one line and pasta with a breadstick in the other. In the middle of the room there was a salad bar filled with greens and various fruits. The salad bar was self-serve with tongs for each food item, while the lunch ladies stood behind the counters to give students whichever option they chose. The walls were covered with posters for the school sports teams or information about the food pyramid and how much of whatever type of food should be on the plate.

I took a step back, realizing I was a bit too close to the person in front of me, only to bump into someone else.

I turned and said, "Sorry."

As I turned, I realized it was Ashley.

"Sorry, I didn't know you were there," I said.

"It's fine, it happens more often than you think," she said.

I just gave her a slight nod, not sure what else to say. She walked closer and stood next to me.

"You're new, right?" she asked.

I nodded again.

"You don't talk much do you?"

"Don't want to bore you with mindless chatter."

"Good, because I don't like mindless chatter.

So, let's talk about something more important."

I raised an eyebrow, "Like what?"

"How about where you're from? That accent tells me you're probably not from the south."

I nodded, "Guilty. I just moved here from Colorado, and lived in a few other places before that."

"Like where?"

"You're really that curious?"

Her face flushed a bit, "Sorry, I hope I didn't get on your nerves. I just like to listen and learn about people."

"No, it's fine," I said quickly, "I just didn't expect it."

She stayed quiet for a moment.

"Anyway, I've been to Maine, Jersey, Illinois," I paused and thought for a moment before saying, "Pennsylvania, and Rhode Island. And I was born in New York."

"So, what you're saying is you're a city boy."

"Born and raised," I said with a grin, "but I don't miss it."

"Why not?"

"Too many people. Sometimes you just need some peace and quiet for once; living out of town helps with that."

The group started to move forward. We looked up and followed. A group of about thirty students were allowed inside before the rest of us were cut off again and told to wait.

"What about you?" I asked.

"Never lived anywhere other than here."

"What about your family? What are they like?"

"Well, I have an older brother, and it's just us and my dad."

Something about the look in her eye told me

not to ask about her mom. Whatever it was, it was a hard subject.

"What about you?" she asked, snapping me back to reality.

I took a deep breath before saying, "I...I'm adopted. That's why I moved here actually."

Her eyes widened slightly, "I'm sorry, I hope I didn't –"

"Don't worry about it. You didn't do anything wrong."

I smiled a bit to reassure her. The line started forward again and we were allowed to get our food. Coincidentally, we both went toward the burger line. I looked around the room and saw to the far left were fridges full of water bottles, juice, and sports drinks. A few feet away from the entrance sat a freezer like in small grocery stores, which was full of single serving ice cream cups.

Never seen that in a school before.

The lunch lady gave me my food. I thanked her and started toward the only exit, a few openings next to the fridges with several registers for students to pay for their food.

"They won't let you leave if you don't grab fruit," Ashley warned.

"Can they do that?"

She shrugged and said, "Don't know if they technically can, but they do."

She walked to the fruit section and grabbed an orange. I grabbed an apple.

"Thanks," I said.

"No problem. Do you know your ID number?"

I gave her a confused look, "No. Nobody told me about an ID number."

"Do you have your schedule with you?"

I checked my pocket, then mumbled under my breath when I realized I had put it in my backpack during class.

"Do I really need it?" I asked.

"Yeah, that's how you put money in the school lunch account."

"Great."

She hesitated, then said, "I'll cover you today."

"You don't have to do that. I can just go back and get it."

"And where do you think you're going to put that tray? They'll just throw it away and you'll have to start all over. Besides, you can cover me next time."

I looked at her face for a moment, then said, "You're not really giving me a choice, are you?"

"Nope."

She took the tray from me and walked toward one of the registers. She held a tray in each hand and easily set them down on the counter before punching a number into a machine to pay. I followed her quickly. While the lady at the register waited, she asked, "Hungry today Ashley?"

"No, he just doesn't know what he's doing," Ashley replied with a grin.

"In my defense, I am new," I said.

The woman smiled at me and said, "Don't worry, the first day is always the hardest."

She pressed a few buttons on the register, then said, "Y'all have a good day."

We thanked her, then grabbed our trays. I started to walk in another direction, but Ashley stopped me.

"Where do you think you're going?" she asked.

I turned back and gave her a confused look. She turned her head and motioned for me to follow her as she said, "You can sit with me and my friends if you want to."

Why is she being so nice to me?

"Uh, sure," I said.

She led me to one of the large tables with eleven kids already sitting down, with about half a dozen seats to spare. Most of them had trays too, except for a couple with thermoses filled with soup and another with chips and a sandwich from her lunch bag. I quickly recognized a few familiar faces.

"Well, well, well, are you following me or something bro?" Melvin teased as he looked up at me.

"Actually, I think you're following me more since you keep asking to help me find my classes."

"Alright, guess I gotta give you that."

Ashley had already sat down by then. Not knowing where else to go, I sat in the empty seat next to her, which happened to be across from Diego, with Natalie to his right and Melvin to his left.

"I see you've met my bonehead of a brother," Ashley said.

Melvin put a hand to his chest and said, "Ash, you hurt me."

She rolled her eyes. Melvin reached over and stole a fry from her tray.

"Get away from my food you jerk!" she yelped. Melvin laughed at her reaction.

Another boy next to Melvin said, "Is this the guy you've been telling us about Mel?"

"Yeah guys, this is Logan."

He held his hand out to me and said, "Adrian."

I shook it, not wanting to offend anyone after the fight I already had that morning. Adrian was somehow taller than Melvin, even sitting down. He was lean and muscular, with dark skin and hair that was long on top and cut to fade as it got closer to his ears. He gave me a welcoming smile that matched the warmth in his brown eyes.

I realized I was making a face when Melvin asked, "What's that look for?"

"Nothing, I just..."

Adrian cocked his head and asked, "You have a problem with me?"

My eyes widened as I realized what he thought and I said, "No! Not at all!"

The rest of the group had turned to me by then.

Fantastic. Now I made them all mad.

"I'm not like that, seriously Adrian."

"Then what is it?" Melvin asked.

"Well, hopefully this isn't offensive, but I'm just wondering how you and Ashley are related because of your...how do I ask this in a way that doesn't get me killed?"

Ashley choked a bit on her water from laughter. Adrian started laughing too as he realized what I was asking.

"Oh, I get it bro," Melvin said, "Ash and I are half siblings. We have different moms."

Ashley rubbed my shoulder a little as if trying to help me relax.

"None of us would've been offended if you'd just asked the question Logan," Adrian assured me.

"Hey, you never know anymore," I said.

"Amen to that."

Adrian took a drink from his own water bottle and turned to the girl sitting to his left.

"Ash told me she had an older brother, but if you're both seniors, how –"

"I got held back in eighth grade. I was having trouble with some classes and getting into trouble instead of doing my homework."

"Yeah, until you found me and I whipped you into shape," Adrian said.

"Actually, it was football."

"Yeah, but who got you to even try out?"

"Whatever man."

While they kept bickering, I looked over the rest of the group. Ashley tapped my shoulder and asked, "Do you want to know their names, or just stare at them?"

"Dang, you guys don't let up, do you?" I asked.

"They do eventually after I tell them to shut up," someone said.

I turned to look at the girl next to Adrian again. She was a skinny girl with black hair wearing a camouflage jacket and shirt, with jeans and a red ball cap.

"That's Vivian."

She gave me a peace sign, then snatched Adrian's water bottle and drank what was left in it before giving it back. He shook his head and stood to find a water fountain to refill it.

"And she's dating Adrian," Ashley added.

"Well, I hope so. I'd be a little concerned if not since she drank out of his water bottle," I said.

I looked at the jacket again and saw a patch with a name stitched on the shoulder.

"What's your jacket say?" I asked.

"Lee. It's my last name," Vivian replied.

"Wait, isn't that your dad's jacket?" Ashley asked.

"Yeah, but I forgot mine and it's too cold to sit for three hours in Mr. Heath's classroom!"

"Does your dad know you took it? You know how much that jacket means to him."

"Yes mom, he knows I took it," she said sarcastically.

Ashley shook her head and pointed at a brown haired boy two seats to her left with his head on the table, barely awake.

"That sleeping beauty over there is James."

"Shut up Ashley," he grumbled.

James looked almost childlike. He did not have any facial hair, which highlighted his slightly rounded facial features. It did not help that he was wearing a bright, light blue T-shirt with cartoon characters I had not seen in almost ten years. The blond girl next to Ashley giggled and played with his hair.

"Come on babe, let me sleep," James moaned.

She rubbed his shoulder before laying her head on it. Compared to James, her features were very angular. Her eyes were like September, a mixture of brown and green that only appeared as autumn began. She wore a short sleeved loose shirt similar to Natalie's with tight-fitting shorts and a pair of white flip flops.

"Why is he so tired?" I asked as I finished my fries and moved on to my burger.

"Because the genius here decided that during his junior year he was going to take six advanced courses at once."

My eyes widened and I looked over at him, "Dude, what made you come up with such a bad idea?"

"We don't talk about it, alright?" he grumbled.

I chuckled and took another bite.

"And his girlfriend here is Brandie," Ashley continued.

Brandie waved slightly, then closed her eyes and cuddled with James. Ashley pointed across from the two of them and said, "That's Alice and Bryan."

Alice gave me a small wave but did not look up from her book. Bryan peeked over her shoulder a bit, trying to see what she was reading. Bryan was notably shorter than the other guys in the group. He was shorter than Brandie too, who was the tallest of the girls. He wore a dark blue button up shirt with little white whales scattered across it with black slacks and loafers. He also had a pair of black rectangular glasses on his face and undercut hair. Alice had short, light brown hair with eyes of a matching hue. She wore a vibrant yellow blouse with black pants and combat boots. She also wore a little silver bracelet on her left wrist and two silver rings on her left hand, one for her pointer and middle finger.

"Alice, let me see," Bryan complained.

She huffed and scooted the book between them, then said, "Next time remember to bring your own book Bryan. You read too slow."

"Hey!" he yelped, "It's not my fault I'm having trouble learning a second language!"

Their eyes frantically tore through the book.

"They've got a German test today, and they both forgot about it until I reminded them," someone said.

I turned to see a girl who had been drawing in a sketchbook, sitting at the opposite end of the table from me. She had short auburn hair and eyes the same color as the graphite she was using, as if someone had carefully drawn them. She wore a short blue dress and flats with silver earrings and a matching locket.

"My name's Peyton," she said with a warm

smile before returning to her work.

The boy at the far end of the table stood with his tray and started toward one of the trash cans, then the tray return.

"Who's he?" I asked.

"That's Ulysseus, Peyton's brother. He's a freshman, but Mel and I have known the two of them for years," Ashley replied.

Ulysseus was very different from the other members. Almost out of place. He wore a black leather jacket and dark blue jeans, with black hiking boots. The jacket was completely zipped up, as not to show anything underneath, including the pendant on the silver chain around his neck, which you could only see if the light hit it just right. He had black crew cut hair and stubble on his face outlining what could become a full beard if he let it. As he started back toward the table, I noticed the little nicks on his hands and a small scar in his left eyebrow that was slightly lighter than the rest of his skin. But it was his eyes that were the most disconcerting, because compared to everyone else, his seemed cold and distant. A brilliant blue that may have once been filled with joy seeming to show a hardened soul that had been shattered. I knew those eyes. I saw them in the mirror every day.

New Bonds

The members of the group chatted amongst themselves the rest of lunch, aside from Ashley. For some weird reason she wanted to keep asking me questions, but I slowly started to open up more. It was not long before the bell rang, telling us to go back to class. I walked with Diego, Natalie, and Ashley back to class. We sat down at our desks while Mrs. Carey started going over the answers for the worksheets. I took a corner scrap from my notebook and scribbled a note on it, then slid it over to Ashley. She gave me a confused look, then glanced at Mrs. Carey before reading the note. She glanced up at me, then wrote a reply before giving it back. I opened it.

When does class end? I wrote, and her reply was, *When it ends. Maybe you should check your schedule for more than just your ID.*

I grinned, then checked to make sure no one was paying attention before playfully nudging her shoulder. She smiled, then looked back at the front board.

When we finished checking the practice problems, we were given our homework and told to go ahead and start with the class time we had left. By the time I got my textbook out and found the right page, the bell rang. Then I noticed that Ash had not done any more than write down which problems were homework before packing up.

Maybe I do need to look at that paper more, I thought.

Everyone left in different directions. I looked at my schedule for my next class.

Why does this room number have an A in front of it? I thought.

I looked around and none of the nearby classrooms had letters.

Maybe I didn't read it right.

I looked again.

Nope, definitely an A.

I rubbed my forehead as I started walking left, hoping maybe I would just miraculously find it, but that was not likely.

"Need help?" a girl asked.

I looked up to see Ashley again, realizing I had almost started going down the stairs without paying any attention.

"I think I can figure it out," I said.

Liar.

She raised an eyebrow and said, "Really? Because you just about fell on your face. And you have more wrinkles in your forehead than my dad after a bad day at work."

We continued down the stairs as we talked. I noticed that she looked genuinely concerned for me.

"I'm fine, it's just been a rollercoaster of a day," I said as we reached the first floor. We stopped in the lobby so we could talk without aimlessly wandering.

"Then let me help make it easier," she said, holding her hand out for my schedule.

I looked at it again, then huffed and handed it

over. She skimmed over it, then said, "Oh, hey that's actually my next class. Come on."

She handed it back to me and started to walk out the main door of the building. I quickly followed her.

As we started down the concrete steps, I said, "I better not find you using that ID number since you know where it is."

She rolled her eyes but smiled. I smiled back at her.

"Did you figure out what number it is?" she asked.

"Haven't looked at it long enough."

She rolled her eyes again. When we started walking across the courtyard, she pointed to it, a long number next to my name.

"Hold up, the number you typed in at the cafeteria wasn't nearly that long. Don't tell me I have to type all of that in."

"No, just the last five numbers."

"Good, because I'd rather bring my lunch than put in ten numbers every time I need to pay for food."

"Yeah, but then you'd miss out on my engaging lunch line conversations."

"I don't know if I'd put it that way."

She lightly elbowed my side and I chuckled.

"Just wait until I get to know you a little more," she said, "It'll get better."

She led me to the arena building, then down the stairs and down a hall to a smaller gym in the corner of the building.

"Melvin's in PE with us too, so you won't have to listen to my boring conversation topics," she joked.

"Aw, come on. I was only teasing."

We stepped in the gym as the late bell rang. It was then I realized that Ashley had been tense the entire walk and started to relax a little.

"You okay?" I asked.

"Yeah, just a time freak. I don't like being late."

There was not much in the small gym. A small basketball court took up most of the room with a set of bleachers along the wall near the door. Then there was a small gap between the bleachers and the far wall that had a cart full of basketballs and another with dodgeballs.

Melvin saw us come in and waved us over. Ulysseus sat quietly next to him, closing the music app on his phone and removing his headphones.

Ashley and I sat on the seats in front of them. Melvin and Ashley started talking about a phone game they were both playing. Ulysseus looked at me, as if studying me, which made me nervous.

"Sorry," he said, "Not tryin' to make you uncomfortable."

His accent took me by surprise. It was distinctly different, even from his sister's, and I couldn't figure out why.

"I don't think we've properly met," he continued, then held his hand out to me as he said, "I'm Ulysseus."

"Logan."

I shook his hand, his grip much stronger than I expected. The ends of his lips turned up slightly, as if he were trying to force a smile, or hadn't done it in a long time.

"Yer accent's strange lad," he said.

I raised an eyebrow and replied with, "I could say the same for you."

He grinned, showing his teeth slightly.

"Where are you from?" I asked.

"My dad's family is from Ireland. Peyton and I lived there for a few years before our parents passed, then we moved here. After eight years here, Peyton and I talk more like these two, but my roots slip in every now and then."

"Did you let them rub off on you?"

"You just wait. A year or two and they'll have you saying all sorts of incoherent garbage," he said with a grin.

Melvin turned and said, "Says you. The day I met you, you called me a 'melter that haven't a baldy notion how to wind your neck in.' I still don't know what that means."

Ulysseus laughed and said, "It means you're frickin' annoyin' and don't know how to shut up."

Melvin pulled him in a headlock and gave him a noogie. Ulysseus yelped and tried to get out of the hold. When Melvin let him go, Ulysseus gave him a light punch on the shoulder, then fixed his hair.

"He has a point though," Ashley said.

"You want one too?" Melvin asked her, leaning forward to grab her.

"No!" she shouted before jumping away.

I laughed and leaned against the bleachers. Ashley sat back down next to me, then nervously looked at the other groups of students.

"Everythin' alright Ash?" Ulysseus asked.

She nodded, then took off her jacket and shoved it in her backpack. While her back was turned, a familiar and unfriendly voice said, "Look who it is."

I turned to see Damien less than a foot in front of me. Behind him stood three more lamebrained meatheads.

Seriously? This idiot again?

I stood, ready to defend myself again. He flashed a wicked grin.

"Look fellas. Li'l tenderfoot thinks he can take me on."

"Damien. Leave him alone," Melvin warned as he stepped between us.

"Gonna make me, cap?" Damien taunted.

The high pitched screech of a coach's whistle filled the room. I turned to see a short, muscular man with dark hair and dark beige skin. His face was clean-shaven and his eyes were a dark brown. He wore a red and white athletic wear shirt with black gym shorts and a pair of black tennis shoes. On his crew cut sat a pair of thick, black sunglasses. A silver whistle fell and hit his chest, held around his neck by a thin cord with the campus colors. He held a plain brown clipboard under his left arm as well.

"Alright everyone, let's get to it. Today, we're playing dodgeball for the first half of class. After that, you can either keep playing or walk upstairs around the arena."

Really? The biggest first day at a high school stereotype ever? Seriously?

He blew the whistle and everyone stood and started picking teams. Melvin and Damien were selected as team captains by the coach and started pointing to people they wanted on their teams. The coach waved me over and I walked to him.

"I haven't seen you here before," he said, then looked at the paper attached to the clipboard. It was the attendance sheet, with most of the names already checked off for the day.

"Heard I was getting a new student today. Wood, right?" he asked.

I nodded and he put a checkmark next to my

name for the day.

"Well, I'm Coach Hunter. And a word of advice for you, watch out for that Nash kid. He's got a mean throwing arm," he said, his head leaning slightly toward Damien.

"Thanks," I said, but he had already started walking off to get the dodgeballs.

I hurried to stand with the rest of the students that hadn't been picked yet, and Melvin quickly pointed at me. By then, he had already picked Ashley and Ulysseus too.

"Damien always plays dirty," Ulysseus whispered to me, "Always stealin' the balls on our side of the court and things like that. Keep an eye on him."

I nodded, then said, "No offense, but how good are you at this game? You don't really move very quickly."

"That's because I don't normally have a reason to. I can't throw very far, but don't doubt me yet."

Surprisingly, nothing really abnormal happened for most of the class. Damien targeted me of course, but I was great at dodgeball at my previous schools. In the entire seventeen years of my life, I had only been hit with a dodgeball twice. I was not about to let Damien make a third.

Then came the last match. Ulysseus and I were the only members left of our team. Damien was the last man standing on his. His eyes were filled with rage because after four matches out of five, his team still had not won, and he could not stand it.

Ulysseus stood a few feet ahead of me to the far right of the court, his eyes locked on Damien.

"You can do it Ulysseus!" Ash shouted.

"Gee, thanks," I yelled back jokingly.

"Come on guys!" Melvin yelled, clapping his hands in encouragement.

Damien had all the dodgeballs on his side of the gym. He chucked one at me. I sidestepped to avoid it. The next flew toward Ulysseus and he ducked.

"That all ye got?" Ulysseus shouted.

Damien's jaw clenched. He grabbed two more dodgeballs and threw them aimlessly, making them fly past us toward the wall. He threw another at me and I jumped over it before it hit my foot. Damien's face turned red. He had one ball left. I steadied myself and prepared to move as he started walking toward me, stopping at the line in the middle of the court, but before he threw it, he changed targets and it flew at Ulysseus, about a foot away. He was ready for it, and expected it. He reached out and caught the ball before it hit his chest, then spiked it back at Damien as if it were a volleyball. Damien stumbled back after the ball hit him from the force and shock. The coach blew his whistle, then the bell rang. Melvin gave Ulysseus a pat on the back as we grabbed our bags and headed out the door.

"Too bad Melvin didn't dodge very well today. We missed out on his throwin' skills," Ulysseus said.

"Nah, you guys did fine without me," Melvin said quickly, as if wanting to change the subject.

Ashley rolled her eyes at him and leaned closer to me. She said, "He gets embarrassed because he thinks he's a cliché."

"Why?" I asked.

"Thanks blabbermouth," he grumbled, then said, "I'm QB for the football team."

"I figured you were probably a pretty import- ant member of the team, and considering that nickname you have I'm guessing you're the team captain too."

He nodded and said, "Yep, biggest cliché of all time."

"No, I'm pretty sure there's worse," Ulysseus said as he scrolled through his phone.

"Well, still, I don't like being a cliché."

"It's only a cliché if you do it because dad wanted you to, and you're doing it because you like it," Ashley pointed out.

He looked at her thoughtfully, then said, "Yeah, that's true."

"Then why are you ashamed of it?" I asked.

Ulysseus glanced at Melvin, then back at his phone. Ashley looked down a bit as we walked through the hall. They knew something I did not.

"No offense man, but we did just meet today. Stick around a while and I'll tell you," Melvin said, giving me a pat on the shoulder before walking quickly past us and up the stairs.

After one more lecture, school was finally out for the day. I walked outside, my phone in hand looking for a new, loud song to listen to on the bus ride home. I stood behind the back building, rock and roll ringing in my head as I waited amongst the other students for my bus to arrive. Other students used crosswalks to reach the student parking lot behind the bus line. My head started nodding slightly with the beat of the song. Suddenly there was a hand on my left shoulder. At first, I thought it might be Damien, but I realized the hand was smaller and only lightly touched me rather than holding me in place. I took one earbud out as I turned to find Ashley standing behind me.

"Hey," I said.

"Hey. I've been hollering at you."

"Sorry," I said awkwardly, holding the earbud up slightly, "I like loud music."

"Obviously. What song is it?"

"Want to hear?"

She nodded and I handed her the earbud. Her eyes lit up as she exclaimed, "I love his song!"

I chuckled. We listened to it until the steel strings faded out.

"So why are you standing out here?" she asked.

It was then that the big yellow monster pulled up, and I pointed to it.

"There's my ride," I paused before walking and said, "Guess I'll see you tomorrow."

My foot barely touched the first step when she stopped me.

"Logan, wait."

I turned.

"How about I drive you home instead," she offered.

"Really?"

"Yeah. We all know the bus sucks," she replied.

I thought about it for a moment, then smiled slightly, "Yeah, sure, sounds good."

I followed her to the student parking lot. As we walked, students either gathered in groups to talk or jumped in their cars and drove away, excited to get away from the school. Ashley reached into her pocket to grab her keys. She pressed the unlock button. The headlights of an old burgundy Lincoln MKZ lit up in response.

"Nice car," I said,

She looked me over for a moment, searching for any traces of sarcasm, then said, "Thanks."

We got in the car and I sat back against the seat. Suddenly, music blared from the speakers and I flinched.

"Sorry!" she said as she quickly turned the dial to lower the volume. Her cheeks turned a bit red from embarrassment.

"I see I'm not the only one who likes loud music," I joked.

She smiled a little, then turned the radio up so we could just barely hear it. The CD changed to the next track as she started driving, turning from rock to country in a moment.

"If you don't want to listen to that, you can change it," she said quickly.

"I'm good," I replied.

"Are you sure?" she asked.

"What? A city boy can't like country music?"

She gave me a small smile, then backed out of the parking space.

We were both quiet for a while, listening to the music in the background. Ash was the one that broke the silence.

"So, where do you live exactly?"

"This place in the woods right outside of town. Over on Phoenix."

She nodded and kept driving.

"So, you said you've always lived in this town, right?"

"Yeah. Mel and I were both born and raised here."

She was quiet again for a moment.

"If you don't mind me asking, what happened to your parents?"

My heart ached a bit. I remembered my parents leaving me the year before. It was supposed to be just another business trip. They were supposed to be back no later than a week. They never came home. I felt my normal mask fading as I tried to hold myself together, but Ash still noticed.

"I'm sorry. I shouldn't have asked," she said.

I lifted my head back up, "It's fine."

I bit my lip, trying to give myself something else to focus on, even if it hurt. It seemed better than getting angry.

She quickly moved past the subject, "How long do you plan on staying here?"

"Until further notice," I said, looking out the window so she couldn't see my face.

The car stopped and the stereo went silent. Cautiously, she reached out and touched my arm.

"Are you sure you're okay?" she asked. When I didn't reply, she said, "I'm sorry, maybe I shouldn't be –"

"No, it's fine."

I put my hand on hers before she pulled away. I could not explain it, but something about her made me feel better. As if I could tell her anything and she would never tell another soul. It was weird after only a day, but I already knew that I could trust her. Even if my mind seemed to nag me about the past.

"Hopefully this doesn't come off as rude, but why are you being so nice to me?" I asked.

"You have a way with words, don't you?" she said sarcastically.

"Ash, I'm serious."

I held her gaze for a moment, then she shrugged and said, "Because I'm not really a mean person. Besides, you seem nice enough, and I've got a good feeling about you."

She pulled her hand away and started driving again while I let her words sink in.

That is not at all what I expected.

She stayed silent for a moment, then said, "I have trust issues too."

I turned to look at her but said nothing.

"The way you were acting in Stat told me you probably did, and your question confirms it," she paused again, "And if you ever need to talk, I'm here for you."

I gave her a perplexed look before sitting back again and saying, "I just met you today Ash. I'm going to need more time to get to know you."

"That's fine. Like I said, I'm here whenever you're ready to talk."

"Why?"

"Because I know what it's like not to have that."

A while later, we turned onto my street. Rows of oaks rested on either side of the dirt road, their branches casting shadows that only allowed glimmers of sunlight to touch the earth. The wooden walls were split by the occasional home and a single farm with a field of cattle. I looked out the window and watched a calf drinking from a watering hole before trotting after its mother.

"I've never seen them this close before," I said.

Ashley raised an eyebrow, "You mean the cows?"

"Yeah. City boy, remember?"

"How have you not seen one before?"

"I've seen pictures. Sometimes on the road when we moved, but like I said, never this close."

"Maybe you can hang out with us sometime. My dad has a couple cows and a horse at home. Mel and I help him take care of them while he's at work."

"What does your dad do?"

"He works in television. He writes scripts for comedy shows. He just got his own talk show too."

"That's really cool. Does he work from home a lot?"

"No, he tried to once. Apparently, Mel and I are a lot louder than we think, so he works at his studio most of the time."

I looked out the window again, but we had already passed the farm and the wall had reappeared.

"So, where do you guys live?" I asked.

"Not far. About five, maybe ten minutes from here."

I looked forward and we both stayed silent for a few minutes as she drove.

"How much farther before we reach your place?" she asked.

I pointed and said, "It's right there."

She looked at a house to our right and said, "Wow, you live there?"

She pulled over at the curb next to a large three story house made with grey bricks and surrounded by a white fence. At the top floor, there was a large balcony connected to the master bedroom. A bright blue Mercedes sat in the driveway, despite the two car garage behind it. Well-kept hedges lined the front of the porch, an American flag waving in the wind above them. The lawn was neatly trimmed with a small flower garden tucked in the corner.

"Yeah, that's me," I said, slightly embarrassed.

"It's really cool," she said, "I'm surprised Jared adopted someone."

"Thanks."

I grabbed my bag and climbed out of the car

before adding, "Thanks for the ride."

I closed the door and slung my bag over my shoulder, then started toward the house.

"Hey Logan."

I turned back to her.

"Do you need a ride tomorrow?"

I raised one hand a bit and said, "I appreciate it, but I don't want you to have to go out of your way, really."

"It's not out of the way. Like I said, I literally live a couple houses down."

"Okay, well, if you're sure."

She nodded and said, "So, see you at seven?"

"Yeah. See you at seven."

We waved at each other, then she took off. I started marching toward the house again. I put my key in the lock and stepped inside, only to immediately be slammed onto the floor. Two massive figures landed on top of me licking my face. I shoved them off only to have Daisy the golden retriever start licking my face again, with Oliver the pitbull licking the back of my head.

"Come on guys, at least let me get in the door," I said with a grin.

I stood back up just as Jared, my new guardian, walked into the room. He hit his knees with the palms of his hands, calling the dogs to him. Oliver and Daisy charged full speed to meet him. He laughed and scratched behind their ears before looking back up at me.

Jared was a tall man with short brown hair and grey eyes. He had a short, well-trimmed full beard and a smile that put anyone at ease. I remembered him telling me that he had taken the day off at work so he could check on me when I got home, so he was not wearing his normal business suit. Instead, he wore jeans and a dark blue flannel with his muddy yard work boots and a blue ball cap. The sleeves were rolled up, revealing his tattoo painted arms. One was a large black cross on his outer right forearm painted in the center of an ink gauntlet. I remembered seeing the bald eagle head on the same arm at his shoulder. On his inner left arm were three dates above his elbow, on the outer forearm was the quote, "Justice will not be served until those who are unaffected are as outraged as those who are – Benjamin Franklin" written in cursive.

It was always a bit surreal to see Jared. To think about all the things that he had told me about his past. He had adopted me about a month before spring break, and we spent a few days getting to know each other better. He grew up out in the boondocks, or "the boonies" as he calls it. He grew up doing stupid things with friends while hunting and fishing in the woods, his arms and legs covered in scars from things anywhere from car and motorcycle crashes to an old friend accidentally shooting him in the leg while deer hunting. He did not go to very good schools growing up and did not have a good relationship with his own parents, which he explained on my second day in town.

I remembered us having breakfast at a little diner in town when he told me, "I didn't want to do it forever. I'd done the stupid stuff and had my fun, but when I got older, I knew it was time to get serious. I saw people I'd known for years going to jail for crimes they didn't commit because of the way they acted or the way they looked. Or going to jail for crimes they did commit because they were too stupid to stay out of trouble. I saw others get away with things I dare not repeat because it was swept under the rug for some reason or other."

He paused and took a bite of his eggs.

"I just didn't want to watch it anymore. So, I made a change. Got a ton of student loans and went to a university, then law school. I was smarter than any of them thought, and surprised every professor I met because I looked and talked like white trash, but I still got A's in their classes."

He took a sip of his coffee.

"So, I changed up my look a bit in my third year of college. Started dressing and acting more professionally so I would be taken more seriously. Got through school, got a job at a firm and paid off my loans. Then I moved on to create my own firm here in town and here we are."

"Do you miss it at all? The way things were?" I asked.

He looked at me thoughtfully, then said, "Not really. Don't get me wrong, I still like hunting and doing stupid things I probably shouldn't, but I didn't grow up in a good place. And a lot of my friends from back then weren't good people. Like I said, people got away with things. Not everyone was bad or the stereotypes you see in the movies, but a lot of them were."

I looked down at the table.

"But I don't think I really ever changed who I was, deep down at least. At the end of the day, I'm a human who just wants to help other humans. Maybe that's why my dad didn't like me."

I raised an eyebrow.

"He was, a bit messed up if you ask me," he continued, "Racist, sexist, homophobic, the whole bit. But Momma taught me that we're all human, so if our differences aren't hurting each other, who cares?"

He started to laugh, "Then he kicked me out when I was about sixteen. We had a disagreement because I brought my girlfriend home. She was Hispanic, so he automatically didn't like her. We got in a fight and he told me to leave, so I did."

"No offense, but I'm kind of surprised you didn't turn out like him."

He grinned and said, "I was always a momma's boy. But that's enough about me for now. What about you? What was growing up like?"

"How was school?" he asked, interrupting my thoughts.

I shrugged, "There were a couple of jerks, but nothing I couldn't handle."

He stepped closer and looked me over, a bit of worry in his eyes.

"I can see that," he said, pointing at the black eye that started to swell, "What happened?"

"Some guy wanted me to get out of 'his seat,'" I said, making air quotes with my hands at the last two words.

He huffed and shook his head, "I knew you were a stubborn one the moment I saw you. Did you make any friends at least?"

"Yeah, I think I made a couple of friends," I said with a nod, "I at least met people who didn't want to beat me with a stick the moment they saw me."

He grinned and said, "That's great."

He put his hand on my shoulder and said, "I know it's a bit early, but I'll have dinner ready in about an hour or so if you want to put your things down and get settled."

I nodded before walking up the stairs to my bedroom on the second floor. I opened the door and stepped into the blank slate of a room. Aside from a made bed, a dresser, and a bare bookshelf, the room was completely empty. Jared told me when I moved in that he had left it that way so I could do what I wanted with it. Not that I had any money yet to make it look nice.

I set my bag by the door and laid down on the bed, pulling my phone out of my pocket to listen to some music. I laid there silently until Jared walked in and said it was time to eat.

After an awkwardly quiet meal of chicken and green beans, I walked back to my room. Jared stepped in moments later to talk.

"I hope everything's alright," he said.

"Yeah, it's pretty nice."

"If you want, we can head into town sometime this weekend. Get you some things to, how you say, spruce up the place. Some posters, a desk, whatever you'd like. It would give us a chance to get to know each other better too."

I thought about it for a moment, then nodded and said, "Sounds good."

He smiled, his eyes glimmering with excitement as he said, "Alright, well, I'll leave you be so you can get some work done."

He closed the door softly as he left and I looked at my phone again to start my music once more. On the screen I saw the album cover for Appetite for Destruction. A Guns and Roses album. And just above the artist's name were the words "Welcome to the Jungle."

I looked up and growled, "That's not funny."

Confidants

The week slowly got better. Ash drove me to and from school, leading to car rides filled with chatter, laughter, and music so loud the car shook. Damien continued being an asshole, but I had expected nothing less.

Throughout my classes, I grew closer to several members of the group. I talked and joked around with my tablemates in Statistics. Because of my Chemistry class, I got to know Adrian, Ulysseus, and Melvin after a couple of study sessions. I learned Adrian was a fullback for the school's football team, whatever that means. Ulysseus said he had no real interest in extracurriculars, that he just wanted to finish his classes and move on to college somewhere far away. I was not worried for him, even if he was always stressed about his grades, he was a smart kid. So were Adrian and Melvin, which I saw clearly after discovering they were secret science nerds.

As far as the other members, Brandie and James had been together for two years, and James always found it funny when other juniors asked him how he got a senior for a girlfriend, Bryan being among them.

"Seriously dude, I can't even get a girl our age

to go out with me," Bryan whined one day at lunch.

"Not even you know who?" James teased.

Bryan punched him hard in the shoulder and said, "Shut up!"

This was a fairly common conversation that would take place right before Alice would sit down for lunch, followed by James kicking Bryan under the table and motioning toward her with his head. Even though Bryan had a big crush on Alice, and apparently had for most of his life, he was not brave enough to ask her out. Then after lunch, Adrian would give him a sympathy pat on the back before wrapping his arm around Vivian's shoulders. I do not think he was trying to rub it in Bryan's face, but had only tried to encourage him. Bryan wanted a healthy relationship more than anything, which he made clear he wanted specifically with Alice, even if no one asked.

Peyton and Ulysseus kept to themselves except when they were with the group. They were always a bit nervous and jittery, and it always seemed worse at the end of the day just before Peyton drove them home. Ashley acted similarly sometimes, but only in certain classes. Neither her nor Melvin would tell me why.

The next week stayed about the same, at least until Friday. As Ash and I rode home, a wave of grief washed over me. I stared blankly out the window as she drove. I flinched when she spoke.

"Are you alright Logan? You're making that face again," Ash said cautiously.

I looked at her as I asked, "What face?"

"The one you made last Monday. When I took you home the first time."

"Yeah, everything's fine."

Why do you keep lying to her, dumbass?

Because everything was not fine. Everything I had been burying inside for the last year was getting too strong to hold onto. I could feel tears forming and trying to escape as I tried to make them stop.

Do not cry. Don't you dare cry in front of her.

Ashley pulled the car over and cautiously reached for me.

"Sorry, it's nothing," I said quickly, rubbing my eyes in an attempt to hide the tears.

"It doesn't look like nothing," she replied.

It was a different side of Ashley. Void of sarcasm, or jokes, or teasing of any kind. She was serious and soft spoken, trying to put me at ease. I had not been around someone like that in a very long time.

"Hey, I already told you. If you want to talk, I'm here," she said after a moment of silence.

"Are you sure?" I asked cautiously.

"What are friends for, right?"

She rested her hand on my arm to comfort me. I turned to look at her and saw the genuine concern in her eyes.

"Well, you remember that I'm adopted, right?" She nodded.

"Well...my parents disappeared a little over a year ago."

I paused to collect my thoughts. Ashley rubbed my arm gently, never taking her eyes off of me.

"And for a long time, I was really close to them, growing up, ya know. Then one day a few years back they started ignoring me. I think I was maybe twelve. My dad only talked to me if he was pissed off and wanted to yell at someone."

I stopped and quickly apologized for the swearing, but she just said, "Believe me, I'm used to it. It's fine."

I nodded a little, then looked forward.

"And I was going through a lot. I always got bullied for some reason or other. Sat in the wrong seat, said the wrong thing, maybe someone just decided they didn't like me that day. I'd get beat in the halls, ambushed in stairwells, no one really cared. I didn't have any friends to back me up because we moved too much. Then I came home where my dad just yelled at me. And mom was so tired and stressed out from helping him with his work that she just slept when she was home. And sometimes I wonder if maybe they were working so much because of me. What if –"

"Stop," she said.

I looked at her, a bit surprised.

"If you and your parents were that close, they wouldn't just leave you."

"But Ash, that was before –"

"Logan, stop. They were stressed and didn't know how to handle it, and that has nothing to do with you."

I did not say anything, and a tear started to roll down my face. I grit my teeth and rubbed it away forcefully.

"Come here," she said.

I gave her a slightly confused look, but then she wrapped her arms around me into a hug, but it was a bit of an awkward hug because of the middle compartment of the car. She rubbed my back gently, and I put one arm around her.

"It's okay to cry," she said, "There's no one else here, and I won't say anything."

Another tear rolled down my cheek, but that was all.

"I'm sorry," I said with a shaky breath, "I just miss them so much."

"Don't apologize," she said softly.

We stayed that way for a while, until I finally pulled away to wipe my face and rub my eyes a bit more. She put her hand on my shoulder.

"If you need anything, just tell me. Okay?" she said.

I nodded, then looked at her again, "Thank you."

She nodded in return, then said, "I get what it's like to lose a parent. Not both, but I have an idea of what you're going through."

"Your mom?"

She nodded again.

"What happened?"

"She died from cancer about two years ago. Chronic lymphocytic leukemia," she said slowly.

"I'm so sorry," I said, watching her in case she got upset.

"It's okay. I'm better than I was before. I still miss her of course, it just doesn't hurt as much."

Despite her claims, I could see the pain in her eyes. Her hands started shaking and her lip quivered slightly just before she bit down on it. I reached for her hand and took it, squeezing slightly. She squeezed mine back. Then we sat silently for a while longer until she checked the time on her car's digital clock.

"We should get home before someone worries," she said, then pulled her hand away from mine as she composed herself. I nodded and sat back. As she started driving again, my eyelids felt heavy, and despite my best efforts to keep them open, I soon fell asleep. In what felt like moments later, Ash was shaking my arm to wake me.

"Logan. Logan, come on, you're home."

I opened my eyes and turned to her, "Sorry about that."

"Stop apologizing," she said gently, "You've been through a lot."

I nodded, "Thank you again. I know we're still getting to know each other, and you didn't have to listen. I kind of put a lot out there."

"You're welcome. Like I said, what are friends for?"

She gave me a small smile. I could not help but smile back. I grabbed my bag and stepped out. Ashley rolled down the passenger side window.

"What are you doing later tonight?"

I shrugged, "Homework, I guess."

"Do you think you could get out of the house for a night?"

"Is something going on tonight?"

"There's a basketball game at school, if you want to go."

I smiled sheepishly as I admitted, "I don't really know a lot about the sport."

"That's fine, I can teach you. Or we can just hang out and talk for a while if you want instead."

I could not stop myself from grinning a little more as I said, "That sounds fun. What time?"

"I could come pick you up at six thirty if that's okay."

"That sounds great."

"Alright, I'll be back in a bit."

She rolled the window back up and drove off. Once she was a good distance away, I hurried inside the house. I jogged upstairs to my room, which had changed drastically within the last two weeks. In the far left corner sat a new wooden desk to do my homework, with a small lamp and a couple of my textbooks resting on it. My bed had a new set of blue sheets and pillowcases with a thick comforter that was slightly lighter. A refurbished nightstand sat next to the bed with a digital alarm clock and the book I had been reading on it. The bookshelf had a few new books, a CD, and a couple of DVDs I had grabbed while Jared and I were out. I had put up a poster for one of my favorite movies, *Smiths and Soldiers.* Jared had also helped me put up a small flat screen TV he had sitting in a box in storage that he had never used.

It was four thirty. I threw my bag on my bed, then hurried to the bathroom to look in the mirror, closing the door behind me. I nervously rubbed my palm along my clean-shaved chin. My heart beat quicker for some unknown reason. I rubbed my tired blue eyes, then splashed water on my face to wake up.

That afternoon dip is terrible.

I dried my face with the hand towel, then fidgeted with my short brown hair, trying to miraculously fix it and never being satisfied. In between the furious preening, I brushed my teeth at least three times despite the fact I already had that morning.

At about six, I was still in the bathroom, now staring blankly at myself in the mirror at all the little flaws that made me human. I heard the front door open and close as Jared came home from work.

"Logan, I'm home," he said, his voice louder than normal so I could hear, "Had a bit of a late day at the office. This new case is ridiculous."

I did not respond, just ran a hand through my hair once more. I heard the familiar sound of his leather dress shoes as he walked up the stairs.

"Logan?" he called.

I heard him step closer until he stood just outside the bathroom door. He knocked lightly.

"Are you okay in there?" he asked.

"Yeah. Everything's fine."

"Alright, well I brought dinner from Peg's Diner."

He started to walk off, but I opened the door and stopped him before he went far.

"Actually, Jared, there's something I want to ask you," I said nervously.

He turned back to me. He was wearing his grey suit and tie with a white dress shirt, his tie already slightly loosened since he was not at work anymore. He raised an eyebrow as he waited for my question.

I sighed, "Is it alright if I go out for a bit tonight?"

"Something going on?"

"Yeah, there's a basketball game at the school tonight. I'm going with a friend."

He carefully looked over my face, then chuckled when he saw my hair and asked, "And would this 'friend' happen to be a girl?"

I said nothing, and apparently that was the only answer he needed. He grinned and said, "You work fast."

I gave him a look of shock, "It's not like that."

"Like what? A date perhaps?"

I rubbed my hands over my face and walked to the left, straight toward a small white couch at the end of the hall. He followed me and stood nearby as I sat down.

"I don't know what it is," I said, "Right now, it's just two people hanging out."

"Right. Says the teenage boy who has probably been messing with his hair for half an hour. Am I right?"

"If you add about an hour, then yes."

He laughed a bit.

"Shut up," I growled.

"It's okay to like a girl you know. It's okay to go out with one too."

He sat next to me and said, "Just don't get any ideas beyond that."

I looked at him and raised an eyebrow in confusion, then realized what he meant, "Whoa, it's not like that at all!"

He gave a hearty laugh and put a hand on my shoulder, "I know you well enough to know you're not like that. I just like to see you squirm."

"You're sick," I said with a glare.

"Hey, I'm a parent now. It's my job to embarrass you in any way that I can."

I put my head in my hands and groaned, feeling hopeless. Jared's brow furrowed.

"Are you alright?" he asked.

"Other than being extremely nervous, yeah just peachy."

"What are you so worried about? I mean, I know it comes with the territory, but you've done this before."

I lifted my head and my fingers intertwined in front of me. My foot tapped on the floor.

"Haven't you?"

I shook my head, "There wasn't ever anyone I was really interested in. And even if there had been, we moved too much because of my dad's job, so I wouldn't have bothered."

He patted my back, "Want some advice?"

I turned to him, "Guess it couldn't hurt."

"Well for starters, it's okay to feel nervous, especially if you haven't dated before. Perfectly normal, just try to keep a clear head and don't say anything stupid."

"Well, gee, I didn't think of that," I said sarcastically, "Any other advice oh wise one?"

He grinned, "Yes. On a more serious note, just be yourself. You being yourself is what caught her interest, so stick with it."

"Okay, but again, I don't even know if it really is a date."

"Then don't treat it like one. Put yourself in a mindset of it being just two friends hanging out. If it turns into a date or if she gives you signals that hint that it is a date, you go from there."

"How will I know if she's giving me a signal?"

"Son, women are a very complicated form of the species, but trust me. You'll know if she wants you to think it's a date."

I looked forward again nervously.

"Look," he said, "I haven't been on a date in a while, but some symbols can be very simple. If she stands closer to you than normal, or puts a hand on your arm. If she's really confident she might hold your hand or put her hand on your leg."

"Doesn't that stuff mostly happen in movies?"

"Where do you think they got it?"

I thought about it for a moment, then nodded. "Are you walking there?"

"No, she's driving actually."

"Well, if this continues, we may have to get you a car so you don't end up using all of her gas."

I rolled my eyes, but grinned. He clapped me on the back and stood.

"Stand up," he said.

I did as I was told. He straightened my hair for me, then we walked downstairs. I sat in the living room trying not to stare at my phone for the last fifteen minutes I had to wait. Oliver walked up to me and jumped on the couch, bumping my hand with his nose until I scratched his velvety ears. His head rested in my lap and he dozed off while I rubbed his back.

Soon it was six thirty. She still had not arrived. All kinds of thoughts raced through my mind.

Maybe I heard the time wrong? What if she changed her mind? Maybe I heard her wrong and I was supposed to meet her there?

I slipped my phone out of my pocket to check my texts. I opened our chat.

Ur picking me up, right?

A few minutes later, my phone vibrated.

Sorry! I fell asleep and lost track of time!
I'll be over in a few minutes

I let out a sigh of relief. Oliver squirmed a little before settling back down.

"You're not going to let me get up, are you?" I asked.

Oliver's nose nuzzled my belly and he huffed. I smiled and patted his shoulder.

"Glad you and Ollie get along," Jared said as he walked toward his recliner, a glass of tea in his hand. "He tends to get nervous around new people."

"Why?"

"I found him at a shelter. His previous owners weren't good people. Poor fella has a scar on his hind paw from a beating. That's why he limps sometimes when that leg gets tired."

He looked at us thoughtfully before continuing with, "Maybe you two get along because you're so alike."

Then there was a knock at the door. Oliver's head shot straight up as he let out a guttural bark. Daisy ran into the room from her bed in the kitchen and followed suit. I took Oliver's distraction as an opportunity to stand up.

"Is that your new girlfriend?" Jared teased.

I punched his arm as I walked by. He laughed and sipped his drink as he opened a book. I hurried to the door. When I opened it, Ashley stood there and gave me a small smile. She had changed since she dropped me off, now wearing a green T-shirt with the school's mascot, along with black shorts and tennis shoes. I started to get nervous again, thinking that I was dressed inappropriately in comparison. I was still wearing the jeans, black T-shirt, and shoes I had worn at school. She did not seem to notice my discomfort.

"Ready to go?" she asked with a smile.

I nodded and followed her out, but Jared waved me over to him before I left. I leaned closer and he murmured, "Have fun Logan, but not too much fun."

"Not helping," I growled.

He grinned while I walked back to the front door, closing it behind me as I walked to Ashley's car. I jumped in the passenger's seat and buckled in while she started the engine. Just before we started the long drive back to school, she gave me a funny look.

"Are you alright Logan?"

"Am I making a face again? I promise I'm feeling better."

"No, you just look nervous about something."

"Really? Wouldn't know why."

We got back to the school a little early for the game. Ashley led me to two seats at the left end of the arena that were aligned with the middle of the court.

"These are my favorite seats. You can see everything here," she said excitedly as we sat down. Then she spent the next few minutes telling me the basics of basketball so I could at least follow along with the game.

As people started filing in, I turned to her and asked, "Do you need anything to drink?"

"Yeah, a water would be good actually."

"Well then, I'll be right back."

I walked to the concession stand on the opposite side of the arena and bought two water bottles. Once I returned, I gave her one and sat down again.

"So, let me make sure I understand this," I said, "Every shot is two points, unless the player is behind that line," I paused and pointed to the so-called three-point line, "If they make that, they get three points. If someone does something they're not supposed to, somebody gets free throws which are one point apiece."

"You pretty much have it. Free throws happen when someone commits a foul, which could be grabbing, pushing, running with the ball without dribbling, things like that. Then someone on the other team gets at least one free throw depending on the foul."

"Seems simple enough."

"Oh really? Coming from a guy who's never played the game."

"And you have?"

"Yeah, actually, I used to be on the team."

I gave her a look of surprise, "Impressive. Why did you stop?"

Her face fell and she looked back at the court as she said, "I got hurt. A few months before mom died. I haven't been able to play competitively since."

I rubbed her shoulder, "You had a really bad year, didn't you?"

"Trust me, you have no idea."

"You know the talking goes both ways, right?"

"What do you mean?"

"I mean, if you need to talk, I'm here for you too."

She gave me a small, half-hearted smile, "Thanks."

Then it came. A bone-chilling voice that made us both flinch, "Well, well, well. Look who it is."

Ashley's muscles tensed a bit. I turned to see Damien standing over me with his arms crossed.

"Didn't peg you for a sports guy," he said.

"What do you want, Damien?" I asked suspiciously.

"Me? I have to want something to come by and say hello?" he asked, his voice laced with mock innocence.

"Seems like every time you say hello to me, I end up with a fist in my face."

"Oh, come on now. Don't exaggerate."

"I'm not exaggerating and you know it. So, what do you want?" I growled.

"Well, if you insist."

He took the empty seat next to me before continuing, "It seems we have a little problem."

"Which is?"

"Well, by the look of things, it seems that you're out with my girl."

I turned to look at Ash. Her jaw clenched tightly.

"Damien. I dumped you a long time ago. There is nothing between you and me. Besides, Logan and I are just friends."

Not a date. Got it.

He shifted his gaze toward her, then grinned and said, "Well good." His hand clapped my shoulder and squeezed hard, "As long as we've established that."

He stood and shot me one final glare before walking away. Once he was gone, I turned to Ashley.

"You dated that jackass?" I asked.

Her cheeks flushed with embarrassment, "It was a long time ago, and he wasn't like this back then.

Once he started acting like that, I dumped him. Especially since he –"

She stopped and her eyes widened.

"What? What did he do?"

"Nothing. Forget I said anything."

I was curious but decided not to push her.

"Let's just watch the game," I said.

A buzzer went off and the players started dashing across the court. Soon Ashley started to relax and eased back into her seat.

We walked silently back to the car after the game. Our team won, which was good, but Ash seemed distracted again. She started to climb into the driver's seat, but I caught the door before she closed it. She looked up at me.

"What's going on?" I asked, "Ever since Damien came by you seem a little off."

She shook her head, "Logan really, it's no big deal. Don't worry about it."

"A little late for that."

She sat silently in thought, avoiding my gaze. I crouched down beside her.

"Come on, you can tell me. What are friends for, right?"

Hesitantly, I touched her hand. Every part of her tensed as if in terror. I pulled away.

"Ashley?"

She turned to look at me again, her eyes seeming conflicted. We stared at each other for a long moment as I waited silently for her to respond. She shook her head and looked at the pavement.

"It's not something I like talking about," she said, "I'll be fine, really."

"Okay, if you're sure."

I knew she was lying. Even with her trying to look away from me I could see tears forming in her eyes at the thought of whatever was wrong, but I knew it was time to let the subject go. At least for the time being.

She looked up and grabbed the steering wheel with one hand, the door with the other.

"Come on, let's go," she said, waiting for me to move out of the way.

"Maybe I should drive," I suggested.

She started to get annoyed, "Logan, I told you I'm fine."

"I know, but I think you need to just sit for a bit. I get that you don't want to tell me what's going on, but I'd rather not risk us getting into an accident in the process."

She glared at me.

"You're not going to move until I get out, are you?" she growled.

I raised an eyebrow and looked up as if in thought, "Hmm, nope. Don't think so."

She huffed and rolled her eyes as she got out of the car. I got in the driver's seat while she walked around the front to get to the passenger's seat.

"Do you even know how to drive?" she asked as she sat down.

I pulled my wallet out of my pocket to show her my license, "I just don't have a car. I'll be careful, I promise."

"Okay," she said. When she buckled in, she added, "Obviously I'm not going to win this argument."

"What can I say? I come from a long line of

stubborn people."

"Ah, so you're the jackass."

I turned and glared at her, smiling slightly. She grinned and gently pushed my shoulder.

"Come on. If you don't start driving soon, I'll be asleep before we even get out of town," she joked. The Ashley I knew was starting to come back.

It was not long before she fell asleep though. Music played softly from the radio, just loud enough to hear without waking her up so I had something to occupy my thoughts. I could not help but glance at her every now and then as I drove. She did not make a lot of noise, just some shuffling when she moved a bit in the uncomfortable seat.

I wish it was a date, I thought sadly.

My text tone went off.

Who is that?

I suspected it might be Jared checking in, so I pulled over to the side of the road to look at the messages. Surprisingly, it was from Melvin.

Hey bud, sorry to bug y'all.
Is Ash still with you? She's
not picking up her phone.

The text tone went off again. Another message from Melvin.

Come on man, don't tell me
this is what I think it is.
That's my sister dude.

I rolled my eyes.

Why does everyone think I have some ulterior mo-

tive? I thought angrily.

It's not what you think it is.
I was driving. Do you really
think I would do that?

Hey man, you never know.
I'm the big brother, gotta
protect her when I can.
Where is she?

She fell asleep on the drive.
I guess her phone's on silent
because I didn't hear it

R u bringing her home?

Yeah, we're about twenty minutes
out. Can you text me your address?
Ash said it was near mine, but I
haven't been by yet.

Sure, hold up a sec.

He sent me the address and I thanked him, then punched it into my GPS. Ashley made a strange sound. I turned to see her shaking in her sleep with her brow furrowed.

"Ash," I whispered.

She did not respond, just made another sound, then slowly relaxed back into her seat.

I should get her home, I thought as I pulled back onto the road.

I had just turned onto our street when she woke up. She moved a little at first, then yawned and stretched.

"Where are we?" she asked, eyes barely open.

"On our street. I had Melvin text me the address so you could sleep."

She rubbed her eyes and turned to me, "Don't we need to go to your house first? So you can, I don't know, get home."

"I can walk. It's only two houses down."

"Yeah, with big blocks of woods between them," she said, giving me a look of concern.

"I'm not worried about it, Ash. It's still not that far."

"I don't like that idea," she said quickly.

"Why not? It's not hard to backtrack a straight line."

"That's not the problem. There could be bears or wolves out here, and it's pitch black. The houses are far apart and sometimes their porch lights aren't on so you won't be able to see."

"You know smartphones have flashlights, right?"

"Logan, be serious," she grumbled, "I don't like the idea of you being out here by yourself this late."

"Why?"

She hesitated, as if collecting her thoughts in her hazy state, "Because you're my friend. I wouldn't be able to forgive myself if something bad happened to you."

I looked at her for a moment before looking back at the road, then said, "Fine, if you're that uncomfortable with it. Are you awake enough to drive home?"

She nodded and sat back, rubbing her eyes once more.

"Don't drift on me or I'm walking home," I warned.

"I won't. Just drive."

We sat silently until we reached my house. I saw that Jared had left the porch light on for me as I pulled into the driveway. Once I stopped, I got out and Ashley walked around to the driver's seat. She closed the door and rolled the window down so we could talk for another minute.

"Be careful, alright," I said.

"I will," she replied, still looking a bit sleepy.

"This might sound weird, but can you text me when you get home? Just so I don't worry," I asked awkwardly.

"Yeah. I'll let you know when I'm home."

"Good. See you later?"

"Yeah. Bye Logan."

I waved as she pulled out of the driveway. She waved back before driving down the street. I smiled a little, then walked to the front door to go into the house.

In the living room, Jared had fallen asleep while reading his book, which had fallen open faced on the floor. I quietly picked it up and slipped his bookmark in, hoping that was where he had stopped, as I put it on the coffee table. I checked to make sure I had locked the front door, then snuck upstairs to change. I slipped into a pair of shorts and a grey tank top before getting in bed. I checked my phone for a text. Still nothing. I heard a scraping sound from my closed door. I set my phone down on the comforter and stood to open it. Oliver dashed in and lunged onto my bed, claiming a spot for himself.

"What, your dad fell asleep in the chair so you're taking my bed?" I whispered.

He looked up at me, then huffed and snuggled down into the comforter.

"Guess that's a yes."

I walked back to the bed, leaving the door open in case Daisy wanted in too, or Oliver decided to leave. I laid on my side and held my phone with one hand, using the other arm as a pillow while I waited. A few minutes later, my phone vibrated.

I'm home dork.

> *I'm glad. Thanks for actually remembering to tell me.*

What's that supposed to mean?

> *Uh, ur forgetful, I thought that was obvious lol.*

Shut up :)

> *Ok. Get some sleep.*

I will. Goodnight

> *Night*

After that night, Ashley and I started hanging out more often. Usually, we just went with other members of the group to dinner and a movie or to the mall, but we got a lot closer. When we were alone, we would tell each other everything. From basic interests to secrets and fears. She became my best friend. In the process, I got closer to other members of the group too, especially Melvin and Adrian, who were both protective of Ashley. Melvin's reason was easy to assume, but Adrian would not tell me his reason. I assumed it was because the guys were such good friends. Plus, Vivian was keeping an eye on me too, being one of Ashley's oldest friends.

About two weeks after the basketball game, Vivian grabbed me by the arm and pulled me into an empty hall.

"What the heck Viv?"

"Oh, shut up you wuss."

I pulled my arm back and asked, "Where are you taking me exactly?"

She rolled her eyes, "Nowhere in particular, but we need to talk."

"About?"

"Ashley."

"What about her?"

She looked around to make sure we were alone, then said, "Look, I'm just worried about her. She's...having trouble coping with some things, and I don't know if you trying to date her is helping."

I raised my hands in surrender, "Whoa there, I never said I was trying to date her."

"You didn't have to. That look you give her is the same one Adrian gives me. You like her, so don't try to deny it."

"I'm not denying that I like her, but I'm also not going to push her. She told me before that she has trust issues. I don't want to mess anything up by pressuring her."

She eyed me suspiciously.

"What's going on with her?" I asked cautiously.

"If she didn't tell you, I'm not going to either."

"Fair enough. Look Viv, I'm not going to pressure her, or hurt her, or whatever other bad thing you think I'm going to do."

"Right, because you wouldn't ask her out."

"I mean, I've thought about it. I was just waiting until we got to know each other better."

"Well, wait a while longer. She doesn't need any more stress."

She started to storm off, but I said, "What makes you think I would add stress to her life?"

She froze, then looked back over her shoulder and said, "Because she's never had the best luck with dating."

"Is that why she's been acting weird?"

She nodded slightly.

I walked up to her and said, "I get it. You're just trying to protect your friend, but we've gotten really close. And I don't understand how dating would ruin that for us."

She turned to face me, then said, "Fine, if you want to try it go ahead."

She stood on her tip-toes to get in my face before adding, "But if she says yes and you hurt her, I promise, I will kick your ass."

She turned and marched off again.

Dang, she's scarier than she looks.

Due to my newfound fear of Vivian killing me in my sleep, I decided to wait a while longer before I asked Ashley out.

On the last Friday before finals week, I sat on a large concrete block behind the school, waiting for Ashley to get out of her last class so I could drive her home. I pulled out my phone and started playing a game, then flinched when someone sat down beside me. I looked up to see Ashley grinning ear to ear.

"I'm guessing class went well?" I said, closing my game.

She showed me a piece of paper in her hand.

"Passed my test with flying colors," she said happily.

I took the paper and looked it over. It was a test paper for her advanced history class. It was a long essay examining a historical document of her choice. Even though she had been worried all week that she might have gotten a C on the paper, she ended up with a ninety five. I was not surprised.

"That's fantastic!" I said as I handed it back.

She chatted excitedly about it, and I listened. Truly, I did. She had picked apart the Emancipation Proclamation. But since I was not in the class, I did not really understand why she had to analyze it, other than it was for an assignment.

She stopped suddenly as something caught her eye.

"What?" I asked.

"Let's go."

"Everything okay?"

"Yeah, but we should go now."

She stood and motioned for me to do the same. I did, but we did not get far before someone started shouting.

"Ashley! Over here!"

Ash muttered something under her breath before turning to look at the girl behind us.

"What do you want?" Ashley snapped.

The girl we saw was the pure definition of stereotypical emo. Her hair and nails were jet black and she wore dark makeup on her face. She had rings in her ears, lip, and nose, as well as a silver bracelet on her left wrist and a silver chain necklace. She wore a *My Synthetic Allure* tee with dark, tight fitting jeans and black shoes.

"Aw come on Ash, is that any way to treat an old friend?"

"We haven't been friends since junior high."

She waved Ashley off, "Details, details."

"You didn't answer my question. What do you want?"

"That's just like you, always so eager to get to the point."

"And you're so eager to avoid it."

The girl gestured to me, "Who's your friend?"

I cleared my throat, "Logan."

I hoped the uncomfortable moment had passed. I was sorely mistaken.

"Christina," she said with a grin. I immediately knew what was coming next as she started to look between us. She pointed and asked, "Are you two –?" She did not finish the question.

Ashley's eyes dilated a bit in surprise, "No."

She looked unsure of what to say since she had been taken off guard.

"We're just friends," I said, maybe a bit too quickly.

"Really? Because I've seen you around school. You two hang out an awful lot to be 'just friends.'"

I glanced at Ash. She said nothing, an icy glare aimed at Christina.

Christina looked over her shoulder, then turned back to us and said, "Well, looks like my friends need me. Maybe we'll see each other again soon."

It was not a question. It was a statement made as she gave us a final smile and walked back to her group.

"Is that why I was supposed to hurry?" I asked.

"Yes," she growled.

"I'll go faster next time."

"Good."

She marched toward the parking lot. I followed close behind, feeling like I was somehow in trouble. At the very least she was irritated during the walk to my new car. Well, new to me. Jared had taken me to get a car a couple of weeks after the basketball game. I picked a used car so it would not cost as much, and I got a job at a movie theater a few days later, determined to pay him back at least half like I had promised when we bought it.

I unlocked the small black Camry as Ashley approached the far corner of the lot. She got in and set her bag on the floor, sinking back into the grey seats as she closed the door. I hurried in on the other side, tossing my backpack in the back seat before I sat down. Ashley's jaw was tight when I started the car.

"You're going to hurt your teeth," I warned.

She closed her eyes and took a deep breath, her jaw slowly loosening its grip.

"Let's just go home," she said softly.

"Hello? Hello? Anyone home?"

I blinked twice, realizing Ashley's hand was waving in front of my face. Apparently, my mind decided to wander while we sat at a stop light. Drivers behind me were honking their horns and probably cussing me out. I started forward.

"Sorry, I was just thinking," I said.

"About what?"

I tapped my fingers against the steering wheel nervously.

"Just something I've been thinking about for a while."

"And what would that be?"

I drove a little farther in silence. My nerves were trying to get the better of me. She waited patiently, giving me a curious look.

Guess there's no turning back now.

I stumbled over my words as I said, "Would you, maybe, possibly, if you're free –"

"Oh, for goodness sake Logan, just spit it out already!" she said, interrupting my rambling.

I took a deep breath. My grip on the wheel tightened.

What is wrong with you? Why are you so nervous?

To be fair, I had never asked a girl out before, but I still did not understand why I could not get the words out. It looked so easy seeing other guys do it.

I pulled the car over so I would not have to try focusing on too many things at once. Plus, I did not want Ash to feel like I had trapped her there.

I turned to her and said, "Ashley, will you go out with me?"

She did not say anything, just turned away to look out the window.

Welp, that's a no, I thought to myself.

When she did not give me an answer, I said, "We can just go if you want. You don't have to –"

"Don't."

She quickly got out of the car and started walking. I froze for a moment, stunned by the reaction, then got out to catch up with her.

"Ash, wait!"

She didn't. She just kept marching forward.

Idiot! What did you do?! How could you possibly screw up one simple question? I thought angrily.

I jogged ahead and gently put my hands on her shoulders to make her stop. She did not struggle. She did not try to walk around me. But she also refused to look up at me, facing the grass under our feet. I did not know what to say, so I just said the first thing that came into my head.

"What did I do wrong?"

She looked up at me slowly. Her beautiful smile had disappeared, leaving only a straight line at her lips. Her body trembled slightly and her eyes were full of fear and anger.

"Nothing. You didn't do anything," she said, her voice forcing the words out.

"Then what's wrong?"

She shoved past me, "I don't want to talk about it."

I ran in front of her again, "Ashley, stop."

I didn't touch her this time, just put my hands up between us as I said, "If you don't want to talk, that's fine, but please let me take you home."

We stared at each other for a minute or so before she finally turned around and walked back to the car. I got back in the driver's seat as she fastened the seat belt. She zipped up the navy jacket that she had worn the day we met and sat as close to the door as possible. She did not look away from the window for the rest of the ride, still shaking the whole way. I caught the reflection of her eyes in the window. Even though the anger had already been drained, they were still filled with fear.

I wanted to do something, anything to make her feel better. She was my friend. My best friend. All I could think was that I should have said nothing at all.

As we got close to our street, she started talking again.

"Please stop the car," she said weakly, her voice cracking.

In her reflection, I could see the tears in her eyes that she was trying to hold back.

"Just stop somewhere. I can walk the rest of the way."

I tapped the brake.

"Logan. Stop the car. Now," she said angrily, her voice rising.

I did as I was told, but took the key out of the ignition. She got out and started walking off again, backpack in tow. She did not turn at our street, just kept walking straight forward while looking at the dirt below us. I did not try to stop her, just walked close behind.

She later dropped her bag in the ditch by the dirt road and turned to walk into the tree line, then deeper in the woods. I stayed close behind her, knowing I would annoy her but still unwilling to leave.

"Go home Logan," she shouted.

I stayed a few paces behind her. By the time she had yelled at me we were deep in the forest near a small clearing. I did not want her to be in the middle of nowhere alone. Especially not like this.

Her arms crossed in front of her as she walked, as if she were trying to calm herself. Once we were in the middle of the clearing, she stopped but did not dare to turn around.

"Why won't you just go away?" she asked half-heartedly.

"Why won't you just talk to me?"

"Because I don't want you or anyone else to see me like this."

I reached out and gently rested my hand on her shoulder, but she jerked away. She was shaking even harder than in the car.

"Ashley, please. Talk to me," I begged.

She tried to stay quiet. To hold back the tears. But she could not anymore. Her legs gave out from under her and she fell to her knees, sobbing uncontrollably.

I crouched down next to her and slowly wrapped my arms around her quivering figure. She did not fight it. Instead, she buried her head in my chest and continued to cry.

"It's okay," I said softly, gently rubbing her back, "Just let it out. I'm right here."

I kept trying to calm her, but nothing worked, so I just silently held her close until she ran out of tears. When she finally stopped crying, she was still trembling, but seemed to feel a little better. She took a few deep breaths as she nestled her head closer to my chest. Then she pulled away and tried to stand, but her legs were shaking so hard she ended up back on the ground.

"Just rest for now," I said softly.

She nodded and laid down in the grass. I laid down beside her, gently taking her hand in both of mine.

"Do you want to talk about it?" I asked.

She bit her lip and tried to roll away from me. I gently caught her arm.

"Please stop that," I said, "Just tell me what's going on. It's not healthy to hold it all in."

She looked up at me.

"You can be a real pain in the ass, you know that?" she said weakly.

"As you remind me time and again," I said with a small smile.

She gave me a slight smile back, but it was

gone a moment later. She sniffled a little before she started talking again.

"Do you remember when we were at that game? When you found out that Damien and I used to date?" she asked.

I nodded.

She sighed, "We were together for almost a year. And everything was fine at first, great actually. He was sweet and caring. He listened to me and helped me, and we were together all the time."

She smiled a little at the thought, but her face fell again as she continued, "Then one day he started acting more aggressive, and not just on the football field. I thought it wasn't that big of a deal. He has a crazy strict dad who wants to control everything about his life, so I thought maybe he was just having trouble with it and taking his stress out more openly, but he wasn't hurting anyone. Sure, he yelled at some of our friends, but they said they thought it was the same thing."

She bit her lip a little.

"Soon he started getting more aggressive toward me too. It started with yelling like he did with everyone else, so I didn't think much of it. Then we were fighting more. A lot more. And it got more... malicious. A lot of bad things were said."

She paused again. I gave her hand a gentle squeeze.

"Then one day he started acting normal again. He was sweet and considerate again, like before. I didn't understand why or what was going on, and he wouldn't tell me either."

She stopped and took a deep breath.

"Take your time, it's alright," I said, now holding her hand in one of mine, with my other hand gently rubbing her forearm.

She took another moment before continuing, "Then one night we went to a movie, just the two of us. And it was a great night until he started talking about how no one was at his house...and how he wanted me to go home with him to..."

She stopped and looked away. I rubbed her arm a little more as she started shaking again.

"Did you?" I asked.

"No! No, I wasn't ready for anything like that!" she said quickly, her eyes suddenly much wider, "And that's what I told him...but he didn't like that answer."

My muscles tensed. Somehow more tears started to glint in her eyes.

"He got angry. He hit me hard over and over again. I tried to run, but he grabbed me and nearly pulled my arm out of its socket. I think I even blacked out for a minute. By the time he was done, I had a black eye and I was covered in bruises. Everything hurt."

"Did anyone try to stop him?"

She shook her head, "The lot was empty. No one else even saw it happen."

A tear escaped and she tried to take deep, choked breaths. I shushed her softly and pulled her closer, rocking her slightly in my arms.

"And when he finally stopped, it was like he came out of a trance. Like he'd just realized what he was doing. Suddenly he was worried about me and about what he'd done. He just kept apologizing for all of it."

I paused a moment before asking.

"So, what did you do?"

"I screamed at him. I told him to leave me alone. To get away from me. Then I walked home. Damien asked me to let him drive me home, but I was scared of what he would do if I got in the car. So, I just kept walking, and he followed me. I guess to make sure I actually made it back. When I got there, no one was home because mom was still in the hospital. Damien got out of his car and tried to follow me inside, but I told him to go away. That I wanted nothing to do with him. Then I locked myself in the house. After that, I just sat in my room and cried the whole night."

I rubbed her back gently.

"He still comes by the house though. He doesn't really go away. He always wants to be around Melvin for some reason or another, so I have to go out or hide somewhere in the house when he's there or I have a breakdown."

I raised an eyebrow.

"Wait, Melvin doesn't know?"

She shook her head.

"Why didn't you tell him?"

"I didn't know how," she said, her voice cracking again, "They've been like brothers since they were little. I didn't know what to do."

She started to cry again. I rocked her in my arms once more. Then she raised her hands up to cover her face, feeling embarrassed.

"Please don't tell anyone. Especially not Melvin."

"Okay," I murmured.

I reached for her hands and gently pulled them away, but she quickly moved them back over her face.

"Damien's the only person I've ever dated. I was sixteen and we'd only been together for a year and I just –"

I shushed her and gave her a gentle squeeze, cutting off her rambling.

"I understand. You don't have to explain yourself. It's okay."

Soon she calmed down and snuggled against me.

"Logan, it's not that I don't want to go out with you," she said slowly, "I just...I can't go through something like that again. It's been haunting me for almost a year because I couldn't tell anyone."

I pulled back a little and put a hand under her chin, gently lifting it to look at her face.

"You told me," I pointed out.

She bit her lip again, unsure of what to say.

"Are you scared I'll be like him?" I asked.

She sniffled and nodded timidly. She tensed as I pulled her closer, but I shushed her and rubbed her back again until her muscles eased.

"I promise, no matter what, I will never do anything like that to you. Ever. And I know my word probably isn't much to you after everything you've been through, but I think you should know that."

She sniffled again and nuzzled my shoulder.

"One night," she said.

"What?"

"I'll go out with you for one night."

I pulled away, raising an eyebrow, "Really?"

"Yes, but I have some conditions."

"Like what?"

"I want to drive."

"Totally fine. Anything else?"

"I want to pick where we go to dinner, if that's okay," her voice was almost too low to hear.

I smiled and nodded, "That's fine, just don't break my bank account. Believe it or not, selling popcorn doesn't pay much."

She gave me a small smile, "Maybe the popcorn smell is supposed to be payment enough."

"Maybe," I replied with a grin.

She rolled onto her back, staring silently at the sky.

"Hey," I said

She turned her head.

"If at any point you are uncomfortable during the date, we'll stop. Immediately. We can go home and we never have to do it again if you don't want to."

She seemed surprised but nodded. I started to get up, but she stopped me.

"Can we just...stay here for a minute?" she asked nervously, "I don't want dad and Mel to be worried when I get home.

"Yeah, whatever you want."

I laid back down. She curled up to me again.

"You sure don't seem worried about me right now," I teased.

She laughed a little and said, "Don't ruin the moment Logan."

I smiled and wrapped an arm around her, gently holding her shoulder. I was shocked that she had yes, especially after everything she had told me. I thought if I got an answer at all, it would be one of those "I'll think about it" kind of things I heard women say in movies before never actually thinking about it. I never thought I would get a yes.

I am still not sure how long we stayed there. We watched the birds fly overhead while snuggling together. At one point, she sat up and looked around, as if waiting for something, then settled down again.

"I like it when you're comfortable around me," I said, "Makes me feel cozy."

"Shut up you dork," she said with a grin.

The next time she sat up, she said, "We should go. Mel will start calling me before long."

"He's really overprotective, isn't he?"

"What makes you say that?"

"The fact that every time you and I are together alone for more than a few minutes, he's texting me about 'Where are y'all at man?' and 'Dude, remember, that's my sister. This better not be what I think it is,'" I said, making a poor imitation of Melvin's voice as I quoted him.

Her cheeks turned red and she asked, "How often does he do that?"

"Literally every time you and I are out alone or get separated from the group."

Her face turned a shade brighter with embarrassment, "I'm going to kill him!"

I burst into laughter and hugged her, "So, you do like me."

"Shut up Logan!"

She tried to wiggle out of my grip but I held her close to me. Her skin was so hot from the embarrassment it radiated off of her.

"How long have you liked me for?" I asked curiously.

"I'm going to kick your ass Logan," she growled.

"You might have some problems with that

since I've got you already."

She glared at me. I smiled before letting her go.

"Let's just go home," she said, walking away quickly to move past the subject. I stood and matched her pace.

When we were close to the road, I grabbed her bag out of the ditch and put it on the dirt road. She stepped over the trench and grabbed it while I crawled out.

"When do you want to go out?" she asked awkwardly as we started walking again.

I thought for a moment, then said, "Are you free tomorrow night?"

"Yeah, I'm off work, so that'll be good."

"Where do you want to go to dinner?"

"Not sure yet. Depends on what else you have planned."

"Yeah, I was mostly just waiting to see if you would actually go out with me first."

"Well, you have a day to figure it out."

"Yeah, but I still don't know about everything we could do."

"You're smart. You'll figure it out."

When we reached the car, I started driving again and took her home. She slowly started dozing off.

I pulled up onto the driveway and turned to her. She was sleeping peacefully, to the point I didn't want to wake her up, but I knew I had to. I shook her shoulder lightly until she lifted her head.

"You're home sleepyhead," I said softly.

She rubbed her eyes a little and picked up her bag.

"Are you okay now?" I asked.

The fear was gone. She was smiling again.

"Yeah. Yeah, I'm okay."

She could tell I did not fully believe her and added, "Really, I'm fine. I feel a lot better after that."

She yawned and added, "Being emotional just makes me tired."

"Well then, go get some rest," I said, "If you need to talk, you know where to find me."

She opened the door and gave me one more closed-mouth smile before walking onto the porch.

First Impressions

Call me crazy, but I spent the rest of the evening planning. I even asked Jared to help me, seeing as how I kept second guessing myself. There was always the classic dinner and a movie option, but I was worried about setting her off again if the movie was later at night. I did not tell Jared that of course. I just told him I wanted to do something different.

"Does she like history?" he asked while we sat at the kitchen table, trying to put a plan together.

"Yeah. It's her favorite subject."

"Alright, start from there. There's a little history museum at the edge of town that you can go to, then go to dinner and just talk. Simple and gives you plenty to talk about."

I nodded and wrote down the address, slipping it into my jacket pocket when I went to bed that night.

The next morning, I jumped out of bed and looked through my closet, trying to find something better to wear than my go to. I decided to wear jeans with a set of boots and a navy button-up shirt. After setting it all out on the bed, I walked downstairs to eat breakfast.

Jared was already downstairs eating his morning oatmeal while sitting in his recliner. I looked in the fridge for eggs. Oliver ran behind me and bumped my calf with his nose. I turned and scratched his ear, then grabbed the carton and washed my hands. I then grabbed a bowl and cracked two eggs in it to beat them.

Jared took a sip of coffee and turned to me.

"Ready for your date?" he asked.

"I think so. Then again I could still mess it all up."

"You'll be fine. Stop worrying so much," he said between bites.

"Easy for you to say. How many dates have you been on?"

"Fewer than you think. I haven't been out in years."

I grabbed a pan from the cabinet and poured the eggs in to scramble.

"Why not?"

"To put it simply, there's no one around here that's really my type and interested in me."

"Well, no offense, but you're almost forty. Your dating pool is getting smaller."

He chuckled and said, "Yes, I guess it is."

I finished cooking my eggs, then put them on a glass plate and filled the pan with water as I set it in the sink. I added a slice of cheese to my eggs, then grabbed a fork from the drawer and sat on the couch. Jared continued sipping his drink.

Oliver still followed me, now attracted by the smell of fresh eggs and cheese. He jumped on the couch and tried to take a bite.

"Hey!" I yelped as I yanked the plate away from him.

Jared nearly spit coffee back in his mug as he watched Oliver chase my plate until I stood. I tried to step away from the couch, but he reached up, placing his front paws on my arm and standing on his hind legs. I pinched a chunk of egg out of the pile and threw it on the floor. While Oliver leaped after it, I hurried to sit at the table.

"I should've warned you," Jared chuckled, "Eggs are his favorite."

"Well thanks, that would've been good information five minutes ago."

"I know, but it was so much fun to watch."

By then, Daisy had run into the room and was sniffing around Oliver, trying to figure out what he just ate. She followed the scent until she reached me, then put her paws on my thigh in an attempt to pull herself up onto my lap.

"Alright, I'm eating upstairs if you need me," I said as I stood.

"That's probably best."

He called the dogs to him, giving me enough time to get to my room and close the door. I turned on the TV and ate my eggs, then sat back for a bit to watch the rest of the episode. When it was over, I walked to the bathroom to brush my teeth. Moments after I started, my phone vibrated and I checked it to see a text from Ashley. I smiled a little and opened the message.

We never talked about it, but what time do I need to come by?

6 ok?

Sounds good to me. See you tonight :)

See you tonight

I set the phone down on the nightstand.

I hope she's feeling okay today, I thought.

I was going to go out in the backyard for a bit, maybe play fetch with the dogs, but it started raining in the afternoon. I decided to take a shower and shave to get ready instead. After shaving, I buttoned up the shirt and flattened the slight creases that had formed while I put it on. I checked my chin and jawline, making sure I did not miss anywhere while shaving, then walked downstairs again.

Jared walked in the back door as I reached the first floor, wearing a set of his yard work clothes covered in mud and rainwater. He closed the door, then turned and looked at me.

"Wow, somebody cleaned up," he joked.

"First impressions, right?"

"First impressions? I think it's a little late for that, don't you?"

I rolled my eyes, "You know what I mean."

He nodded and said, "You look nice."

He took off his gardening gloves and threw them in the laundry room.

"How long until you have to go?"

"She should be here any minute now."

"You're not picking her up?" he asked, a bit surprised.

"She insisted on driving. I'm covering the rest of the date."

He nodded once again, "Well, I'm going to get cleaned up. Good luck and have a good date. Make sure you're back by ten."

"I will, thanks."

He looked at me one last time, pausing to

straighten the collar of my shirt, then began the trek up to his room on the third floor. I sat nervously on the couch, waiting for Ashley to knock on the door. My palms started sweating. I wiped them on my jeans.

Relax. It's going to be fine.

I remembered my jacket was still upstairs and hurried up to grab it. It was a black leather jacket with a hood. One of the only things I had left from when I lived with my parents. I put it on while I walked back downstairs, making it just as Ashley knocked.

I took a deep breath and ran my hands over my clothes, then walked to the front door. When I opened it, I froze. Ashley stood there with that brilliant smile, wearing a pair of skinny jeans, an olive green blouse, black combat boots, and a black jacket. She had the hood on to defend against the pouring rain, but I could still see that under it she was wearing a light layer of makeup, something she almost never wore.

"Hey," she said.

"Hi," I replied nervously.

Hi? Really? That's all you can say to her right now?

I cleared my throat and added, "You look really nice Ash."

"Thanks, you do too," she replied.

Then I heard a low grumble. We both looked down to see Oliver standing defensively next to me.

Oh no.

Ashley did not back away or run in terror like I thought she would. She crouched down and put her hand close to Oliver's nose so he could smell it. He sniffed it for a moment, then the wrinkles in his muzzle smoothed and he started to lick her hand.

She scratched behind his ears, then his side. His back foot started tapping on the ground.

"How did you do that?" I asked.

"Ollie and I know each other, it's just been a while since the last time I came over."

Oliver licked her hand again as she stood, then hurried off inside the house.

"Ready to go?" she asked.

"Uh, yeah. Whenever you are."

She started back to her car. I put on my hood and closed the door, using my house key to lock it. I hurried into the passenger seat.

"Where are we going?" she asked.

"Jared suggested this museum near town, if you're interested."

"Oh boy," she said, her voice containing a hint of sarcasm.

"What's wrong with that?"

"If it's the one I'm thinking of, I've seen it about a dozen times. Jared and my dad have been friends since Jared moved onto the street ten years ago. They're a couple of war buffs and they took Mel and I a lot growing up."

Wish I knew that sooner, I thought, scrambling to figure out something else we could do, but I still did not know the town very well.

"If you want, I have a suggestion instead," she said.

I turned to her, "And what's that?"

"Well, there's an arcade in town if you want to go. It only costs a few dollars to get in."

"What about actually paying for the games? I don't really have a roll of quarters on me."

"No need. They wire the machine so all you

have to do is press a button, and the machine reads it the same way it would if you put a coin in."

I smiled, "That sounds really cool actually."

"Well, I am the cool one between the two of us," she joked with a grin.

"I don't think so. I'm just still learning about this town."

"Excuses, excuses."

We talked the whole way to the arcade. It was in the middle of town, halfway between our street and the school.

"It's that building there. Just a heads up, it's usually packed on Saturdays," she said as she parked, pointing at the building.

It was nestled in the far corner of an outdoor shopping mall and while the walls were plain white, the windows were amazing. One window was covered with a painting of arcade characters clashing with one another. On the next window, there were more seemingly causing mischief. I smiled at the familiar images of a knight, a gorilla, ghosts, and spaceships in flight.

"This is sick," I said eagerly.

"I told you," she said as got out of the car.

I got out and followed her to the concrete awning in front of the building. We took our hoods off and she preened her hair.

"I'm definitely not saying we should go somewhere else, but aren't we a little overdressed for an arcade?" I asked.

"Logan, people literally come here to play games before prom in dresses and suits."

I raised my eyebrows, then said, "Then why did we all go to dinner before prom instead?"

She laughed and said, "Blame Melvin, he was the one in charge of the group plans."

"Okay, we need to have a serious sanity check done on your brother."

"I've been telling dad that for years."

I took a few steps ahead to open the door for her.

"Look at you going out of your way to make a good impression," she teased.

"Well, I am still hoping for a second date."

"Let's get past the first one, hotshot."

"So, I'm hot now, huh?"

"Don't put words in my mouth you dork."

She hurried inside. I followed close behind, grabbing a few dollars from my wallet to give to the man at the small podium near the door. Ashley suddenly grabbed my arm and pulled me down a long row of vintage arcade machines.

"Ash, where are we going?"

"You'll see."

We reached the back of the building. To the right were more machines lined up along the wall. To the left there was a snack bar. In between there was a couch with a TV sitting in front of it. And there it was on the floor. My favorite console. One I had not seen since I was eight.

"No freaking way," I said.

"I remember how much you like these," she said with a smile.

I hurried to the empty couch before someone else could get to it. The retro console was surrounded by five cartridges for games I had not seen since I was a kid. Games my family had until my dad sold them for extra money when he lost his investors. Frustration hit me for a brief second as I remembered him getting rid of the games rather than drinking a few fewer glasses while out with his friends.

"I wish you had told me this was here sooner," I said as she sat down beside me.

"Yeah, but then you would have spent all your time here instead of doing your homework."

"Touché, but if you were that worried about my homework, you would've hidden this until after finals next week."

My eyes skimmed over the games sitting out.

"Well, are you going to play it or just stare at it?" she asked.

"I'm trying to decide on a two player game, but I don't know if you want to face me in *Crash Companions*."

"And why's that?"

"Uh, because I would definitely win."

She smirked, "Really? You think so?"

"Oh, I know so. *Crash* is my jam."

"Somebody's a little cocky."

"Alright, fine. You want to play, let's do it. But it's your funeral."

"We'll see about that."

We decided to play two out of three so we would not hog the console all night. I won the first round. I thought I would win the second, but realized she had held out on me in the first. In the second she continuously threw my character off of the platform. I could not land a single hit.

Then the final round came. We each had one life left. I was determined to hold up to my promise to beat her. But I have to admit, she was really good at the game. I glanced over at her. She had a wide smile and rapidly hit the buttons, practically button mashing, but she actually knew what the button combinations would do. By the time I looked back at the screen, I realized my mistake. With a final blow, my character was knocked out of frame.

"Yes!" she shouted.

"Dang, Maleshi has never failed me before."

She turned to me and said, "Aww, don't feel too bad."

She ruffled my hair. I pulled away, still smiling despite the loss.

"Stay here, I'll be back," she said.

She stood and walked over to the bar, returning a moment later with two bottles. She sat back down and held one out to me.

"Maybe this will make you feel better."

I took the glass bottle and opened it, taking in the familiar smell of root beer.

"First date and you already know me so well," I said.

I took a big swig of it, then said, "I thought I was covering this part of the date and we were splitting dinner."

She shrugged and said, "Well, if you really want to make up for it you could pay for my dinner too."

I grinned and said, "Root beer in exchange for dinner. Sounds fair."

She took a drink from her bottle.

"You know I planned on paying for your dinner anyway, right?" I added.

"I figured. You seem like that kind of guy, but I feel bad not paying for something."

"That kind of guy? What does that mean?"

She leaned close, "The kind of guy who likes it more, traditional. If that makes any sense."

"You really do get me, don't you?"

She smiled and took another drink. I cautiously put my arm around her shoulders and pulled her against me. She nestled closer.

"Maybe I don't. Is this traditional for first dates?" she joked.

"What can I say, I'm a cuddler," I paused, leaning closer to whisper, "Don't tell anyone. It's our secret."

"I think we have a lot of those already. I'll just add it to the vault."

"You're the best."

"Thanks, I know."

"You're also a pain."

"So are you. Any more obvious facts you want to point out?"

"That you're very pretty and I like hanging out with you."

"Aww, you're still a dork. But I like hanging out with you too."

I chuckled and gave her a gentle squeeze, then said, "Alright, what are we playing next?"

We walked around with our drinks, playing about a dozen more games before we left. The one thing that made me happier than the date itself was her demeanor. She was happy. She was talkative and laughing. The Ashley I knew, but with a few added surprises. I knew she played video games, but I did not know how extensively until that night. We talked about the games and characters we loved. Discussed storylines, different games within our favorite series, movies connected to the games, and anything else we could think of. Even surprise twists and endings from games we had both already finished playing, taunting each other with knowledge the other did not have. We were there for hours before we started rubbing our eyes from staring at those screens for way too long.

It was dark out when we finally left. She walked a little closer to me than normal as we stepped outside, her hand brushing past mine. I did not dare to take it, just in case it freaked her out. She unlocked the car and we got in.

"So where are we going for dinner?" I asked.

"Honestly, right now I just want a cheeseburger."

"You keep adding all these brownie points you'll never get rid of me," I joked.

She drove us to a little fast food place near the arcade. We got a burger each and an order of fries to share, sipping on water instead of tea or sodas. We sat across the table from one another as we ate, starting a new conversation once we finished.

"Ashley, can I ask you something?"

"You mean other than the question you just asked?" she replied with a grin.

I smiled a little, "Yes, other than that."

She nodded, "Go ahead."

"After everything you told me, about your previous relationship, why did you say yes?"

Her smile faded, but the look she had yesterday did not come back, luckily. Instead, she gave me a thoughtful look, as if trying to figure that out herself.

"I think it's because you're different from Damien."

"Good different, I hope."

She nodded, then continued, "You're smart, thoughtful, and..." She stopped, as if lost in thought.

"And what?"

"I don't know, it's just different. I trust you a lot more than I ever did Damien. Besides, you're actually interested in how I feel. What I'm thinking. You tried to help me, make me feel better."

"I thought you said he was good in the beginning."

"Yeah, way before we actually really got to know each other. Before we started talking about more serious things. Even when my mom was sick and I wanted to be with her, he always wanted it to be about him. He'd half listen thinking it would get him out of having to really try. With you, it's different. Because you do try, and I don't think it was all just to get a date with me."

I smiled a little.

"I just hope I was right," she said.

"Ash, I would've listened whether that question came up or not."

"Why?"

"You and Melvin were the first people I connected with when I came here. And you were the person I, for lack of a better term, latched on to. When we met, all I wanted was to be your friend."

"Alright, so here's a personal question for you. When did you become, for lack of a better term, interested in me?"

"Just interested, or...?"

"Okay fine, when did you know for sure that you wanted to go out with me?"

I thought about it for a moment before saying,

"Do I have to answer?"

"I answered your question, it's only fair."

I snapped my fingers jokingly, "Dang."

I thought for a bit, because I really had not thought about it before.

"Well, don't leave me in suspense here," she said impatiently.

"Well, I have to think for a minute. I mean, I kind of had a crush on you back at the basketball game, but I'm trying to think of when I knew one hundred percent."

"Really? That far back?"

"Yeah, but again, I wasn't completely sure then."

I thought hard about it, then looked into her eyes and said, "That movie night a few weeks ago. The one at your house, when it was just you, me, Melvin, Adrian, and Viv."

She laughed.

"What did I say wrong now?"

"Nothing, it's just, I looked terrible that night! I was so tired I came down in my pajamas, looked like a slob, and didn't even make it through the movie!" .

"And yet, I thought you were still so beautiful."

When I realized what I had said, I froze. She blushed a bit, suddenly looking nervous.

"Maybe I should shut up now," I said quickly.

"It's okay. That's really sweet actually," she said.

Slowly, her hand moved across the table toward me until it was resting on my arm. Then she blushed even more and moved away, seeming to suddenly realize what she was doing.

Finally! You said something right, I thought.

I checked my watch, then looked back at her. It

was a little past nine-thirty.

"Not that this hasn't been fun or anything, but we should probably get home. My curfew's at ten, and if you don't get home by ten thirty Melvin's going to start blowing up my phone."

"Trust me, he's not patient or forgiving when it comes to that," she warned, "I was five minutes late for a dinner event one time and when I looked at my phone, he had already sent me about fifteen gifs of cartoon characters tapping their feet impatiently."

I laughed and we threw away our trash, then started home.

By the time we reached our street, the rain had finally slowed to a drizzle. She parked at the curb in front of my house, then walked with me to the front door. As we walked up the driveway, I tried to make conversation.

"Did you have fun?" I asked, suddenly nervous again.

"Yeah, I had a great night Logan," she replied.

"Would you, maybe, want to do this again sometime?" I asked as we walked up the porch steps.

"Not next week with all the testing, but yeah. I can safely say that I would like to go out again."

I raised an eyebrow at her, "With me, right? There's not anyone else you'd want to go with instead."

Her eyes narrowed. I laughed.

"Yes you, ya big dummy," she said as she punched my shoulder playfully.

"Good. Just checking."

I did not know what else to say, or what to do, so I nervously stood near the door with her. Then

I leaned forward a bit for a hug, but she quickly pushed me back.

"Whoa there," she said.

"Great, what did I do now?" I asked, irritated with myself once again.

"I hope you weren't planning on trying anything just now."

I gave her a confused look, then raised my hands as I said, "No, no, just a hug, that's it. Nothing more."

When I felt the heat on my face, I was glad that the porch light was dim.

"Good," she said, "Because you'll have to try a lot harder than one good date."

The serious look disappeared, replaced by a mischievous grin. She was messing with me.

"You jerk!" I said.

She laughed, then leaned over for a hug. I hugged her back, then told her goodnight and watched her walk back to the car. She waited a moment for me to step in the door before driving home.

Days to Forget, Nights to Remember

I filled in the final scantron bubbles, then the bell rang. The last bell I would ever have to hear. Final exams were over for seniors. We were set free until graduation night in a couple of weeks, and during that time everyone else would have more time to study, prepare, and, of course, be constantly stressed out about their grades.

I stood and handed my test forms to Mrs. Carey, wishing her a good summer break. Then I grabbed my bag on the way out the door. I did not go far, waiting for Ashley since she was the only other senior in our Statistics class. Sadly, Diego and Natalie were juniors, so they could not escape the mountains of homework yet.

She stepped out a few minutes later, but I stepped in an indentation in the wall to hide. She looked around for a moment, before walking in my general direction, unaware that I was waiting for her. She looked down at her phone as she passed me, typing a message to someone. I slowly followed behind her. Then my phone chimed. She turned around to glare at me.

"You were going to try to scare me, weren't you?" she asked suspiciously.

"I have no idea what you're talking about. Do you really think I would try something like that?"

"Yeah, one hundred percent I believe that."

I pulled my phone out of my pocket and saw the message from Ashley in my notifications.

Where did u go?

"That's sabotage," I said.

She grinned and stepped forward, giving me a warm embrace. I tightly hugged her back.

"How do you think you did?" she asked.

"I mean, I think I passed, but I wouldn't ask for more than that."

"I didn't think it was that bad."

"Stat makes my brain hurt, okay?"

She squeezed me tighter and said, "I'm just glad we're finally done."

"Yeah, until college starts."

"Shh, let's not talk about that right now."

She reluctantly pulled away and we walked down the hall together. We still had not started holding hands yet, so we just walked close together, trying to stay quiet in case other students were finishing up their classes or tests.

When we walked outside, the other seniors in our group, Melvin, Adrian, and Vivian, were all standing outside chatting excitedly.

"What's going on out here?" I asked.

They looked over and greeted us, then Melvin clapped me on the shoulder as we joined them.

"Hey Logan, Ash told me that you guys went to an arcade for your date last weekend."

I raised an eyebrow, unsure of what he was

getting at, "Yeah we played some games and spent pretty much the whole time talking about them."

"So, would you consider yourself a gamer?"

"I guess."

"Melvin, would you just tell him?" Vivian said.

"Alright, alright, take it easy," he replied, then turned back to me as he continued with, "Look man, this group has a bit of a tradition. Usually, this weekend would be a couple weeks before finals for all of us, which is when we get together and play videogames to chill before testing. Obviously, we're all done, but we're still doing it to hang out with the rest of the group. And since you're new, I decided to buy a new game we can all try together, if you want to play."

"What game is it?"

"It's a new VR game called *Seventy Five Lives*."

"With the most basic name they could've possibly chosen," Vivian chimed in.

"Yes, but it looks like a good game. You have to go through seventy five levels that take place in different locations and time periods from history until you finish, well, all seventy five."

"It's pretty cool," Ash said, "Melvin saved up a bunch of money to buy the equipment for everyone so we can all play together."

"Have any of you actually played it yet?" I asked.

"No, that's the one annoying thing. It's not actually out yet, but I preordered it and it's coming next week. So, we'll have to wait longer than usual, but we're still going to stick with tradition," Melvin said.

"How many people can play at once?"

"The whole group can play at the same time as long as we have all the gear, which I made sure to get all thirteen sets."

I gave him a confused look, "How is that even possible?"

"Some new tech the company developed. Basically, every order has a group code that they add in. If everyone types in that code, we can all play together. It's all in the description."

"When does it come in?"

"Friday, so we can play on Saturday. That gives me time to get the game room setup," Melvin said excitedly, "And from the photos they've released, the graphics look amazing! Completely lifelike!"

"So, what do you say Logan?" Adrian asked, "Are you in?"

"Sure, sounds fun," I said.

We talked more, a little about the game, but more about how we thought our exams went, then we began parting ways to go home.

Ash, Melvin, and I walked together to the lot while Vivian and Adrian walked to the front of the school. Vivian was always picked up by her parents or taken home by friends or Adrian since she could not drive. Her parents were picking her up that day, and pickup was only allowed at the front of the school.

Melvin and Ashley had carpooled to campus, but when they got to his red truck, Melvin paused.

He stopped Ashley and said, "Who are you riding home with?" He already seemed to know what her answer would be.

She turned to me, "Mind if I tag along with you?"

"If he's okay with it," I said, "I'm not too keen on having my ass handed to me if not."

Melvin laughed, "It's fine. If y'all go out though, you know what time she's supposed to be back by."

I nodded, and he waved goodbye as he drove away.

"Do you want to do anything, or just go home?" I asked as we walked to my car.

"Well. I don't want to go home just yet, but I don't really know what we should do either," she replied.

"It might seem predictable, but how about dinner and a movie?"

She smiled, "That sounds perfect. You can't mess with the classics."

We got in my car and I started the engine.

"Well, it's only four. Do you want to walk around the mall a bit before dinner?" I asked.

She nodded, then buckled in. The mall was only a few minutes from the campus. I parked near the doors in the nearly empty lot. That was no surprise, since malls were starting to die out. We walked inside to find the building just as empty as the parking lot. The only people around were retail associates, food service associates, and a few scattered shoppers. Ashley and I walked a few laps around the inside of the mall, mostly window shopping other than a few stores we stopped in to look around.

When we finished our walk, we still had a few minutes before seven, and the movie was at eight. We sat on a bench in the mall, but we did not talk. We just sat close and listened to the sound of shoes tapping the tiles.

We decided to have dinner in the food court

since we were already there. We ordered some pizza from one restaurant. Ashley glanced over at another restaurant as we sat down. I looked over to see a place called The Ivory Lotus.

"Do you want to try that?" I asked.

She shrugged and said, "I don't know. I just thought maybe we could balance it out a little bit, if you want."

"I'll try anything. What do they have?"

"From what I heard it's supposed to be all natural food. A lot of vegetables and things like that."

"Veggies and pizza. I'm in."

"Look, now you're the one getting brownie points," she said.

"Brownies are good too," I joked, "Where did you see those?"

She rolled her eyes, smiling slightly.

I stood and walked over to order a steamed vegetable platter, then brought it back for us to share.

"You know most people would think this combination is crazy, right?" I said.

"Yeah, but that's not my problem. My only problem right now is that I'm hungry."

We ate our food quietly. Ashley was the one who broke the silence.

"Are you still planning on going to college here?" she asked nervously.

I nodded, "Yeah, are you?"

"That's the plan."

"Do you think you'll go live on campus or stay at home?"

"I don't know. It's not like I live very far. I would just drive the same amount I do now. Plus some of the scholarships I applied for don't specifically have to go toward housing or tuition. I could use some of it to pay for books instead of a dorm. Maybe even get a new computer for school."

"That would be nice to start with."

"What about you? Are you staying on campus?"

"Probably not. I don't qualify for as many scholarships as you do. Jared offered to cover the cost if I wanted to, but I'm not going to take it."

"Why not?"

I shrugged, "I just don't think there's a need to. I don't live very far away either, so I'm not too worried about it. Besides, I don't want some stranger looking at all my stuff when I'm out. And even if it doesn't happen, that's all I would be thinking about."

She took a drink of water. I remembered a question that I had wanted to ask her for a while.

"Can I ask you a weird question?"

"Go ahead," she said curiously.

"So, you and Melvin are in the same grade because he got held back, but if you're only about a year apart, how did the two different moms thing happen?"

"I was waiting for this one," she said, then took another drink before continuing, "Mel is about a year and a half older than me. His mom had a thing with dad before he met my mom. They weren't married, but they dated for a long time. From what dad told us, they broke up before finding out she was pregnant. And when they did find out, she was scared of having to raise him, especially by herself. She wanted to give Mel up for adoption, but dad asked her to give him custody instead so he could take care of Melvin, and she could see him any time she wanted to."

"Sounds like a pretty good deal."

"He thought it was, and she agreed to it. But as soon as she signed full custody over to dad, she disappeared."

"What do you mean?"

"She just took off. Dad said he didn't know why, but whatever the reason, she's never come back and dad hasn't heard from her since."

My eyes widened in surprise, "That's crazy. How did Melvin feel about it when your dad told him?"

"Surprisingly, he took it pretty well. He said that he understands that she was probably just scared."

I took it in for a moment, then she added, "Plus he said that my mom being there made things okay. She treated him like her own kid and he never thought of her as anything other than his mother."

"That's pretty cool. I'm glad it worked out for him."

"Me too. I'd rather have a goofy brother who's loving life than one who's miserable and obsessively looking for his birth-mom. It would probably drive him crazy."

"So how did your dad meet your mom?"

"Actually, it was around when dad started working in television. He changed jobs after breaking up with Mel's mom."

She paused for another drink.

"My parents met at a local station and became friends. Then they got to know each other better and started dating about a month later. When Melvin was born, he made the custody agreement, but didn't tell her until after."

"That sounds like a bad idea."

"Yeah, remember that," she said with a wink.

I raised an eyebrow, "What does that mean?"

"It means that you better not leave me out of the loop on anything."

"Yes ma'am."

She grinned, then said, "Mom wasn't that upset when she found out though. They had already talked about how his ex-girlfriend was pregnant, they just didn't know she would abandon Mel like that. And they already talked about having a family, so she had no problem with taking him in. Dad proposed a few days later. Long story short, she said yes, they got married soon after. Then mom got pregnant with me. Nine months later," she paused while lifting her hands up dramatically, "Here I am."

I grinned, then hesitantly said, "I'm sorry about what happened to her."

Her smile fell, but not completely. Like the face of a person with hope despite the hurt they felt.

"Me too, but I think she would be happy that I met someone like you."

I smiled, unsure of what to say. She reached for her phone and her eyes widened slightly.

"We better go or we'll be late," she said.

"Time spaz," I teased.

"Shut up."

We threw our trash away and walked outside. Our movie was supposed to start at eight, and it was seven fifty. Ashley walked at a quicker pace than normal and I had to speed up to match her pace.

"Ash, it's okay if we're a little late."

"And miss the previews?"

"Uh, yeah. I'm fine with that."

"I'm not. They've had some good movies out lately and I want to know what's next."

The theater was just across the street from the mall, so we walked rather than wasting the gas. We hurried across the crosswalk then slowed.

Once we were in the theater parking lot, I said, "Race ya," then dashed to the front doors.

"Logan!"

She ran after me but could not quite keep up. When I reached the front door, I stopped and turned. Her pace slowed as she came closer.

"Looks like I won," I said with a grin.

"That's because you took me off guard."

"Right, sure it was."

She rolled her eyes and said, "Whatever."

We both stood awkwardly for a moment, neither of us sure what to do next. She cleared her throat and said, "The movie's about to start. We better hurry."

I nodded and held the door for her, then jumped ahead to pay for the tickets. Ashley walked to the concession stand and bought us drinks and popcorn, then we walked to theater eight. As we walked down the hall, I noticed she had started walking with a slight limp, but considering she was trying to hide it, I decided not to mention it yet.

Since the movie had already been out for a couple of months, the theater only had a few other people inside. Either crazed fans or those who still had not seen it yet. We picked a couple of seats toward the back, staying quiet so we would not disturb anyone. Once we were settled, we whispered softly, talking about the movies that were coming out. Previews for a comedy, an action film, and a horror movie all flashed across the screen one after the other. Then the movie finally started. I stopped eating the popcorn. My eyes were glued to the screen, my attention only shifting long enough to take a drink every now and then.

But now I don't really remember what was happening in the movie, just that something happened somewhere in the middle. My brow furrowed as something touched my hand, then wrapped around it. Fingers became intertwined with mine. I turned a bit to see that they belonged to Ashley, but she would not look at me. I could see the stress in her eyes as she waited for my reaction. Her cheeks became slightly brighter. I smiled, then sat back again to watch the movie. Soon she rested her head on my shoulder, and all of my focus on the film was gone. All I could think about was her and how I did not want to move, just so she would be comfortable. My thumb gently massaged the back of her hand. Her muscles softened as her worries dissipated. I was too focused on the snuggling to pay attention to anything else. I missed the rest of the movie that night.

We were together every day after that. The next few days mostly consisted of us hanging out at her house or mine. Of course, being at her house led to me meeting her dad. It was not the most comfortable night of my life.

Mr. Evans was a lean man that towered over me, which told me where Melvin got his height from. His black hair was filled with patches of grey, acquired after years of stress from work and raising two children. He had a fairly friendly demeanor, but his eyes told another story. The kind of story that ended with my ass kicked if I hurt his daughter. I did not even sit too close to Ashley the day I met him because he was so intimidating. Things only got worse after he sat in an armchair and began cleaning a rifle right in front of me, despite Ashley's complaints. Eventually, he asked me general questions about where I was from, my hobbies, what my major would be, and so on. Although, it was hard to focus with what I assumed to be a loaded firearm only about two feet away from me. Not that I was afraid of guns. Just the man holding it.

At one point, he stepped out to go to the bathroom. I relaxed slightly since the gun was just sitting against the chair and not being held. Ashley rubbed my shoulder and I flinched when she touched me.

"Relax," she said, "He's just trying to scare you."

"Oh, really? I hadn't noticed."

"Don't be a smartass," she warned.

I rubbed my forehead and said, "Sorry, I'm just nervous."

"Oh, really? I hadn't noticed," she said mockingly.

I glared a little, but she scooted closer and said, "Just relax. I don't think it's even loaded."

"If it's not, then your dad plays some sick mind games."

"Yeah. You're a guy, and dads want to scare the crap out of them. You better get used to it."

I heard the bathroom door open and flinched. Ashley started to sit back, but gave my hand a light squeeze before moving further away.

I nervously looked around the living room while we waited for him to come back. The floor was covered in tan tiles surrounded by slightly darker walls. Ash and I were sitting on a brown sectional sofa with a few throw pillows that matched the tiles. Soft red throw blankets were folded and draped behind us. A large television sat on top of a simple, wooden entertainment center that seemed to be handmade. A coffee table with a couple of vacant coasters rested between the sofa and the entertainment center. To my right sat Mr. Evans' armchair, which matched the sofa. To the left were tall windows revealing the backyard. In between the windows and on each side of the television were photos of Ashley's immediate and what I assumed to be extended family.

Mr. Evans still had not returned, so I stood to pace a little and get rid of my nervous energy. Ashley watched me quietly. As I walked, one photo in particular caught my attention. I took a step closer. Ashley and Melvin stood at the front of the photo, seemingly no older than twelve when the photograph was taken. Melvin was wearing a grey suit that showed off a frame much smaller than the one he had at the present. Ashley wore a glittering blue dress and small heels. Behind them stood Mr. Evans and presumably Mrs. Evans. She looked to be only slightly shorter than her husband. She had dark wavy hair like Ashley, but it was much shorter and thinner. Her eyes were a deep brown that glittered because of whatever light source was used when the photo was taken, or maybe the flash of the camera. She wore a long black dress and Mr. Evans wore a black suit with a little blue handkerchief in the breast pocket. In the background I could see what looked like the inside of a church, with white tables and decorations far away from the figures.

Ashley stood and walked up next to me. I

pointed at the picture.

"Is that your mom?"

She nodded and stood a little closer.

"When was it taken?"

"A few years ago, at a cousin's wedding. It was right before she got sick."

I turned to her and noticed the glimmer of tears forming. I wrapped an arm around her shoulders and gave her a light squeeze.

"I miss her," she said weakly.

"I know," I replied softly.

I wiped a tear away from her cheek, then pulled her in for a tight hug. She squeezed me back. As I held her, I could feel a small pool forming on my shoulder. I leaned forward to rest my chin on her shoulder and swayed slightly. She nestled closer, as if to hide from the world. I didn't stop her.

Then I looked up a bit and saw Mr. Evans. He looked longingly at his daughter from the hall, no doubt filled with the desire any good father would have to hold their child and tell them that everything would be okay. Then his gaze shifted to me. Our eyes met for a brief moment. I was afraid of what he might say or do. But he only gave me a nod, then turned and walked back down the hall for a moment to leave us alone.

Does that mean he approves? I wondered.

Ashley started to pull away and I loosened my grip. She rubbed her face to wipe away a few more tears, still sniffling. She wrapped her arms around her chest, as if hugging herself, or trying to hold the emotions in. I reached out and touched her shoulder. She took a deep breath to calm herself.

"Thank you," she said, obviously still feeling

vulnerable.

"I'm here for you," I said simply.

Then Mr. Evans walked in again, swiftly and with purpose. Ashley quickly stepped out of the room to wash her face. I sat back down on the sofa while Mr. Evans returned to his armchair, but he didn't pick up the gun. He looked down the hall and waited until the bathroom door shut, then turned back to me.

"That was good, what you just did," he said awkwardly, as if unsure of how to react.

"Thanks," I responded nervously, "I was just trying to make her feel better."

"Yes, I know. I appreciate it."

We sat in tense silence for a moment, then he cleared his throat.

"I don't know what she has or hasn't told you, but my daughter has had to deal with a lot of...unsavory company in her life," he said in his silky southern accent, "She's been hurt by a lot of people she thought she was close to. And most of it happened around the time my wife passed."

I nodded, quietly taking in his words.

"Please understand that I act this way to protect her. I know more than she thinks, and I know that the last boy she was with hurt her, even if she won't give me all the details. And to be frank, I thought you would be just like him. But it seems I may have misjudged you."

"Was he so bad he wouldn't even hug her?"

"Not often," he paused before continuing, "and when he did, there was something off about it."

"What do you mean?"

He hesitated, seeming to believe he had said

too much already, "He just seemed to do it because he thought he had to. Not because he wanted to."

His fist clenched and he added, "I knew his father well growing up, and they're more alike than I would have ever thought, but not the good qualities."

I waited a moment before saying, "Well I'm sorry you both had to deal with that."

He studied my face carefully, then said, "Look Logan, Ashley has spent a lot of time trying to assure me that you are different. And to some degree, I do agree with her after seeing what you just did. But know that this doesn't mean that I like you."

Wow, great visit, I thought.

He huffed, "But if you make her happy, maybe I'll start to tolerate you."

He stood and walked into the kitchen. I sat there dumbstruck.

Well, I guess that's something?

Mr. Evans went upstairs to his home office soon after Ashley came back.

"Remember you two, I'm right upstairs so don't go doing anything irresponsible," he hollered.

Ashley put her hands over her face and shouted, "Dad, get out!"

He chuckled as he closed the office door. Ashley still had her head in her hands.

"He's gone now," I said.

"I don't care. I don't want to look up again."

I grinned and wrapped my arms around her. She melted against me as we sat back on the couch. We watched a movie to end the evening before I went home.

The days after that were filled with more movies, talking, and snuggling when our parents were not immediately there to embarrass us. Even Jared was poking fun at me the nights Ashley was over. Especially the night we fell asleep on the couch at my house. We were still exhausted and recovering from stress filled study sessions and just happened to doze off while watching TV together. He said something about "Don't think you'll get away with a sleepover with your girlfriend that easily," or something ridiculous like that. Just to make me want her out of the house as soon as possible so he couldn't continue.

On Thursday morning my phone rang. I checked the caller ID and saw Ashley's photo on the screen. I smiled as I answered the call.

"Good morning," I said.

"Hey. Are you busy today?"

"Not unless you made some plan for us that I didn't know about."

"Don't worry I didn't. I have a question for you though."

"Shoot."

"Would you be willing to go to the gym with me today? I usually go with Viv, but she has a family thing to go to."

"I'm sorry, I'm not willing. You'll have to drag me there in chains," I joked.

I could almost hear her eyes roll, "I think by the time we got there the workout would be done, don't you?"

"Yeah, probably."

"So, will you? Please? I haven't gone in a few days and I'm getting antsy about it."

"Yeah, I'll go. What time?"

"I have to go to work for a bit first. But could

you meet me at the gym around five?"

"I'll be there."

"Thank you. I've gotta go, my shift's about to start."

"Okay, have a good day."

"You too."

Jared had already left for work, so I went out to the backyard to play fetch with the dogs until they were worn out. They ran ahead of me when I opened the door and crawled into their beds to sleep. I checked the time. It was nearly three thirty. I walked up the stairs to my room to change into a plain black t-shirt, shorts, and tennis shoes. Afterwards, I walked back downstairs to fill a water bottle, then hurried out the door to drive into town.

I was excited to go to the gym, which might sound strange to some. I had not been to one since I lived in Denver, not that I was out of shape. I did things like pushups and sit ups in my room, or sometimes I would go on morning jogs to keep in shape. But I had always enjoyed using the machines and the free weights to get stronger. I would play basketball on the indoor court at my old gym too, so I hoped this gym would have one as well.

I parked in the lot for a gym called "Down to Workout." It was some gym that was actually fairly large for a business with a name so haphazardly made it could not be real. Yet, there it was. Painted above the doors in bright blue letters with a mustard yellow background.

My eyes skimmed across the crowded parking lot, searching for Ashley's car. I checked the time to see it was just twenty after five and leaned against my car, giving her a few more minutes before I called to check on her. She beat me to it.

"Hey," I said.

"Hey. Where are you at?"

"The gym parking lot, you?"

"I just parked. Meet me at the door?"

"Yep, see ya there."

I hung up the phone as I walked up to the glass doors and waited. Moments later I saw her walking toward me, still wearing her work clothes with a gym bag in one hand. I pulled her in for a quick hug.

"I wouldn't hug long," she warned, "I'm already gross from work."

"Bad day?"

"No, just busy."

"That's okay, I like the smell of cheeseburgers."

She pulled away and said, "That's just gross."

"No, it just means you smell like cheeseburgers."

"That's not making me feel any better. I'm taking a shower as soon as I get home."

"Well I hope so. Sweat might make you smell like a soggy cheeseburger. Now that is gross."

She punched me in the shoulder and I laughed, then said, "I'm kidding!"

"You're such a pain in the ass," she growled as she opened the door.

"Oh, come on. You must like it to some degree or you wouldn't put up with it," I said while following close behind.

"Whatever."

"See, you didn't deny it."

She shook her head, then said, "Come on, we need to sign in."

While she talked to the woman at the front desk, I looked around the gym. Immediately to my left sat a few vending machines about a foot away from the desk, with doorways to the men and women's respective locker rooms. On the far side of the main floor, treadmills were lined up side by side in front of a line of windows. To my right there was a gap, then a few ellipticals and two stairmaster machines. Behind the cardio equipment were weight machines, from back press and leg extension machines to a cable pulley machine. The far side of the right-hand wall was lined with mirrors, and in front of them were racks with dumbbells, weight plates, and kettle bells of various sizes. The racks were near a row of various benches set up on the right. The left-hand was mostly empty space by the wall, aside from a pullup bar, a few stability balls, and some mats.

Ashley tapped my shoulder and said, "I'm going to go change in the locker room really quick."

I nodded, then did a few stretches while I waited. She walked back out of the locker room wearing a tank top, shorts, and tennis shoes. I looked her over, just for a moment, but she caught me.

She snapped her fingers and said, "Hey, eyes up here."

I felt my face heat up with embarrassment. She smiled a little, then said, "I'm going to use some of the weight machines. I won't be far if you need me."

"Okay, I'll be over here."

She walked toward a leg press machine. I walked to a treadmill to warm up while I tried to figure out what I would do afterwards. I noticed Ashley stretching a couple feet away from the machine so she would be out of the way. I did not look for long though, knowing I might get caught again if she turned around.

It wasn't long before I lost her in the evening crowd as the gym filled with people coming in after work. I tried to just focus on my own workout, not wanting to get in Ashley's way if I tried to stay too close to her. I spent most of the night using free weights, something I had not used in a very long time. It took a while for me to find my sweet spot with the weight since I had lost a bit of my strength from the year before.

After about an hour of lifting, I was exhausted. I decided to just wait for Ash to finish her own workout and found out that there was an indoor basketball court. By then, most of the crowd had already gone home, so the court was empty. I grabbed a ball to dribble and take a few shots while I waited. I was happy to find that the skills I had built up in Denver had stuck after a few practice shots. I had so much fun that I didn't even realize the time until I looked at a wall clock. It was nearly seven. I put the ball away and looked around the main floor for her.

Did she leave?

I did a quick walkthrough and found her sitting on a bench and breathing heavily.

She looks worn out. She was probably waiting on me.

I felt bad at the thought and started toward her. As I stepped closer, I started noticing more. She had a tight grip on her left knee and her muscles were tense. She was grimacing, her teeth clenched as she stared at the floor. I rushed over and crouched down beside her.

"What happened?" I asked.

She came out of her trance, a fearful look joining the pain in her eyes.

"Nothing," she said a bit too quickly, immediately letting go of the knee. Her foot fell to the ground. She winced on impact.

I reached for her knee, but she quickly turned away.

"Really, I'm fine. Just go back to exercising," she added.

She looked pale, almost sickly.

"Ashley."

I gently held her chin and turned her face toward me.

"What happened?"

She swallowed hard, looking skittish.

"I...I..." It was as if she couldn't get the words out.

"It's okay. Talk to me," I said softly.

Her muscles were still stiff, her nerves on edge. I sat next to her and began gently rubbing her upper back to help her relax. The tension slowly eased.

"Please don't be mad," she said weakly.

My brow furrowed, "Mad about what?"

"I...I need to go home. I hurt my knee, really bad."

I crouched back down and reached again, but she started to turn away.

"Ash, I can help, really," I said.

She eyed me warily before giving in. I felt along the sides of her knee.

"Just keep your feet flat, okay?"

She nodded, remaining still while I massaged

at and just above her knee.

"What are you doing?" she asked, suddenly skittish again.

"Ash, just trust me."

I continued to knead the muscles while she watched. She took a couple of deep breaths before the pain started to ease.

"How did you know how to do that?"

"My mom taught me," I said, "She studied to be a doctor when she was younger, but she never had the chance to finish. When I lived in Colorado my parents and I went hiking a lot, so she started teaching me some stuff in case of an emergency."

"Why didn't she finish?"

I shrugged, "She said it was because of dad's job. We just moved too much for her to get through the couple of courses she had left. Plus, after they had me someone had to be home, and he was working twelve hour days. Sometimes more."

"It's too bad she didn't get to be a doctor."

"Yeah, but she always told me she didn't regret it. She said raising and getting to know me was a lot better than she ever imagined the job would be, and sometimes you have to weigh the options. The opportunities against the things you might miss out on."

I continued rubbing her knee as I spoke.

"And she always planned on going back after I finished high school anyway."

I stopped briefly, lost in thought, then continued.

"So, what else did she teach you?" she asked, trying to shift the topic.

"Just some basic things. Treating hypothermia,

shock, burns, heavy bleeding. I could stitch someone up if I absolutely had to, but I'm not great at it. She took me to some classes to get CPR certified too."

"That's really cool."

"Yeah, I'm not a complete knucklehead."

"I never said you were."

"No, but I bet you've probably thought it."

"No, if I think of anyone as a knucklehead it's Melvin."

"Oh yeah, that's right."

We both grinned, then I stood.

"Do you feel better now?" I asked.

She nodded, "Much better."

"Then let's get you home so you can rest."

Her eyes widened slightly, "No, I'm alright. Just go back to your workout."

I sat down with her again.

"Ash, a few minutes ago you said you had to go home."

"And now my leg feels better, so I'm fine."

She tried to stand, but I caught her.

"Ashley, take it easy. That massage is only going to help so much. You need to get home."

"Logan, really, I'm fine."

"No, you're not. Besides, I'm worn out. We've already been here for over an hour."

"That long?"

"Yeah, it's past seven."

She had a frantic look in her eyes, as if preparing to run. I slowly held my hand out for her to take as I stood once again.

"Please Ash."

She hesitated, then cautiously grabbed my hand. I helped her stand, but her knees buckled and she fell forward. I quickly caught her at the waist. Her body stiffened as if bracing for the fall.

"It's alright, I've got you," I said as I helped her steady herself.

I took her left arm and wrapped it around my shoulders, then put my arm around her waist to steady her as we walked.

We felt a slight chill as we stepped outside, despite the fact it was May. She shivered a little and I rubbed her hand with my thumb to comfort her. Unsure of where her car was parked, I started to help her walk to mine. She immediately started to panic.

"I can drive myself Logan," she said hastily.

"Ash, you're hurt. I can't just leave you by yourself."

"I'll be fine, really," she said as she started to pull away.

Afraid she would fall and make things worse, I stopped walking and squeezed her slightly, just enough to keep her stable against me. She started to quiver and her eyes were full of terror.

"Okay, what is going on?" I asked.

Apparently, my tone was more forceful than I meant for it to be because she trembled uncontrollably and looked up at me, unsure of what to say or do. Like a wounded animal. I rubbed her hand again soothingly. It was easy to forget how scared she could be. That everything that happened in her past made her much more fragile than she let on. Her head suddenly lowered, as if she were afraid of even facing me.

I took a deep breath and murmured, "Ashley, what's wrong?"

She would not stop shaking. She would not

look at me. She didn't have to. I could tell when she was about to cry.

I looked around the lot for anywhere to sit, but there was not so much as a small bench to let her rest and give us a chance to talk. I turned back to her and cupped her cheek, turning her face toward mine.

"Let's just go to the car and sit. We don't have to go anywhere if you don't want to," I said softly.

After a moment of hesitation, I leaned forward to kiss her forehead. Her eyebrows furrowed for a moment in surprise. I eyed her nervously, unsure of how she would react. She just nodded in response. We started forward again. I unlocked my car and helped her into the backseat. After closing the door, I hurried to the other side to get in with her.

She was already in tears by the time I sat down. Immediately, I wanted to hold her. To tell her everything was okay. Anything to make her stop crying. I reached out for her slowly, but she cowered away. I pulled my hand back.

"Ash, it's okay," I assured.

Cautiously, I took her hand and gave it a gentle squeeze. After a moment, she squeezed mine back and looked at me, then turned away again, unsure of what to do. I let go of her hand and slowly wrapped my arms around her. She was somehow shaking even harder than before.

"Please just don't hurt me," she whimpered.

I gently turned her head toward me.

"What makes you think I would want to hurt you?" I asked.

She didn't answer, averting her eyes to avoid my gaze. Her muscles tightened as she seemed to brace herself for the worst.

"Ashley, I promise. Nothing bad is going to happen."

Silent tears started rolling down her cheeks. I carefully wiped them away, then pulled her against my chest. I rocked her gently and nuzzled her hair, despite the sweat smell. Soon she started to feel more at ease. She began pressing against my chest, trying to snuggle closer. I rubbed her back soothingly.

My eyes widened when the realization hit me.

"What did he do?" I asked firmly.

She did not want to answer, but at least the crying had finally stopped.

"You're safe, I promise. I won't let anything happen to you. Just tell me," I whispered.

She looked into my eyes as if she were searching for something. Maybe anger, or frustration, but I stayed calm, only worried about what was going on in her head.

"Do you...do you remember when I told you about my knee?" she asked.

"Yeah."

"It was at a championship game for the school. There was an accident and I broke my kneecap because of it. I...I got lucky because it was a stable fracture, so it healed pretty easily. When my doctor said I could walk again, she gave me some exercises to help me get my strength back. So, I started going back to the gym. And that's when I started bringing a guest...I was scared of being alone or their being only strangers around if something went wrong. I asked Damien to start going with me and everything was fine at first, but then..."

She stopped and started shaking again. I ran my fingers through her hair.

"It's alright, just take your time," I murmured.

She took a deep breath and said, "Then, after about a week, he started getting mad. I could only do so much for so long, and I would be done really quickly. I never said he had to stop. I told him I could just sit and rest, but he wouldn't listen...and when we went outside to the cars, he would scream at me. Tell me I was weak, or that I wasn't trying hard enough. Or that I was ruining his day even though I was in so much pain. Then he started to...to hit me for it. He even kicked me a couple of times in my bad leg."

"What did you do?" I asked.

"Nothing," she said shamefully, "He's so much bigger, and I was hurt. I couldn't do anything."

She sniffled. I shushed her softly.

"He'd be upset if I took too long too and did the same things. I just got to a point where I was doing too much too quickly so I wouldn't upset him. It made everything worse though. The pain just got more intense because I was pushing too hard. Between that and the hitting, I had to get knee surgery."

I sat silently for a moment before asking my next question, "Is that why you were scared to get in the car? Did he wait until then to hurt you?" I asked.

She nodded, "Or on the way to it when no one was around."

I squeezed her a little and whispered, "You're safe now. You're going to be just fine."

I rocked her slightly in my arms to comfort her. I took her hand again and held it, gently rubbing her fingers with my thumb.

"Is that what you were talking about? When

you said he was being malicious? I thought you said he was just saying bad things."

"I said that a lot of bad things were said. I never said that worse things weren't done."

"I'm so sorry."

She was quiet at first, then started talking again, a slightly crazed look in her eyes, "I should never have joined the team. I wouldn't have gotten hurt and I could've kept going. He would've left me alone. Maybe none of it would've happened if I had just..."

"Hey, look at me."

She slowly turned her face toward mine.

"None of this is your fault. You got a sports injury. They happen all the time. And the things Damien did to you aren't your fault either."

She pulled away and rubbed her eyes, taking a few deep breaths.

"I'm sorry," she said quietly, "I shouldn't have acted like that."

"It's okay."

I scooted a little closer.

"But just know, I'm never going to hurt you. And I'm here for you."

"Why?"

"Why what?"

"Why do you care so much?" she asked, looking at me over her shoulder, "Why would you ever want anything to do with me?"

I lightly rested a hand on her shoulder and said, "Because you're my best friend."

She slowly turned toward me.

"Even if we weren't dating, I would still care just as much," I added.

She didn't say anything, just sat in thought for a moment, as if trying to take in the words. Then she pulled me into a warm embrace and rested against my chest. I nuzzled her hair again.

We snuggled in the seat a little longer, then I checked the time on the dash clock.

"How's your knee?" I asked.

"Still hurts," she croaked.

"Okay. Are you ready to go home?"

She nodded and pulled away. I got out of the car and walked around to help her out. By the time I got there, she was already trying to do it on her own and lost her footing. I managed to catch her, but not before her bad knee hit the asphalt below. She yelped on impact, then began muttering a string of curse words in an attempt to take her focus off of the pain. She started to turn pale again.

"Do you need me to take you to a doctor?" I asked as I pulled her to her feet.

"No. Just take me home. I'll be fine, really."

I helped her into the passenger's seat before hurrying to the other side. Not long after we got on the road, she started moaning and wincing from the pain. Steering with my left hand, I reached with my right for her hand to hold. She squeezed it a little bit in return.

I pulled up into her driveway. Mr. Evans' car was gone, but Melvin's truck was sitting nearby. I helped Ashley out of the car up to her porch. She fumbled with her keys before handing them to me so I could unlock the door.

I pushed the door open and shouted, "Melvin! I need help here!"

He appeared from the hall at the top of the stairs. His normal smile disappeared when he saw his sister doubled over in pain. He rushed down the stairs, leaping over the last few.

"What happened?" he asked, quickly taking Ashley's face in his hands to look at her.

"She hurt herself while we were working out, and she fell when we were about to leave."

"The knee?" he asked, trying to get her attention.

Ash was shaking, exhausted from the pain. She could not answer him. When he realized that, he turned to me.

"Did she fall on her left knee or not?" he asked, his voice slightly panicked.

"Yes. She told me to bring her back here."

"Get her to the couch. I'll get something to help with the pain," he said before running into the bathroom.

I helped her stumble over to the couch and let her lay down. I rested her head on a soft pillow, then took another to elevate her knee. Melvin hurried past us into the kitchen, then ran back with a cup of water and two pills. He crouched down and held the medicine out to her. She wrinkled her nose as she turned away from him.

"Ash, it's Tylenol. Take it," he said firmly.

Her jaw clenched and she glared at him. He glared back. I started to feel uncomfortable. It was as if there was a silent argument between them that I should not have been there for. Melvin huffed, but didn't back down.

"Logan, do me a favor please?" he said, careful not to look away from her, "Grab a bag from the drawer by the fridge and fill it with ice, then get a hand towel from the one by the sink."

I stood and walked into the kitchen, doing exactly as he instructed. When I walked back into the living room, she was drinking the water and the pills were gone. Melvin stroked her hair and spoke softly while her stiff body started to relax. I gave him the ice pack and he wrapped it in the towel, then set it on her knee.

"Hold that there," he said.

I took the ice pack from him. Then he turned back to Ashley and told her, "I'm gonna get the bandage and be right back."

He turned and ran back up the stairs. I scooted closer to her and held her hand. She squeezed mine, as if to reassure me that she would get better. Neither of us said anything, but she gave me a small smile and her thumb rubbed the back of my hand.

Melvin returned moments later with a compression bandage. I moved out of the way, still holding the bag of ice. He lifted her leg and carefully wrapped it.

"Do you want me to call Dr. Baker and ask if she'll see you today?" he asked worriedly.

Ashley shook her head and said, "It's not that bad. I just need to rest a bit."

"If that's what you want," he said halfheartedly.

The three of us sat in the living room together until Ash started to doze off. Melvin lifted her and carried her down the hall on the main floor. I followed and realized the hall was longer than I thought. At what I thought was the end, it turned left. There were three more doors within that section of the hallway. At the first one, Melvin asked me to open the door for him. He stepped into a fairly small room with tan walls. The furniture was made of dark stained wood, including the bed frame. The dresser and gaps on her shelves were covered with framed photos of her friends and family members. The shelves were also filled with various books, movies, and CDs. Her bed had two pillows with brown cases, a comforter, and three or more fleece blankets. The fleece blankets were covered in different colors and patterns, with characters from multiple shows and video games that would never be seen together otherwise.

I stood outside of the room while Melvin set her down on the bed. When she began to shiver, he wrapped her in one of the fleece blankets before stepping out of the room.

As he closed the door, he said, "Thank you for getting her home."

"Of course," I replied as we walked back to the living room.

Melvin sat down on the couch. I sat beside him. He began repeatedly rubbing his hands over his face, a tic he had whenever he was stressed.

"What was that all about? With the medicine?" I asked.

He huffed with irritation before speaking, "Did she tell you about her injury?"

"She said it was some kind of basketball accident."

He nodded, "Yeah. Before the championship a couple years ago she was pushing really hard during practice. She was pushing more outside of practice. Then during the game, she tried to make a shot and jumped, but she landed on her knee. She collapsed on the floor and couldn't get up. Everybody thought she was just resting or recovering from the fall, so dad and I weren't worried at first. Then the ref and a few of her teammates were with her. The coach was there soon after and had called an ambulance because Ash wouldn't let anyone touch her leg. Dad just about lost his mind. He ran to the court to get to her and helped the coach move her to a back room until paramedics got there. I don't think he let go of her hand except when the paramedics put her on the stretcher and when they took her to the emergency room."

He put his hands down in his lap.

"They had her on a lot of pain medication after that, but Ashley's never done well with medicine. She used to read about all these cases where people got addicted to pain medications, even the over the counter stuff. It really scared her, so she was always trying to avoid taking it after we got her home. There was a point that dad and I had to watch her until she swallowed it just to make sure she was really taking it, not just hiding it in her mouth to spit out and flush later."

I took in his words while he paused in thought.

"It's always been an irrational fear of hers," he continued, "And I've tried telling her that as long as she doesn't use too much and only uses it when she needs it, she'll be fine. She still doesn't listen. And those first couple of weeks you could tell when she didn't take it. She was in so much pain, and wasn't thinking straight. That's why we started watching her and checking her mouth before walking away."

We stood and he walked me outside. Once the front door was closed, he said, "I hope that you knowing all of this isn't going to drive you away from her."

I raised an eyebrow, "Why would it?"

"I just know that a lot of guys don't want to take the time to be with someone with the problems she has."

I shook my head, "Everyone has problems, right? And things like an injury are out of her control."

"I mean about the medication thing too."

"Maybe she was taking it a little far in the condition she was in, but I think that everyone fears that to some degree, at least once in their life. Especially as strong as some of them are."

He grinned and nodded, "Okay, good."

We began slowly walking together toward my car. He thought for a moment, then said, "I just wish she would stop doing this."

"Doing what?" I asked.

"She's pushing herself too hard," he said, shaking his head, "and she knows it. Her doctor's been on her about it since the accident. She should've been back to functioning normally months ago, but she keeps getting hurt when she works out. Probably doing things she knows she's not supposed to."

"Like what?"

"No squatting and deep knee bending is what Dr. Baker said. She also said to avoid stairs if possible. Her room used to be upstairs but dad and I moved her stuff into the room she's in now so she wouldn't have to use them as much. She still insists on using them at school though, it drives me crazy. And she even has the doctor's note that is required to use the school's elevators."

"What elevators?"

"There are a few that they put in place. There's at least one in every building, but some are a little out of the way to get to."

"Why wasn't she using them then?"

"I don't know, but if she keeps this up, she'll never heal. She already had to get surgery once because of this."

I leaned back against my car and looked up toward the sky.

"So, as far as the exercises, does using leg press count as a deep knee exercise? I assume it probably does but correct me if I'm wrong."

"No, you're not. It definitely counts. Was she using it?"

"Yeah, she was pushing pretty hard too."

I turned to catch him rolling his eyes, "Like I said, she knows she's not supposed to be doing that and she has to hold off until her knee is stronger. If I had known she asked you to go, I would have let you know that. Usually, Viv keeps an eye on her, but I know she had a dinner thing or something like that."

I shrugged, "All I know is she had a family thing. Ash probably asked me to go because I didn't know about all of that."

"She's too smart for her own good sometimes," Melvin said. He paused for a moment before adding, "I just don't understand why she does this."

I thought about what Ash had told me, about Damien calling her weak. I wondered if he had harassed her for trying to avoid those exercises.

"So, did you guys have any other plans tonight?" he asked.

I shook my head, "No, but I had made plans

for tomorrow. I want her to feel better before we do anything though."

"What were you planning?"

"I was going to ask her to go for a walk with me tomorrow and surprise her with a picnic. It probably sounds dumb, but I thought she might like it."

He smiled, "She'd love that. Ash has always liked that sort of thing."

"Good to know. Too bad it'll have to wait."

He patted me on the back.

"You'll get your chance."

We said our goodbyes and I drove home to rest.

I awoke the next morning to the sound of my notification tone ringing. I rubbed my eyes and grumbled, then picked up my phone. Ashley was texting me.

Hey sleepyhead :)

> *Hey. How do u feel?*

Better. I'm on my feet a little this morning

> *That's great!*

Mel's been watching me He won't let me out of his sight other than to use the bathroom, which is annoying

> *At least u know he cares... even if he's a little annoying about it lol*

Speaking of Melvin, he told me you guys talked last night about the plans you made. He felt bad

and if you want to come over
he'll make up for it

It's not his fault

I told him that. He said he still
felt bad because we didn't get
to do anything
It's also his night to make dinner
and he's an amazing cook, so if
you want to come over we can
stay here for dinner and a movie...

That sounds really nice.
Ur dad going to be home too?

No. He's out of town, but
Melvin will be at the house.

U sure? He's not going to
sneak up behind me and scare
the crap out of me?

Don't you trust me?

No, not at all lol

Lol

Neither of us said anything for a moment.

So...what do you say?

That sounds great. What time?

You could come at 6 if that's ok

I'll be there

We texted a little longer, then Ash said she had to go. I said goodbye and that I would see her that night. All I did before walking to her house was take some time to relax at home. That afternoon, Oliver sat on the bed with me while I watched TV and took a nap. When it was time to go, I changed into a pair of shorts and a t-shirt because of the extreme heat outside.

I jumped onto her front porch to knock on the door. Melvin let me inside.

"Your fella's here," Melvin teased, then walked to the kitchen.

I closed the door and stepped into the living room. Ashley turned to give me that beautiful smile. She seemed much calmer than the day before. I smiled back as I sat down on the couch beside her. She was wearing a dark blue t-shirt and athletic shorts. She had a sleepy look in her eye, as if she had not been awake for very long, and she was huddled under a fleece blanket that matched her shirt. She scooted closer to me. I wrapped her up in a hug.

"Logan, can we talk?" she asked timidly.

"Yeah, what's up?"

She pulled away from my grasp to look into my eyes, "I don't think that I've been fair to you in this relationship."

My brow furrowed, "What do you mean?"

"I just feel like I keep hiding things from you. Things about me. And then, when I finally do tell you, it's after I have a complete breakdown that you have to deal with. And after that, I get scared that maybe you'll use them against me somehow…I don't know, I just think I'm having trouble trusting you after everything."

I thought for a moment, "I get why though."

"I know, and that's great, but I don't want this whole thing to just be me being scared and acting crazy because of something that happened a long time ago. I don't want to drive you away, and I definitely don't want this to seem like it's all about me."

"You don't get upset all the time though. When we went to the movies the other night, the afternoon walks, the times when we're hanging out at my house or your house. You're perfectly fine."

"Yeah, but yesterday was especially bad. I didn't mean to get scared or to cry, but I just lost control."

I held her hand, "Everyone needs to let it out sometimes, and you've been bottling it all up for a long time. It's not healthy."

"I know, but I still don't want to unload it all on you. I don't want you to try to carry all of that weight."

"I don't want you to carry it all either."

"But it's still not fair to you."

I thought for a moment, knowing what I wanted to say, just not sure if I should say it, or even fully how to. She watched me nervously. I worked up the nerve to say what I was thinking.

"I'm not saying that I'll be able to carry all the weight, but if you're in this relationship for the long run, I want to help ease some of it off your shoulders. I want to help you move past some of the stuff you've dealt with so you'll feel better later on. Does that make sense?"

She nodded slowly.

"Good, because I was kind of just saying what I was feeling, but my brain doesn't always know the difference between that and mindless rambling," I joked.

She grinned.

"So, are we okay?" I asked.

"That's really up to you, I guess. I don't want to be a burden."

"You're not. And if you need to talk, just let me know. It could be two in the morning and I would still pick up the phone."

"Well, hopefully it doesn't come to that. Eventually I need to sleep."

"Me too, but if it happens, I will pick up."

"Thank you."

We hugged each other, then let go and turned toward the television. She had been watching a sitcom. I remembered her telling me it was one of her favorite shows. Something about these four guys who would dare each other to say or do embarrassing things. The person who lost the most challenges ended up with some kind of punishment the other three would choose. I had never seen it before, but she insisted that we watch some of it before Melvin finished dinner.

Ashley leaned closer to snuggle up against me. I wrapped an arm around her, but Melvin walked in moments later.

"Get a room you two," he said laughing.

"We had one until you walked in," Ashley replied.

"I guess that's true. And hey," he paused to point at me, "don't get any ideas over there."

"Why is it that everyone thinks I've got some underlying scheme planned?"

Ashley raised an eyebrow, "Who else thinks this?"

I looked in the air, pretending to be in thought, "Well, let's see. Your dad, which is kind of a given. Also your brother, another given. But then there's Jared, my boss, your boss, most of our friends –"

"Okay, I get it," she interrupted, "Newest guy

in the group is the one everybody's suspicious of."

"Well, to be fair, I'm pretty sure Jared's joking...not sure about everyone else though."

Melvin motioned for us to come into the dining room.

"Hope lemon pepper chicken's alright. It's dad's recipe," he said.

It was amazing, but that jerk wouldn't share the recipe. Apparently, there was a secret ingredient that only family members were allowed to know. He had also made green beans and mashed potatoes to go with it.

When we finished eating, Ashley walked to a nearby closet to grab a couple more blankets. I watched her carefully in case she fell, but she only walked with a slight limp and came back to the couch to watch a movie. She handed me one, which I set across my lap. She set the other one from the closet on her own lap, then took the blue one and wrapped it around her shoulders.

"You really have a thing for blankets, huh?" I teased.

"What do you mean?"

"I noticed you had a few of them in your room yesterday when Melvin helped you get in bed. And that closet over there is full of them."

Her cheeks turned a little red.

"It's a bit of a weakness," she said, "Especially if they have a design for a movie or show I like. I come by it honestly though."

"How's that?"

"Over half of the blankets in this house were mom's," she said defensively.

I grinned and said, "You don't have to explain

yourself. I think it's cute."

Her cheeks turned a shade brighter, although she tried to hide it.

What are you doing? I thought to myself, realizing that my weird attempt at flirting was somehow working, at least somewhat.

We started watching the movie, but a thought came to the back of my mind. A thought that made me extremely nervous.

Apparently, I was staring off into space because suddenly Ashley was waving a hand in front of my face. I blinked a couple of times and turned to look at her.

"Are you okay?" she asked.

"Yeah, I was just thinking."

Please don't say "about what?"

"About what?"

Dang it.

"Nothing," I said nervously.

"If you say so," she said before turning back to the movie.

You idiot, if you're gonna do it, then do it.

She shifted and sat up before stretching her arms, then leaned back into the couch cushions. She turned to me. I quickly looked back at the screen when our eyes met.

She's right there. Get over yourself and do it.

"Are you sure you're okay? You're acting weird."

"Yeah, completely fine."

Say something smooth. Anything, please just something smooth.

The only thing I could get out was, "Um..."

If I could punch myself in the face right now without looking like a lunatic, I would.

She didn't look away. She didn't give me a look that said I was crazy either, which was a good sign.

She suddenly rested her head on my shoulder and cuddled with me again. My nerves went into overdrive. I had no idea what to do. I froze, almost petrified.

I cleared my throat and said, "Actually, there is something on my mind."

She sat back up and turned to me curiously.

My brain kept shouting *Take it back! Take it back!* But I didn't want to take it back, and it would already have been too late.

I went with my gut and leaned in. She seemed a little surprised.

Please don't tell me I just messed everything up, I thought, making me even more nervous.

I leaned a little closer, hoping and praying that she would kiss me if for no other reason than to keep me from looking stupid. After a moment, she did lean in, but I still ended up looking stupid when my nose bumped into hers.

Way to go ya spaz, you turned your head the same way she did, I thought.

"Uh, sorry," I said nervously, starting to pull away a bit.

She laughed a little, "It's okay."

Before I lost the nerve, I closed the gap between us to kiss her. I closed my eyes, trying to relax. The moment was over all too soon. When I opened my eyes, she was still close. We both smiled a little, nervous laughter coming from both of us. Then she took me by surprise once more with another quick kiss, which ended, again, way too quickly.

My heart thundered with excitement. Her

cheeks were red again. She looked at the floor, trying to hide it. Then she curled up to me and we continued to watch the movie. For a while, neither of us could stop smiling.

It was about eight when the movie ended, but I wasn't ready to go home yet. We decided to watch another one before I had to leave.

I woke up at some point in the middle of the night. The TV was still on, along with a light coming from the dining room.

I rubbed my eyes with one hand, then realized I was having trouble moving the other. I turned and saw Ashley still snuggling against me. We had fallen asleep leaning against each other, which seemed to keep us sitting up rather than falling over.

I smiled a little and kissed the top of her head. She was still sound asleep. I lazily reached into my pocket for my phone, but my eyes widened when I saw the time.

I missed curfew!

I called Jared, nervous about what he would say.

"Hello?" he said.

"Hey, it's me," I whispered, "I'm sorry I missed curfew. Ash and I were watching a movie and we fell asleep."

I planned to say more, but he stopped me, "I know. Melvin called me. He said that he was keeping an eye on both of you. I'm sure he's still up now."

That explains the light being on.

"Okay. Again, I'm sorry and I'll be heading home in a minute."

"It's alright Logan. I understand. Just don't

make a habit of it, alright?"

"Okay."

"Alright, I'll see you at home soon."

"Okay, bye."

I hung up the phone and put it back in my pocket. Slowly, I started to get up, careful to guide Ashley so she would lay on her side. Her eyes opened slightly and she mumbled something inaudible. I shushed her softly. She moved just enough to get comfortable on the couch before closing her eyes again. She shivered a little. I pulled the blankets over her shoulders, then quietly started toward the door. A familiar voice stopped me as I started walking past the dining room.

"Ready for tomorrow?" Melvin asked.

I turned to see him at the dining table drinking water out of a mug.

"Yeah. I'm really excited about the game. Did it come in yet?"

He nodded, "It came in this morning, so I spent a couple of hours setting up the game room before you got here. It took a minute to figure out, but then it got really easy to set up. Especially by the ninth or tenth time."

I chuckled, remembering that Melvin had to set the game up to work for thirteen people. I sat down across from him at the table.

"I'm guessing you were keeping an eye on me?" I said jokingly.

"Yeah, a little bit," he said with a grin. "It's nothing personal you know."

"I get it, she's your sister."

"Yes, there's that, but that's not all of it."

I gave him a confused look.

"I know what Damien did on the night they broke up."

I was surprised, "I thought she said she never told you."

"She didn't. I saw her when dad and I got home from the hospital that night. Dad was too torn up and in his own world. He just went straight to bed when we walked in. I decided to check on Ash before I went up to bed, but I don't think she expected us to be home yet. She was crying when I walked into her room."

"She didn't tell me about that."

He shrugged, "She was probably hoping I just forgot about it. The whole time I was with her she kept saying 'It's nothing,' over and over. And I already knew they had been out because D said he would take her to a movie and to help get her mind off of everything."

He paused to take a drink.

"Then I called Damien up the next morning. I told him I wanted to talk. Then when we met, I asked him what had happened. Eventually he told me that he had hit her, beat her in fact. Of course, it took putting him in a headlock so he couldn't run before his stubborn ass told me anything."

I waited a moment before asking, "What did you do?"

"Well, he was showing off a black eye the next day, and he was walking a bit funny because I kicked him in a very...private place," he replied before taking another drink.

I had to stifle my laugh so I would not wake Ashley. Then, without thinking, I blurted out, "Makes sense. He deserves it after the way he acted."

His eyebrows furrowed.

Uh oh.

"Damien's always been a bit of a hot head," Melvin said, "and his dad isn't exactly the best influence on him, so he's never been good in relationships of any kind."

He eyed me, and I hoped that was all he had to say. But of course, it wasn't.

"Do you know something I don't?" he asked.

I swallowed hard, not sure what to say.

"Logan, what did he do?" he said, his voice firm as he set his cup down.

"I promised I wouldn't say," I said after a moment.

He leaned closer, "Please, I need to know."

"Why?"

He sat back and huffed.

"So I can protect her."

"I don't know how she would feel about this, I mean..." I said.

"I know," he said, cutting me off, "I know that she's strong, and can handle herself, and all of that. But she's still my sister, and I just want her to be happy. So, if there's something else looming over her head, I want to help. Please Logan."

He wasn't angry, he was desperate. I could tell there was something else bothering him too.

"Why though? What's the real reason you have to know so badly?"

"Because whatever it is, it's my fault. It's my fault they got together in the first place."

He looked down at the table, his muscles tense with frustration.

"How so?"

He looked up, "I knew they were interested in each other, but I wasn't sure about her dating Damien. I knew what he was like when no one else was around. He was aggressive and impulsive, but I never thought he was a bad person. Maybe misguided, but never bad. So, I set them up, thinking everything would be fine. Then, a year later, I found my sister bruised and beaten in her bedroom."

His eyes locked on mine, "And if I don't know everything, then I don't feel like I did enough, and it's going to drive me crazy. So Logan, I'm only going to ask one more time. What happened?"

I turned back toward the living room. Ash was still sound asleep and huddled under the blankets. I sighed. Obviously, he was not going to let this go.

"You can't tell her that I told you," I said as I turned back to him, "she wants to be the one to tell you, if she does at all."

He raised a hand, "I promise."

"Damien tried to get Ash to," I paused because I did not know how to say it, "do things she wasn't ready to do. When she told him no, he attacked her."

Melvin's eyes widened with realization, and his giant muscles grew tense. He didn't say anything for a while, then his jaw set as he stood.

"I'm gonna kill him," he said nonchalantly.

I jumped up and blocked his path.

"Melvin stop," I said, trying to keep my voice down.

"Look Logan, I don't want to hurt you, but if I have to make you move, I will."

"Melvin, look at me, it's not worth it."

"How so?" he asked through gritted teeth.

"You and Ashley just finished your classes. Do

you really want to start off your adult life with a record? It happened a long time ago, and Ashley's a lot better now."

"How would you know?"

"Because she told me. We had a long talk when she told me, and she got it all out. Really, she's come to terms with it."

"Then why didn't she tell anyone else? Even if not dad, why didn't she tell me or Vivian? Viv's her best friend, she would know if no one else did."

"She didn't tell anyone because she didn't want it to get back to you. She only told me because she trusted me not to tell you, and look at how that turned out. And she probably knew you would react like this."

He took some deep breaths, then slowly moved back to his seat, lost in thought. After a while, he said, "So, she's feeling better, right?"

I nodded, although I felt like I was lying a little. She was better, but Ashley was to some degree still hurt and afraid because of what happened.

He huffed, then picked up his mug again to drink.

I checked the time on my phone, then said, "I should go. I told Jared I was heading home. Are you going to be ok?"

He nodded, "I'll be fine. Good actually. Now I don't feel guilty about kicking D where the sun don't shine."

I chuckled, then turned toward the door. As I opened it, Melvin stopped me again.

"One more thing Logan."

I looked at him.

"Thank you. And, not just for keeping my record clean tonight," he said with a grin, "I haven't seen Ashley this happy since before mom got sick."

I turned back toward the living room to look at her again as I said, "She's done a lot for me too."

After a moment, he replied, "A warning to you my friend. While I do trust you, if you try anything like Damien did, you won't have to worry about the possibility of having kids in the future."

I turned back to him with wide eyes.

"Do you really think I would do something like that?!"

He laughed, maybe a little too loudly, before saying, "Don't worry, I'm joking...Maybe."

He stood and walked into the kitchen to wash the cup, and I quickly walked out to my car.

Goodbye

I woke up early the next morning to get dressed. We were supposed to meet at Melvin and Ashley's house by eight. I was ready by seven thirty. I said bye to Jared and that I would see him later, to which he replied, "Have fun, just not too much fun." He grinned when I rolled my eyes. Then I walked out the door. My phone vibrated as I stepped outside. It was a text from Ashley.

Are you still coming today?

Yeah, I'm walking over now

Not driving?

I probably shouldn't. There'll already be a lot of cars there. Besides, it's nice out and walking's good for me

I started walking toward her house. Then my phone buzzed with another message.

Melvin told me about last night...
That you told him about Damien

I didn't know how to respond.

R u mad at me?

No. I was a little at first, but he said it was more his fault than yours.

For the record, he wasn't supposed to say anything to u

He said that too, but for the record, he's not good at keeping secrets

Well, that's great to know now

Why did you tell him?

Idk. He was getting frustrated, I thought he would start getting aggressive if I didn't

Lol, trust me, his bark is a lot worse than his bite

Wish I knew that last night

I paused before sending another message.

So, r we ok?

I was almost at her house by then. She did not reply to my message, so I knocked on the door. Ash opened it a moment later.

"Did you get my last text?" I asked nervously.

"Yeah."

"And?"

She gave me a small smile, "Yeah, I think so."

She hugged me tightly. I squeezed her back, only to feel a sudden blow against my abdomen. I stumbled back, holding my stomach. I then realized Ashley had punched me.

"Now we're ok. But a quick tip, don't tell my secrets again if you want things to stay that way."

"Noted," I croaked, "and by the way, you have a killer left hook."

She laughed and gave me another hug, then led me inside the house. She sat on the couch and patted the spot next to her. I sat down cautiously, keeping a bit of distance in case she decided to hit me again. She smiled and leaned closer to kiss my cheek, then held my hand and rested against my shoulder. I wrapped my arm around her, squeezing her tightly as I kissed her hair.

"Whoa, when did that happen?" someone shouted.

I nearly jumped out of my skin as I turned to see who had yelled. It was Vivian, who happened to walk out of the kitchen as Ashley kissed me. She was wearing jeans and a black t-shirt and holding a plate of eggs and toast.

"Oh no, I forgot she was already here," Ashley said.

"So, you weren't even going to tell your best friend?" Vivian asked.

"I was, but I was going to wait until after today."

Vivian pointed at me and said, "I'm watching you," before walking to the dining room.

I groaned and said, "Why can nobody just trust me for half a second?"

"Oh, relax you big baby, she's just giving you a hard time," Ashley teased.

"Whatever."

We sat and talked as the others slowly started trickling in. Peyton sat on the couch next to Ashley and they started chatting about things in the news. Ulysseus slowly paced around the house with a cup of water in his hand and a pair of headphones in his ears. Vivian came back to the living room after eating her breakfast to chat with the girls. I stood and decided to see if anyone else was around.

Soon Adrian came in, who quickly kissed Vivian before hurrying to the kitchen. Brandie and James walked in soon after, hand in hand. Then Bryan walked in groggily, still rubbing his red eyes. A few minutes later, Natalie and Diego came inside while bickering about something, probably because of sibling rivalry. Finally, Alice walked in, her nose in a book as usual. That day, it was about vikings.

The girls were all sitting in the living room talking excitedly about something. When I walked by, I realized that they were grilling Ashley for information on what happened the night before. I scratched a fake itch on the back of my head so I had an excuse to turn it to the side and avoid being bombarded by a small army of women.

I slipped into the kitchen and found that all the guys were making coffee and talking about "the game". All except for Ulysseus. Still the loner of the group, he sat at the dining table, his cup now filled with orange juice. After a moment of hesitation, I sat next to him, but said nothing. I didn't want to interrupt him because he was reading something on his phone, but I was too worn out to talk to a bunch of guys getting charged up on caffeine. I decided to play a game on my phone instead.

Ulysseus looked up from his phone for a moment at the guys and shook his head saying, "They'll be wired to the moon all day."

"What does that mean?" I asked.

"It means those eejits will be driving us mad with all that coffee."

"You don't like coffee?"

"It's not about the coffee. Heck, I already had two cups at home. It's about all of them drinkin' coffee. They get too hyper."

He looked back at the eBook he had been reading. I grinned at his remark before continuing to play the round in my game.

At eight fifteen Melvin ran upstairs. The rest of the guys came into the dining room to sit with Ulysseus and I.

"Whatcha reading General?" James asked.

Ulysseus took his headphones out and grumbled, "I told ye to stop callin' me that."

"Alright, how about Your Majesty."

"That's not funny James."

James wrapped him up in a hug and said, "Relax buddy. I'm only teasing. I'll stop."

"Good."

"What's with the nicknames?" I asked as everyone sat down.

"Ulysseus's name man," Diego said.

I raised an eyebrow.

Ulysseus rolled his eyes and said, "My father had a thing for Homer's writings. He also loved learnin' about Union General Grant. Mom named Peyton and Dad named me. For some reason he decided to try to combine Ulysses and Odysseus. The first bein' a war general who later became president. The second a king who, according to the epic, went on many adventures before finally goin' home and takin' back his kingdom."

"That's kind of a cool combination."

Ulysseus shrugged, "It is nice to have a name that's a little different, unlike James over here. At the same time though, it makes me feel some pressure."

He turned his head, locking eyes with me as he said, "Like maybe my father wanted more out of me."

I thought for a moment, then said, "Or maybe he was trying to give you the confidence to do more for yourself."

He seemed surprised by my comment, as if he had never thought of it that way. Then he nodded and looked back at James, who was tapping on his shoulder.

"So...since I can't call you a general or a king, can I —"

"No James, you cannot call me Mr. President."

James grinned and guzzled down a few mouthfuls of his coffee. Then Melvin came bounding back down the stairs.

"Ladies and gentlemen!" he shouted, "Let us begin our adventures!"

We all looked at each other, then stood and walked into the living room. Melvin stood near the stairwell with his hands in the air, as if waving to get everyone's attention. The girls were still sitting in the living room. Brandie rolled her eyes.

"Stop being so overdramatic Melvin," she said, "Can we play the game or not?"

"Why of course good people!" he shouted in response, "Let us go and play!"

He turned and bounded back up the stairs. James walked up to Brandie and wrapped an arm around her before they went upstairs together. The others walked in groups of two in no special order, all chatting excitedly about playing. Ashley's hand slipped into mine as she put her head on my shoulder.

"Don't fall asleep on me now," I teased.

"I won't, I just like cuddling with you."

I quickly glanced around the room. By then, everyone else had already gone upstairs. I turned and I gave her a quick kiss on the forehead. She opened her eyes and smiled. We flinched at the sound of a loud voice from upstairs, pulling us back to reality.

"Come on lovebirds! Let's go!" Vivian shouted.

"As if you're any better!" Ashley hollered back.

I chuckled and we started up the stairs. She gripped the banister while slowly climbing up the steps.

"Does your leg hurt?" I asked.

"Not as bad, but a little."

I kept holding her hand and watched her as she carefully walked. Luckily, she didn't have any problems on the way up, but she did have to stop to rest at the top.

"Good job," I said, gently rubbing her shoulder.

She studied my face for a moment before saying, "Thank you."

"You know I mean that, right?"

She nodded and gave me a small smile, then started toward a room at the very end of the upstairs hall. I matched her pace, holding her hand again as we walked inside.

It was a large, strangely shaped room. Three of the tall, tan walls were straight and met at sharp corners, taking on a rectangular shape. Meanwhile the wall opposite to the entrance was rounded, as if someone attached the rectangle to a semicircle. The rounded side of the room was lined with a large, curved desk covered with over a dozen desktop monitors. The computer units themselves sat evenly apart underneath the strange table. In front of each monitor rested a desk chair with wheels for each of their respective users.

Between the windows on the two longer walls hung several whiteboards with random notes, quotes, and much more. On the shorter wall by the door, a large flatscreen television had been mounted. There were several full shelves on each side of the tele-vision, and below the screen sat an entertainment center, essentially a larger version of the one in the living room downstairs. I stepped closer to find the cabinet had been filled with various consoles from several decades made by the three biggest compa-nies in console gaming. I looked at the shelves, real-izing they were lined with all sorts of games, at least a dozen for each console, with ESRB ratings any-where from E for everyone to mature and "rating pending". I stared in awe at the collection.

"Dad's been playing video games for years," Ashley explained, "He's had most of these since he was a kid. Mel and I got the newer stuff."

I pointed at the scribbles on the whiteboards and asked, "What's with all this stuff?"

"Sometimes Dad will use this room for meet-ings. Kind of like a home office when he thinks he's been in the studio offices too much. He uses the boards to brainstorm episode ideas and guests."

"I thought your dad didn't like working from home."

"He doesn't when we're home. Usually if he wants to work here he'll wait until he knows Mel and I will be out of the house."

She pointed to the windows at one side of the room and added, "He likes watching the animals outside. Birds, deer, anything that will walk by. Nature helps him stay calm I guess."

"Are you sure it's not the stockpile of video games?"

She grinned and said, "I'm not going to lie, he has had friends over before for game nights up here too."

We turned to look at the rest of the group. They were all huddled together and talking near the computers. Melvin moved out of the crowd toward us.

"What do you think of the game room man?" he asked with a grin.

"It's really cool," I replied, "The best setup I've ever seen."

I turned to Ashley and wrapped my arms around her, then said, "Why did you never bring me up here before?"

"I figured you could wait. Besides, video games can't be the only reason you want to hang out with me."

I grinned and hugged her, then said, "At least I finally get to see all these consoles you keep bragging about."

"Melvin hasn't been letting anyone in here for a week. Not even me. He kept saying 'I'm getting things ready' before he even got the game."

I chuckled and nuzzled her hair. Melvin interrupted by saying, "Jeez, you guys are lovebirds now, huh?"

Ashley pulled away from me and swung a fist at his arm. I laughed when he jumped away in surprise. He held his hands up in surrender and shouted, "I was just kidding!"

She reached up and messed with his hair, which really did not look like it had been combed that morning anyhow.

"Come on, hurry up and quit goofing around guys!" James said.

"You do realize we're going to play a video game, right?" Melvin asked, "We will literally be goofing around all day."

"Not if you keep wasting time," James replied dramatically.
Brandie laughed and kissed his cheek, "Relax babe, it's fine."

I wrapped my arms around Ashley before she could chase Melvin again, swaying slightly.

"Is everything set up?" I asked.

Melvin grinned and nodded, "Come look."

I let her go so we could follow him to the set-up. The computers and accessories had all been pushed against the wall, leaving room for the virtual reality equipment. It was strange though. It was not the typical bulky headset. Instead, each desk was covered in a small sheet of plastic. Neatly placed on each sheet were a set of clear contacts to the left. Below those were a set of flesh colored earpieces, so small they could fit on my fingertip. To the right sat what looked like the average smartwatch. On the right side of it were two buttons, one with the power symbol most devices had, the other a slightly longer button with "START" professionally etched into the metal. On the left, various three character numbers were carved in a similar fashion, and no number was exactly the same.

"Uh, Melvin, what's all this stuff for?" Ashley asked.

"That's what I've been wondering," Adrian chimed in nervously.

Melvin raised his hands and said, "It's a little weird, I know. It threw me off at first too. It's all wireless though. We'll put in the contacts and the earpieces, put on the watch, and go from there."

We all looked at each other warily. Melvin rolled his eyes.

"Guys, it's Alpha Softworks. They promised to bring something new to gamers, right? This is supposed to be just as good as the other stuff, if not better. Plus, I already tried my set on to see how it feels, and it's way more comfortable than a big ass headset," Melvin assured us.

"How does it work with my glasses?" Bryan asked.

Melvin paused to think for a moment, then grabbed the paper instructions he had set to the side. He skimmed through, then looked up and brought it to Bryan.

He pointed at a spot on the paper and said, "It says that if you type in your prescription on the watch keypad, the matching contacts will optimize, so you don't have to wear them."

"So, if I put in -1.25 it'll work?" Bryan asked.

"We can try and see."

Bryan nodded and picked up the nearest watch set, then turned it on. They scrolled through a few menus on the touchscreen until they found it.

Bryan punched in his prescription, then the watch beeped once. He took off his glasses and reached for the contacts, using the reflection from one of the shiny computer screens to put them in. He waited a moment and looked around the room.

"Well, it works," he said with a grin, "It's kind of freaky, but at least I can see."

Melvin grinned, then said, "Come on guys, pick a seat and let's get this party started!"

Melvin quickly took a seat by the set he had already tried on while the rest of us started sitting down. To my right sat Diego, Natalie, Brandie and James at the very end. Ashley sat to my left, then Melvin, Adrian, and Vivian. Peyton and Ulysseus were next to Vivian, but Peyton decided to stand while showing Ulysseus how to put the contacts in. Past them sat Alice and Bryan at the far left.

Ulysseus was the last to get his contacts in. I reached for my earpieces and nervously picked one up. Ashley looked at it hesitantly.

"You okay?" I whispered.

She nodded, "I'm just worried about it getting stuck in my ear."

Melvin waved at us and said, "Watch me."

He picked up one of the earpieces and made sure everyone was watching. He pressed a tiny button on the earpiece, then placed it in his ear. We could see a little bit of it sticking out, similar to Bluetooth earbuds.

"Super easy, and it doesn't get stuck, I promise," Melvin said reassuringly.

We followed his example, making sure to press the tiny, almost undetectable buttons on the earpieces. Then we reached for the watches.

"Do these need to be on a specific arm?" Peyton asked.

Melvin grabbed the instructions again to check, then shook his head. Everyone put their watches on their left wrist except for Brandie and Diego, who put them on their right because they were left handed.

"Alright," Melvin said, "so your player ID is the number on the left side of your watch. The power and start buttons are on the other side. Turn the watches on and tap "New Game" on the screen when it shows up."

I turned my watch to find the numbers "766" carved into it. I turned it back and pressed the power button. The screen lit up and bright blue letters appeared.

Welcome

Then the letters faded and new ones appeared saying *New Game* in the center and *Menu* in the top left corner. I tapped *New Game* and a new selection said *Solo* and *Multiplayer*.

"Press multiplayer and I'll give y'all the code," Melvin said, looking at a tiny slip of paper.

"Where did you get that?" Vivian asked.

"Each set has one. I don't know why, but I guess it's in case you lose one?" he said with uncertainty, "Anyway I just grabbed the first one I saw when I came up here earlier."

I tapped multiplayer and what looked like a search bar showed up. I waited for him to announce the code to the group.

"Everyone ready?" Melvin asked. When everyone nodded, he said, "B0L_UWN10767."

I tapped the box and typed in the code. A final menu showed up with game options, including *Team Data*, *Objectives*, *Rewards*, and *Playback Recording*. Curiosity taking hold, I tapped the playback menu. Three words flashed onto the screen.

Recording Data Unavailable

Weird, I thought.

I tapped the back button and looked at Melvin.

"All we have to do now is press Start and see what happens," he said with a grin, then pressed the start button on the side of his watch.

I pressed the button as well and my vision changed. Everything was suddenly dark and I turned to face forward. Bright green words appeared in the distance ahead of me.

Welcome to Seventy Five Lives

Then a digital woman's voice started to speak. While I knew it came from the earpieces, it seemed like surround sound as she said, "Welcome to Seventy Five Lives. You are about to begin your first life, but first, please enter a username."

I looked down and a digital keyboard appeared in front of me.

"Hey guys," it sounded like Ulysseus, "are we using our real names for this?"

"Yeah," Melvin replied, "It'll make it easier for us to know who's who in the Team Data."

I typed "Logan" and the letters appeared in front of me.

"Welcome Logan," the digital voice said, "Player 766."

My name shrunk and moved to the top left corner of my vision, then the words "Player 766" in smaller print appeared underneath.

"*Seventy Five Lives* is a virtual reality experience that involves no physical movement in the real world. In this virtual reality world, you will be able to move freely and communicate with other players. This experience is meant to feel as realistic as possible."

The voice paused and I raised an eyebrow.

This is getting weirder and weirder by the minute, I thought.

"You will now embark on a virtual journey that will change your life and understanding of the world. Please select start to begin."

The word "Start" appeared in front of me. I felt myself raise my hand and tap it with my finger.

But supposedly, I'm not actually moving? I thought curiously.

The word lit up as I tapped it. I instantly felt a shock run through my body, then the world became dark once more.

When I could see again, I was walking down a tunnel. At the end, the sun shone brightly, revealing a pasture past the mouth of the den. I started running, eager to see what awaited. When I reached the grass outside, I shielded my eyes, allowing them to adjust as I took in my surroundings.

I squinted as something flew toward me from off in the distance. As the object drew closer, I realized it was a large metal orb with what looked like a camera lens in the side of it. A man's voice came out of it, but it was obviously distorted to disguise the person speaking.

"Welcome to Life One," the voice said, "You are just outside of a kingdom long forgotten from the Middle Ages. You are a poor peasant off to see the king with a message from your small village. The rest is up to you. Please complete all objectives if you wish to continue. Are there any questions?"

"Where are my friends?" I asked.

"All players in this world are scattered across the kingdom. Some have different roles and objectives in this life. You are currently on a sub-team with players 767 and 768. Please join your sub-team and complete common objectives to finish the level. Enjoy."

And just like that, it flew off and disappeared. I jumped back a step when bright green letters appeared in front of me.

Objective: Find ID 767 and ID 768

When the words dissolved, a green beacon glowed in the distance. I assumed it was meant to show my destination. I started walking and looked down, realizing I was wearing different clothes. Rather than my usual t-shirt and jeans, I wore a dingy leather tunic and brown stockings with worn leather boots. I also had a belt around my waist that held a scabbard and iron dagger.

When I reached the beacon, it disappeared. It was previously located above an open iron gate that led to a medieval village surrounded by stone walls. As I walked inside the walls, I saw men, women, and children all around me. Their clothes were similar to mine, some in better shape, others in worse. I made sure to pay attention while observing them, trying to see if my friends were nearby. Although I was not sure who players 767 and 768 even were.

My eyes skimmed over the town square. Small shops and food stands sat along both sides of the path to my left. To the right, there was a blacksmith, an inn, a bar, and small houses made of wood and stone. Down the road ahead of me, I saw another gate with a castle just beyond it.

I turned as a familiar voice shouted, "Logan!"

From the blacksmith's forge, Melvin ran toward me and waved to get my attention. His clothes were similar to mine, but he was also wearing a black apron. I smiled as I walked toward him.

"Isn't this great?" he asked excitedly, "This is so realistic!"

"Yeah man, it's really cool."

"Did you find out who else is in our group?"

"Not yet. I just got here."

"I wish I had set up the gear in order, but I couldn't really tell what the ID numbers were until I took everything out of the boxes."

"Too bad. It would be nice to have a hint."

"I don't think you'll need any hints," another voice said.

We both turned and saw Ashley walking toward us. She was wearing full silver body armor, aside from the helmet she held in one hand. An iron sword sat at her hip and she held a shield in her left hand.

Before any of us could say anything else, bright lettering flashed in front of my eyes and I jumped back.

"Are you okay?" Melvin asked, just before having a look of surprise similar to mine.

"What are you guys-" Ashley started, before seemingly staring off into space.

I was unable to see what they saw, but I read the glowing green letters in front of me.

Objective: Slay the Beast

They disappeared the moment I finished reading them.

"Did you guys see that too?" Ashley asked.

"Slay the beast, right?" I asked.

She nodded.

Melvin grinned, "This is awesome! We got our first real objective!"

"That's great, but what exactly are we supposed to fight?" I asked.

"Well, it's only the first level, right? Usually, games give you a few levels or a dungeon that's really easy to get you used to a game. I'd bet money we'll find out any time now," Melvin said.

The shadows on the cobblestone pavement started to grow. I looked at the sky and saw that the sun was going down. The soldiers at the gate frantically grabbed the large wheels lined with chains and pushed them quickly, forcing the gates to close.

"Looks like we're about to find out," I said.

"You there!" a guard shouted, pointing straight at Ashley, "Come and help us turn this!"

She glanced at me for a moment, then put the shield and helmet down and ran to the nearest wheel. She helped the other soldiers unravel the chain link until the gate slammed against the ground. By then the sun was gone; the dark sky revealed a crescent moon.

Ashley walked back to us once the soldiers had dispersed. We watched as they ran up a set of stone stairs that lead to the top of the walls. The troops raised their bows and spears, prepared for whatever was coming.

Then the ground started to rumble beneath our feet. The villagers hurried into the houses closest to them. I turned back to the gate and squinted at a shadow in the field.

The moonlight outlined a distant, four-legged figure charging toward the gate. As it drew closer, its features were unveiled. It was a massive creature, with the head and forelegs of an oversized male lion and the hind legs of a grizzly bear. Each paw had been equipped with long black claws and its mouth was full of sharp, white fangs, several of which were missing or broken. It was covered in various white scars, the most distinct across its left eye. Its pelt was a horrific mess of mud and dried blood.

"Hey, you three out there!" someone shouted.

We turned around to see the blacksmith shouting and waving to get our attention. He was a tall muscular man with terracotta skin and thick white hair with a matching beard. He wore a tunic made of wool and a black leather apron similar to Melvin's.

"Get in here!" he commanded.

The three of us looked at each other for a moment before going inside his house, which was immediately to the left of his forge.

He slammed the door of his one room house shut and looked through a nearby window. We all flinched when we heard a slam from outside. I hurried to the other window and saw the monster bashing its body against the iron. The soldiers on the wall shot arrows and launched their spears at it, but the beast remained unfazed.

The blacksmith grumbled something, then walked to his brick hearth at the other end of the room to make a fire.

"This will keep that monster away. It does not like the light," he said gruffly.

"Why are we hiding?" Melvin said, "We should go fight that thing."

The blacksmith chuckled and said, "You fool. You have no idea what you're up against."

I looked back at the beast carefully. It stood on its hind legs and slammed its massive paws into the bars. My eyes examined the figure, looking for some kind of weak point.

It's like Melvin said, level one is supposed to be easy, I thought.

"Hey, do you know any way to kill it?" Melvin asked.

The blacksmith replied with, "Legends tell of heroes who slayed others of its kind with dwarven weapons, but never revealed how or what happened to these weapons."

"Seems like some pretty important information to leave out, don't you think?" Ashley asked.

Then I noticed something weird about one of the monster's legs. I turned and tapped Ashley on the shoulder.

"What?" she asked.

"Come look at this."

She stood next to me. I pointed as I said, "Look at its back feet."

I stepped back so she could see, then she turned and said, "It has an Achilles heel."

I grinned and nodded, then said, "I'm so happy you made a mythology reference."

"Well, like I told you before, I am the cool one."

I looked back at the monster's left heel. A faint blue light was glowing from its weak point, like the beacon that led me to the castle town.

"Let me see," Melvin said eagerly.

He looked through the opening as Ashley said, "Come on, let's go."

She drew her sword and I drew my dagger. Melvin looked around the room for a weapon.

"You loggerheaded dalcops," the blacksmith growled, "you'll all be dead in minutes."

"We'll see," Ashley challenged, then pushed the door open.

The three of us slowly stepped outside. Melvin found and grabbed a war axe from the forge. Ashley picked up her helmet and shield from the road, preparing for the fight.

The metal bars had already started to give in. I raised my dagger. Then the beast broke through, sending up a cloud of dust as the steel hit the dirt.

"It's through the gates! It broke through the gates!" the guard shouted.

Really? We didn't notice that, captain obvious, I thought to myself.

"Let's go!" Melvin shouted.

I put a hand on his shoulder, "Wait, shouldn't we go out there with a plan?"

"Logan. It's a game. Besides, it's only the first level, so if we have to start over it's not that big of a deal."

"I'd rather not spend hours on the same level if I don't have to."

"Same here," Ashley chimed in, "I'd rather move on and see what else the game has to offer."

"Alright, you've both got some good points," he said, then paused to look at the beast as the dust cleared and added, "We better think fast though."

"I have the armor, so I'll distract it. You guys just focus on getting around to the weak spot," Ashley said, then charged forward.

I heard the blacksmith's door slam shut as we started toward the creature and thought, *Well, no turning back now.*

Ashley took a quick swing at its face and caught the muzzle. It yowled and swung a paw at her.

"Come on! Over here!" she shouted, trying to keep its attention.

Melvin ended up a few paces ahead of me and swung at its leg, but he missed. The beast turned faster than anything of that size should have and rose onto its hind legs. Melvin managed to raise his axe in a defensive position before the bear slammed him down on the ground. It knocked the wind out of him and his eyes widened as he tried to breathe again. Then Melvin started pushing the axe up, his muscles heaving under the weight.

"If anybody wants to help, now would be a great time!" he shouted.

Its open jaws snapped shut mere inches from his face. Ashley charged it again and stabbed its neck, but barely left a scratch. It turned and snapped at her, narrowly missing as she jumped back. I stepped toward her to help, but she stopped me.

"Finish it Logan! Hurry!" she shouted.

I ran around the beast and jabbed at its heel, but the dagger barely pierced the skin and flew out of my hand on impact.

Oh no.

It made another impossible turn and I bolted, trying to come up with another plan. Ashley and Melvin hurried to the blacksmith's house to recover, but I didn't make it that far. It lunged and sliced into my calf, causing me to fall next to the forge. Horrible pain shot through my leg as I tried to find a place to hide.

This is more immersive than I thought.

Melvin was back in an instant, axe in hand. He swung it to try to force the monster back, but there was no fear in its eyes. It grabbed the axe in its jaws and swung its head back and forth until Melvin could not hold onto it anymore, throwing him onto the dirt. The monster threw the axe to the side and roared. Melvin made a slow attempt at standing, but the beast pressed its paws onto his chest to hold him, its face inching closer to his.

Frantically, I looked for something to use as a weapon. All I could find was the hammer the smith was using in the forge. I ran to grab it, then shouted, "Hey ugly!"

The monster turned.

Well, at least it knows its own name, I thought.

I slammed the hammer hard into its shoulder, and the monster yowled in pain, stepping away from Melvin.

I looked down at the weapon, studying it more. The smith said we were supposed to use a dwarven tool, and that hammer looked anything but normal. The handle was covered in a layer of silver that seemed to glow in the moonlight, with the weapon being covered entirely by intricate designs.

What made him think this was a blacksmith's tool? I thought.

I raised it above my head and the monster stepped back. I slammed the hammer down hard into its head. There was a crack and a strained roar from it, but I knew it was not enough to kill it. Its shoulder had already repaired itself. As the dizzy beast tried to recover, I hurried to its hind leg and smashed the weak point with all of my strength. With a final guttural scream, it crumpled into a mass of fur.

I turned to Melvin and held my hand out to him. He grinned as I helped him stand. Ashley ran over and hugged me.

"Quick thinking buddy," Melvin said.

I gave Ashley a tight squeeze before letting go.

Then I felt dizzy and took a step back, reaching for something to hold on to. When I did not find anything, I fell on the ground hard. In one moment, Ashley was beside me, trying to get my attention. In the next, the world turned black.

Everywhere

I awoke and sat up abruptly. My left arm felt heavy. I slowly turned to look, flinching away in shock as I realized my arm was covered by a bionic gauntlet. It was seemingly made of metal and covered with intricate blue and purple patterns, with a set of wires sticking slightly out of the side.

I guess this replaces my watch?

I turned my arm to find a touch screen in the middle of my forearm with a small keypad next to it. I tapped the screen to find the four menus from the watch screen. Then I looked myself over. The medieval rags were replaced by something similar to a black motorcycle suit; a one piece suit made of leather that covered me from the neck down. I could feel an extra layer of padding in the suit that covered my back, chest, shoulders, and arms. My player ID number had been embroidered onto each shoulder with grey thread.

I realized the pain in my leg was gone and pressed my hand against my calf. The claw marks were gone, as if it had never happened. I looked around the room, but it was pitch black other than a spotlight above me. I was sitting on a hard metal floor, but as soon as I stood the floor started shaking.

The plate of steel directly below me turned out to be a platform and pushed me up toward the light.

Great. What now?

The rumbling stopped when I reached the surface. My eyes were momentarily blinded by the sun. When I could see again, I was standing at the center of a colosseum. The arena had walls made of solid steel that were at least two stories high. Above those were rows of metal benches, similar to those at a basketball stadium. The stands were filled with all kinds of people, each of them cheering or waving their fists in the air and wearing suits like mine. Then the walls behind the seats were another story higher. Above that was a roof that closed in the arena, covered with shimmering white lights.

There were holes in the ground all around me. As more platforms reached the surface, I started to see my friends. Ulysseus was closest to me on my left. Ashley stood to my right, with Adrian only a few feet away from her. The others were scattered in other parts of the main floor, but all thirteen of us were there. Each of us wore a different piece of robotic armor. Ulysseus wore a helmet that covered the top of his head, as well as the right half of his face. Adrian had armor covering his right arm from his shoulder to just above his elbow. Ashley had a gauntlet similar to mine on her right arm. In moments, I realized most of the pieces of armor had a match. Vivian had armor like Adrian's on her left arm. Melvin had what looked like the pieces of Ulysseus's helmet that could have been missing; covering only the left half of Melvin's face and the back of his head. Others had boots, greaves, knee guards, and elbow guards. The only person not in a pair was Peyton, who wore the only chest plate in the group.

I heard a whirring sound and looked up. I saw the little orb with the lens from level one.

"Greetings players," the modified voice said, "Welcome to level two. In this level you will learn to fight with your full team in an arena. Some future levels will require similar forms of teamwork to succeed and move on."

More tutorials?

"In order to complete this level, all competitors must work together to win against your opponents. You will be fighting the robotic gladiators. Since you are all normal humans, you have been given a piece of armor that reflects a component of your enemies, distributed as evenly as possible among players. Please enjoy, and I will meet you at the start of the next level."

Then, it flew off once more. All of us started looking at one another, each with a confused look. We all covered our ears as a brain piercing siren blared from every direction. The roaring of the ecstatic crowd was drowned out by the sirens. A new objective appeared in front of me.

Objective: Win the Battle Royale.

Four holes appeared in the walls of the arena, one in each direction. Then dozens of the robots escaped from the passages.

"Uh, guys?" Ulysseus said nervously, taking a few steps back.

"Guess we better figure out how to use our equipment fast," Adrian said as he examined his armor.

I looked at my gauntlet and started pressing buttons on the keypad.

This probably isn't a good idea.

I looked up and saw one of the bots racing straight for me.

But on the other hand, it can't be worse than being torn to pieces, right?

I yelped in surprise as a laser came out of the gauntlet, knocking me on the ground. I looked at the robot from before, but I had disintegrated it. Ashley ran over and crouched down beside me.

"How did you do that?" she asked.

I looked at her gauntlet and saw that it was an exact reflection of my own, down to the placement of the buttons. I looked at my arm and saw that a hole at the top of the gauntlet was releasing smoke. I turned back to find the same opening in hers.

We heard a loud whirring sound from our left. It came from a robot that looked like a mosquito, other than the fact it was bigger than my head and had glowing red eyes. I turned back to her gauntlet and started pressing buttons.

"Aim at that thing," I said.

She nodded and adjusted her arm. When I finished the sequence, the laser shot out of her arm and evaporated the mosquito.

She looked at the gauntlet and clenched her fist as she said, "That's awesome."

"If you two are done goofin' around, I could really use some help here!" Ulysseus shouted.

We turned and saw him being chased by a bronze dome with two arms and sharp claws hovering a few paces behind.

Ashley immediately turned and took aim, "Get

down!"

Ulysseus dove for the ground. Ashley fired at the dome, obliterating it. My eyes widened as she turned to take out several more that were nearby, then turned to me.

"What?" she asked.

"Oh nothing. Just that I don't think I've ever been so terrified of, and yet still attracted to someone," I said dumbstruck.

She grinned and said, "Well, you don't have anything to worry about. Even if you do say cheesy things."

She gave me a quick kiss on the cheek before hurrying off to fight more robots. I swiftly turned and slammed my fist into a robot that had tried to sneak behind me, then fired a laser to finish it off. Ulysseus finally figured out how to use his helmet and shot a bright beam of red light from the piece of the mask that covered his eye.

"Yeah!" he shouted before chasing down another machine.

More robots poured in from the openings of the arena. None of them looked like people, but they came in various shapes and sizes. Some had one eye, others had close to a dozen, some none at all. Many were three-dimensional shapes with appendages. Others resembled various animals and insects. Luckily, none of them were necessarily hard to beat alone.

At one point, Ashley and I somehow ended up back to back with a dozen of the vicious machines surrounding us. We kept firing, but they seemed to be getting smarter, ducking and dodging our shots.

"What do we do?" she asked.

"I'm thinking," I replied.

Moments later, one of them tackled me. It was in the shape of a large dog with jagged teeth and long claws. The animatronic claws tore into my chest, but luckily only shredded the extra layer of padding in the suit. Its teeth came only centimeters from my face. I lifted the gauntlet to block it, but the dog's jaw locked onto my arm and would not let go.

Ash slammed the fist of her glove into the dog's back. When it did not budge, she did it a couple more times, but then another robot grabbed her from behind.

"Ashley!" I cried.

Cracks started forming in my gauntlet. My mind raced frantically, trying to figure out how we could both get away. Ashley fired and evaporated the nearest bots while the dog jerked my arm around, trying to shatter the gauntlet. She turned and tried to aim for the dog.

"Shoot it!" I shouted.

"I can't get a clear shot!"

A bot nearly twice her size grabbed her from behind and yanked her arm back. She fell to the ground and it started dragging her away.

"Logan!" she screamed in terror.

"I'm coming!"

With no other options, I raised my bare fist and slammed it into the dog's face full force. It made a strange sound, as if surprised. I swung repeatedly until it finally let me go. I smashed my gauntlet into its face. A horrid crunching sound erupted from its iron jaws on impact. It twitched sporadically and I heard gears grinding. I fired once, putting it out of its misery, then turned to the others still around me.

"Come on!" I taunted, "You want to fight? Let's do it!"

Adrenaline coursed through my veins as I tore through them, smashing them to pieces or turning them to dust. Soon others started turning, as if facing another opponent. I saw Diego wearing a giant platinum boot on his left leg, crushing the robots to smithereens. I turned in the other direction to find Natalie with a boot on her right leg following his lead.

"Go!" Natalie shouted, "Get Ashley!"

I nodded and dashed out of the crowd. Terror pushed more adrenaline in my system as I frantically looked for her. I heard her cry out and turned to my left. Amid the chaos, the giant bot had her sitting on her knees as it pulled her arm back behind her, close to an unnatural angle.

Out of the corner of my eye, I saw Melvin only a few feet away from her, either headbutting robots or shooting them with the eye laser. He grabbed a smaller one out of the sky, using his natural strength to tear open a back panel and pull out a mess of wires to deactivate it.

As I ran toward Ashley, I shouted, "Melvin!"

He turned to look at me. I pointed in her direction. He looked back at her, gave me a thumbs up, and charged. He tackled the robot, which let go of her automatically, then stood and shot it in the face. He took a look around, then ran off with a grin, seemingly oblivious to the fact his sister was still laying on the ground.

Ashley laid in the dirt, her jaw tight as she clutched her arm. When I reached her, I crouched down to get a better look.

"I'm okay," she said through shaky breaths, "Just a little shook up."

She sat up slowly and worked out her shoulder.

"Are you sure?" I asked.

She nodded. I leaned closer to gently kiss her forehead, but Adrian came from our left and interrupted us.

"I hate to break up your little love fest, but need I remind you we still have some ass to kick out here?" he said before bashing the face of a robot with his armored shoulder.

I stood and held my hand out to Ashley. She took it, massaging her shoulder one more time after I helped her up.

She winced every time the laser fired, as if she felt a sort of kickback from it. It wasn't long before our opponents were either obliterated or fleeing into the shadows of the caves, leaving behind an arena littered with dust and random mechanical parts that had been torn out of the robots.

"That was awesome!" Ulysseus shouted as he dashed toward the others.

While my friends started gathering at the center of the arena, I looked around for Ashley. My gaze landed on her standing off to the side rubbing her shoulder again.

I walked behind her and slowly wrapped my arms around her waist.

"You ok?" I asked.

"Yeah, it's just...weird."

"What is?"

"Well, I know this game is supposed to be life-like, but I never thought we could actually feel pain like that in game..."

"If it makes you feel any better, I think it goes away when we go to another level."

"How do you know that?"

"That bear thing cut up my leg in the last level. There's no pain now, not even a mark."

She moved out of my arms and turned to look at me.

"Why didn't you say anything?" she asked.

"Well, it happened in the middle of the fight, and once we were done, we arrived here. There wasn't really a time to bring it up."

She nodded, then hugged me.

"Are you hurt?" she asked.

"My hand's a little cut up, but I'm fine. That dog didn't get past my armor."

She held me for a moment longer, then felt heavy. Her knees had buckled. I gently laid her on the ground. She stared upward at nothing in particular.

"Ash? You okay?"

Then a familiar dizziness hit me. I fell forward beside her.

I wrinkled my nose at a foul odor that filled the air as I opened my eyes. It was just as dark as it had been when they were closed. That is until lanterns lit themselves aflame, giving off a dim orange glow. I blinked twice, then looked around to see all my friends close by. Some were sitting against a nearby wall while others were lying on the stone floor below. I heard what sounded like running water. I turned my head to see a current an inch or so away from me. Others in the group were lying in puddles of the putrid liquid. The guys were all wearing cotton pants and boots with either a vest or coat. Ulysseus, Adrian, and Diego had small dark hats on as well. The girls were all wearing plain cotton dresses.

"Oh, heck no! Do not tell me we're where I think we are!" Vivian growled.

Then our floating friend flew toward us from down the tunnel.

"Greetings players," it said, "Welcome to London, England in the mid-eighteen hundreds."

"Correct me if I'm wrong," Ulysseus said sarcastically, "I'm pretty sure that London has never been an underground tunnel."

"Which means we're not in London," Bryan said, "We're under it."

Alice turned to him and asked, "What do you mean?"

Then a look of horror crossed her face.

"Yep, I knew it!" Vivian shouted, "We're in a sewer!"

Alice started to fidget a bit, nervously running her fingers through her hair. I raised an eyebrow but said nothing. Bryan noticed and mouthed the word "germaphobe" before wrapping an arm around her shoulders for comfort. I could not really blame her for being grossed out; being trapped in the sewer had to be her worst nightmare, even if it was just a simulation.

"Correct players!" the voice said with what sounded like excitement, "and in this level you will experience your first encounter with chase levels. You are toshers in London's sewer system."

"What does that mean exactly?" Brandie asked.

"It means we're like treasure hunters...that look

for money in sewer waste," James said with disgust.

Alice shuddered. My nose wrinkled. Others in the group had similar reactions.

"Yes, but this is not a search level, therefore you will not be hunting for any treasures today," the bot said.

Alice let out a sigh of relief.

"You see," the robot continued, "This line of work was against the law in this time period, and so to give you a bit of a rush in this introduction, the creators have programmed for the royal guard to chase you out of the sewers. Enjoy, and good luck. I will see you at the next level."

It flew off once more.

"Enjoy? What kind of twisted humor is that?" Alice growled.

Everyone who was still on the ground stood, including myself. We looked down both sides of the hall, then at each other.

"So, what now?" Vivian asked.

I jumped back as the green letters showed up in my vision again.

Objective: Escape the Sewer

Others in the group had similar reactions as they saw objectives in their own vision. None of us were used to that yet.

We heard a scraping sound from above. A light appeared from the ceiling of the cesspool and some-one started climbing down a ladder. Then another, and several more. By the time they stopped, there were two dozen large, heavily armored men only a few feet away from us. They looked around for a

moment, as if disoriented, then one of them pointed at us.

"There! Get them!" he shouted.

"You just had to ask," Adrian grumbled.

"Shut up and run Adrian!" Vivian snapped.

We all bolted in the other direction, trying our
best not to trip over one another.

Soon after we started running, Brandie tripped
over her dress and fell. James was farther ahead, in
the middle of the crowd and could not turn around
to reach her. I hurried back to help Brandie onto her
feet.

"This thing is hard to run in," she griped.

She grabbed the bottom of her dress and tore
off a few inches of the fabric.

"Oh yeah, much better," she declared.

The guards sped up to reach us. I instinctually
ducked at the sound of gunfire.

"Come on, let's go!" I said.

We both started after the group again. Bullets
collided with the stones but were far from hitting
us. Whoever was in charge of the soldiers became
enraged.

"Get a move on lads!" he shouted.

We sprinted through the damp, filthy halls until we hit a crossroad. We stopped as the path split
into three, although I did not realize that we were
stopping until I ran straight into Adrian. He stumbled but stood upright and caught me so I would not
land on the soiled stones. The sound of heavy footsteps behind us grew louder each moment we stood
there.

"Where do we go?" James asked.

"Don't know, but we need to make a decision
before they catch us," Adrian said.

Melvin snapped his fingers, "Idea. Logan, Adrian, and Ulysseus, you guys stay with me. Everyone else go through one of the passages."

Everyone looked uncertain, especially Ashley.

"What? You guys don't trust me now?" he asked, looking a little hurt.

I stepped forward and clapped a hand on his shoulder, "I do. Come on guys, we need to get out of here. I'll take any idea we can get."

They all looked at each other once again before starting down the passage in the middle. Ashley stopped to eye Mel and I.

"I don't like this," she muttered.

"Oh relax," Melvin said, "We'll mess with their heads and meet you at the end. Besides, it's just a game."

Ash and I shared a look that said we were not so sure about that anymore. After a moment, she reluctantly hurried after the others.

Melvin turned back to the three of us with a grin and said, "Alright, here's the plan. We're going to split into two teams. Adrian, you're with me. Logan and Ulysseus, you guys go together. Both teams are going to go down one of the other two tunnels and distract the guards."

Melvin turned as if ready to start running again, but Ulysseus raised his hands again and said, "Wait a minute. You want to split up and do what exactly?"

"Make noises, taunt them, anything to get their attention. We'll do the same and maybe they'll split up so we can either lure them away or take them down."

"Take them down? Are you crazy?!"

"We'll be fine."

"Yeah, you'll be fine! Because you two are a couple of friggin' giants!" Ulysseus shouted, his accent growing heavier.

"What, are you saying I'm not strong?" I joked.

He turned to me, seeming surprised by my remark, "No, I'm not saying that at all. It's just that these two are football players. They're built for runnin' people over and rammin' them on the ground!"

I patted him on the back and said, "Relax, I'm just trying to lighten the mood."

He still seemed frustrated, but he took a deep breath and stopped yelling.

"This is serious," Ulysseus said, "And besides, what if they go down the other tunnel?"

"We just have to make sure they go down the other two."

"But if they don't?"

He looked a little embarrassed. He had not thought that far ahead.

"I'm hearing a heck of a lot of uncertainties in this plan," Ulysseus grumbled.

It was then that we realized the sound of stomping suddenly stopped. We turned to see the guards standing only a few feet away, raising their muskets.

"Run!" I shouted.

"Fire!" the captain screeched.

I ran down the left hand tunnel with Ulysseus close behind. Melvin and Adrian took off down the right hand tunnel. We narrowly missed being shot; I hoped the bullets had not somehow reached our friends running down the center tunnel. The men started shouting at each other, then split into two groups to follow us. We were lucky they were dumb enough to divide in the way Melvin hoped.

"Remind me to kick Melvin's arse when we get out of here!" Ulysseus shouted.

"Noted!" I hollered back.

We ran until we reached another crossroad, this time splitting immediately to our left and right. I looked down both paths for places to hide. Both paths were littered with boxes and barrels of various sizes. The walls were still lined with the lanterns, but they were being spread farther apart. Their positions made the halls dimmer, dim enough to give us time to hide.

"Go that way," I said pointing to our right, "Hide in one of those boxes and I'll go the other way."

"You sure?" he asked, glancing down the left hall.

I nodded, "We've got this. Go."

"Over here!" a guard shouted.

Ulysseus scrambled down his tunnel and I bolted down mine. I looked over my shoulder to see him closing the lid to his hiding place as the guards reached the intersection. The guards shouted something incoherent, and sadly all of them charged after me when their captain pointed toward the left-hand hallway.

"Crap," I said.

I strained my legs to get far enough ahead of them to hide, but it was no use. Soon there were no more boxes or barrels to hide in. There were no side halls to slip in either. Just more empty, dimly lit pathways. The guards still would not let up, and I was running out of energy.

Stupid NPCs and their stupid relentless AI, I thought angrily.

I screeched to a halt as the tunnel ended, opening out into a chasm filled with...well you know. It's a sewer.

The smell became much more horrific. I gagged while searching for an escape route. There were other tunnels that led out of the room, but they were on other sides of the chasm. I found a ledge I could use to reach them, but it seemed too thin for my gigantic feet to walk on. I looked behind me, seeing the guards getting closer, then back at the chasm. I shuddered at the thought of jumping into the horrid mess. I knew I only had one other option, one that was much more desirable than meeting the horrors below.

I hugged the wall and pointed my feet out sideways to clumsily clamber to the nearest tunnel on my right. Two guards screamed in terror as they fell into the darkness below, unable to stop in time. Another poked his head out of the tunnel, searching until his eyes landed on me.

"There!" he screamed, "Get him!"

The soldiers all quickly began trying to follow me. It took all of my willpower not to panic and move faster, knowing I would fall if I did. One of the soldiers slipped and grabbed one of his companions in an attempt to steady himself, but both of them fell. Another slipped soon after, unable to catch himself because of the weight of his armor. There were only seven left.

"Come on!" I taunted, hoping another would fall, "Come and get me!"

I reached the next opening, which was directly above me. Using all the upper arm strength I had, I pulled myself up and inside before running down another, much darker hall.

There were no lanterns to light the way, which probably meant I was not supposed to end up there.

I slowed my pace and felt along the wall as I walked to keep track of where I was going, keeping my free hand in front of me so I would not walk headfirst into stone. Something squeaked and sat on top of my right foot. I froze and forced myself not to kick it, afraid it might attack me. I let out a sigh of relief as it scurried off.

I heard the clicking of boots again. Despite the sound being faint, it would not be long before the remaining soldiers caught up with me. I blindly searched until I found a few boxes piled up in the hall. One in the middle was bigger than the others. Hoping nothing would be inside that wanted to kill me, I hurried in and closed the top. Their thundering footsteps grew louder, then suddenly stopped just outside of my hiding place.

Oh, that's bull. Don't tell me their AI is that smart.

I covered my mouth and nose with my hand to muffle my heavy breathing.

"We're not getting anywhere!" a gruff voice shouted.

"It's your fault! You were supposed to watch where he went!" another replied.

"No, Clive was supposed to!"

"Don't blame me you big oaf!" a third voice snapped, "You're the tracker!"

There was shuffling and screaming, telling me they were fighting. I flinched when I heard something slam and assumed that they were slamming each other into the boxes nearby.

"That's enough!" another voice said, "We don't have time for this. His Majesty expects these sewer hunters to be gone by dawn."

I lifted the lid of the box slightly, just enough to see them. All seven of the remaining soldiers were out there. Two had scratches and bruises that were starting to form, telling me they were the ones who had fought. One guard, a small and very skinny man, stood right in front of my box with his back turned to me.

They lifted their muskets and several lanterns they must have magically gotten, because they did not have them before. They started running down the hall again, all but the skinny man. He was not done looking around but paused to reach for his canteen.

An idea slipped into my mind.

I've always wanted to try this. Now's my chance, I thought.

Slowly and silently, I lifted the lid completely off and set it on the ground behind me. As he started to take a drink, I reached out and put him in a head-lock, pulling him into the box. He squirmed and coughed. I squeezed tighter until he finally passed out, which took a lot longer than I thought it would.

I heard footsteps from down the hall and feared that there may have been a soldier that I had not accounted for. I quickly grabbed the man's gun and lantern off of the floor, then closed the lid to my box. The man next to me moaned, as if waking up. I punched him in the face without thinking, knocking him out again.

The new thumping grew closer, much quieter than the others. Then it stopped and a fist lightly tapped the top of the box. I froze, my heartbeat roaring in my ears.

"Logan?" a voice whispered, "Are ya in there?"

I lifted the lid slightly and saw Ulysseus staring back at me.

"You scared the crap out of me," I said with a

grin.

"Sorry," he said smiling back, then held a hand out to me. I took it and awkwardly crawled out of the box.

"What are you doing here?" I asked as I picked up my new lantern.

"I saw them follow you, so I came to help."

He raised an eyebrow and peeked over my shoulder, then grinned again.

"Obviously, you didn't need it," he said.

I chuckled while I closed the box.

"How did you do that?" he asked.

"Trust me, the movies make it look a lot easier than it really is. I barely got him in there."

"Yeah, well, the fact that you're not very stealthy certainly didn't help," he joked.

"Shut up," I said, playfully punching his arm.

We both looked down the hall as we heard the soldiers shouting about something.

"We better go," Ulysseus said, "They may have just realized their man is missin'."

I nodded and we started retracing our steps. Eventually, we reached the original three-way split and started down the center path.

"Do you think everyone's alright?" Ulysseus asked.

"I'm sure they're fine," I replied.

He nodded but looked down with uncertainty. He pulled up his sleeve just enough to look at his watch, covering it again moments later. He repeated this twice more as we walked.

"Is everything okay?" I asked.

"Uh, yeah. Everything's fine. I'm just worried about them, that's all."

I could tell he was lying. Especially after the

fourth time he looked at his wrist.

"Why do you keep checking your watch?" I asked.

He kept looking at his feet as we walked. I stopped. He stopped a few paces ahead of me but would not lift his head.

"Hey, we're friends, right?" I asked.

He turned his head and looked back at me, then slowly nodded.

"Well, if you need to talk, I'm all ears."

He scratched his chin slightly, a sign that he was stressed out about something.

He huffed and said, "I just keep thinkin' about my grandfather."

"Is something wrong with him?"

"Yeah, but not what you might think."

I raised an eyebrow.

"He's our guardian, for Peyton and I. Our parents died when we were in elementary school. They got hit by a drunk driver one night while the babysitter was watchin' us."

"I'm sorry to hear that."

He shrugged, "It was a long time ago. I still love them, but my focus since then has been Peyton. Our grandfather is not a good man…And to be honest, I don't want to go back. For this day to be over."

He started shaking in fear. I cautiously reached out to touch his shoulder and gave it a slight squeeze.

"I'm assumin' nobody told you about him."

I shook my head.

"He's my mom's father. He's actually the reason my parents met, since she met my dad when she took a trip to Ireland for a foreign exchange program trying to get away from home for a bit. Probably the only good thing that happened because of him."

"Why? What did he do?"

"He's an ex-con, and not the kind that makes a mistake and turns their life around later. He was caught in an armed robbery about when mom was little and went to jail for about fifteen years. He's still bitter about it."

"He's bitter about missing out on your mom's childhood?"

"Yeah right," he scoffed, "The only thing he's bitter about is the fact that he got caught and missed out on that money. Greedy bastard. He was terrible to mom until she finally turned eighteen and left home. My grandparents got a divorce soon after. He's angry at the world for everythin' not going his way. Then when mom and dad died, he ended up becomin' our guardian. He hates that too."

He paused, seeming unsure of whether or not he should continue. I waited.

"Now he drinks. A lot. There were a lot of days Peyton and I didn't eat because of it, which is why she started workin' as soon as she was old enough. It's hard on her with school though and sometimes her grades slip. Plus, she's always tryin' to sneak more food on my plate to make sure I'm healthy, but then she doesn't have enough and gets sick. Sometimes I can get away with givin' it back, but normally she tells me to stop being a thorn in her side and eat it."

He grinned a little at the last sentence, but it disappeared almost as quickly. He started shaking.

"Our grandfather already has a wild temper, but when he really gets drinkin', he's so much worse. Anythin' can set him off and he hits us."

He started scratching his chin again in thought.

"When I was about thirteen, he hurt Peyton really bad before I got home from school. I ended up walkin' home because I missed the bus. Sonofabitch wouldn't take her to a doctor either, and I couldn't take her because I couldn't drive." His voice began cracking as he continued, "So I held her, and I told her everythin' would be alright. I got her into bed to rest. She was bleedin', and shakin', and she wouldn't stop cryin'. I remember runnin' into the bathroom and findin' some gauze and somethin' to make the pain stop while I patched her up. Then I laid in the bed with her until she fell asleep."

He stopped and took a shaky breath. A couple of persistent tears fell to the ground.

"Why was she bleeding?" I asked cautiously.

"Because that bastard cut her with a broken bottle, that's why," he growled.

His eyes were like kindling, lit ablaze by his anger at the memory. Then he closed them, and took a deep breath.

"Sorry," he said nervously.

"It's fine. You want to keep going?"

"In a minute. I think I need to sit down."

We sat against the wall. I set the lantern on the floor nearby. He put his head in his hands.

"I swore that he wasn't goin' to hurt her again after that," he continued, "Because I remember havin' to clean that wound. Luckily, there wasn't any glass stuck in her, but she kept twitching and shaking because it still hurt. Then she slept most of the next day, and we didn't go to school for a week or two. She was feeling too bad and I didn't want to leave her alone with him again."

More tears fell from his eyes as he ran his hands through his hair. I rubbed his back to comfort him.

"That asshole has only gotten worse since then. I make sure I'm home before Peyton no matter what so that if he attacks someone, it's me, not her. It's easier now that she works, but when we were young, I left the buildin' exactly when that last bell rang and ran so I could beat her home. The buses take forever to get out of the parkin' lot, so it's not hard to get home first if I'm fast enough. Now he can see our grades online, and like I said, sometimes Peyton slips a bit because she doesn't get enough sleep or can't keep up with it all. He hates it when our grades slip, and even though it's all his fault, he hurts one of us for it. I make sure to piss him off more when that happens so he takes it all out on me before she comes home from work. Then all she ends up with is him shoutin' at or lecturin' her rather than a beatin'."

He lifted his head and started to pull up his sleeve again, this time up to his elbow. He turned his arm to reveal a mess of scars, some small and curved, others long and horrifically jagged.

"I have more on my back and legs. It's why I wear long sleeves and pants every day, even in the summer. He always seems to have something handy to hit me with."

I remained silent, too appalled to find the right words to say. Ulysseus was definitely an outlier in the group, but he was a good guy. Maybe to his own detriment.

"Peyton's always gettin' mad at me for it," he said after a moment of silence, "She's always saying I should let her take the punishment, at least every now and then, but I don't. I won't. She's my sister, and older or not, I love her too much to let him hurt her like that again."

"Have you talked to anyone about this? The

police, or maybe someone who can get you out of there?"

He shook his head and looked at me hopelessly, "Talkin' to the police while living with a man like that is a frickin' death sentence. Only a handful of people know about this. And I guess that includes you now."

"Who else knows?"

He hesitated, then said, "Melvin and Ashley, and their parents. They only know because he locks us out of the house a lot, especially when we were younger. I think I was eight the first time it happened."

"Why did he lock you out?"

"Drunken bastard loves goin' to the bar but can't bother to give us a set of keys. When we were kids, we once got locked out in the freezin' rain. Peyton and I huddled on the porch until Tonya found us."

"Who?"

He seemed surprised that I didn't know, "Melvin and Ashley's mom."

"Oh."

"Jeez man, you're her boyfriend. Shouldn't ya know that?" he asked, starting to get frustrated with me.

"Ash doesn't talk about her very much."

He sat back against the wall and looked at the ceiling, staying silent for a few moments in thought.

"Anyway," he continued, "Tonya worked at an office for a little while when we were all kids, tryin' to make some extra money before Christmas that year. The office was only a block away from our house and she just happened to see us on her way home. She brought us back with her and we had dinner with them, then she let us sleep in the spare room. She took all of us to school the next mornin'.'"

He smiled a little at the thought.

"After that, Harold and Tonya told us that we could come over and stay whenever we needed to. We would go over there for dinner a lot, and stay the nights we were locked out or just too scared to go back to the house. It was like we had our parents again. It was nice."

I thought for a moment, then said, "You could still tell the police. You have proof that you've been abused, and Jared's a lawyer. Maybe he could —"

He was shaking his head as I spoke. I stopped.

"We can't do that," he said, "After Peyton got stabbed, I told Melvin what happened when we went back to school and he told his family. Harold and Tonya wanted to adopt us, and they were pretty much takin' care of us anyway. Peyton and I were scared though. When they wanted to go to court, we asked them not to because we knew we couldn't lie, and we'd die if we told the truth. I remember Peyton beggin' them not to say anything because she was scared for both of us. Somehow she had convinced them that we would be safer if they said nothing."

He paused for a moment, his brow furrowed and he growled through clenched teeth, "I hate goin' to that house. I hate bein' so close to someone that makes it terrifyin' to even fall asleep at night."

His fists were tightly clenched as he tried to control his emotions. He squeezed his eyes shut as if holding back tears. I felt bad for him. There is no other way to put it. I felt terrible and did not know what to do to help him. Without any other ideas, I reached out and hugged my friend. He tensed slightly, seeming surprised by my reaction, but he didn't pull away. After a few seconds, I let him go and sat back against the wall once more. Ulysseus kept looking forward for another moment, then turned to look at me.

"Hey," he said shyly, "I...I really needed this. Thank you."

"No problem. I'm a hugger, and you looked like you needed it."

He smiled and nodded thoughtfully. Rubbing his eyes as he stood, he turned to me and said, "Come on, we don't want the others to worry."

He held his hand out to help me up. I took it and stood beside him. I grabbed the lantern and we walked silently down the tunnel.

After a long stretch of time listening to the tapping of our feet, we saw a light coming from the ceiling, like a spotlight highlighting the iron ladder to the surface.

We glanced at each other when we heard voices from above and cautiously stepped closer. I realized they were our friends when I heard Ashley growling, "Melvin, what did you do?!"

I grinned and started climbing up the ladder, with Ulysseus close behind. Once I reached the surface, I saw the others only a few feet away. Ashley was fuming and in Melvin's face about something. Adrian stood behind Vivian as if she were a human shield.

"If he comes back here and he's hurt..." Ashley warned.

Melvin had his hands up defensively and interrupted with, "Ash relax. It's a video game, it's no big deal."

The others were chatting amongst themselves, keeping a short distance from the conflict, until Bryan noticed us and pointed.

"There they are," he said.

The others turned to us. Ulysseus walked past me to reach Peyton. She was smiling until she saw his face, which was fine other than his eyes still being slightly red. He pulled her in for a tight hug. As she wrapped her arms around him, she looked at me and mouthed the words, "What happened?"

"Everything's fine," I mouthed back.

She gave him a gentle squeeze and they both let go.

Ashley hugged me tightly.

"Everything okay?" I asked as I wrapped her up.

She said nothing at first, shaking slightly.

"I was worried," she whispered, "I don't know what's going on in this game, I just know something's not right."

I squeezed her gently and murmured, "It's alright. I'm here now. I'm not going anywhere."

Adrian cautiously stood beside Vivian. I grinned.

"Scared of my girlfriend Adrian?" I teased.

"Uh, duh," he said, without hesitation, "The only thing scarier than her is mine."

"Hey!" Vivian shouted, quickly turning to face him.

His eyes widened. He tried to calm her down, seeming to regret his statement. I chuckled and looked down to see Ashley smiling slightly. I rubbed her back and kissed her head.

"You okay now?" I asked.

She nodded but did not let go, snuggling with my chest.

"And I thought Brandie and I snuggled a lot," James teased.

The couple walked closer to us and Brandie asked, "What? You don't want to snuggle now?"

"No, no. I never said that."

He quickly hugged her. She yelped in surprise. I let go of Ashley while she responded, "You can't complain James. You guys have been cuddling for two years."

"Hey, I never said I was complaining," he stated, "I just pointed out something obvious."

"So, the same thing you always do," Brandie said.

He looked up at her, "Who's side are you on?"

She gave him a quick kiss and walked off to some of the others.

Ulysseus suddenly groaned as if in pain. We turned to see him holding his head as he fell forward. Peyton quickly caught him and helped him lay on the ground. I stumbled as my own head started to ache. I slowly sat on the ground. Ashley sat beside me.

"Not this again," Ulysseus said before falling asleep.

"Looks like we finished," Ashley said.

I nodded and let the darkness take over my vision.

Shopping Trip

I slowly opened my eyes, squinting due to the sunrise ahead of me. After blinking twice to adjust to the light, I realized that I was sitting in the driver's seat of a small car and reached for the sun visor. I looked myself over to discover that I was wearing a blue t-shirt, jeans, and tennis shoes. I reached up to my head and found that I was also wearing a black ballcap. I took it off to get a better look, spotting the Alpha Softworks logo across the front.

Plugging that merch, I guess, I thought.

I put the hat back on and took a deep breath, preparing myself for whatever was next. A soft mumbling came from my right. I realized Ashley was still asleep in the passenger's seat. She wore clothes that were similar to mine, aside from her shirt being a dark green and she wasn't wearing a hat.

She muttered something once more, then awoke with a start. I reached my hand out to calm her, gently rubbing her shoulder. She eased back into the seat.

"I'm really getting sick of that," she mumbled sleepily.

"Obviously Ulysseus is too," I said with a grin.

She smiled and rubbed her eyes, then turned

to me.

"What are we supposed to do now?" she asked.

"I don't know. I just woke up too."

She looked me over for a moment, then bit her lip, seeming nervous. I raised an eyebrow.

"What?" I asked.

She hesitated, then unbuckled her seatbelt and leaned closer to me. I was surprised when she kissed me, but that's not why I pulled away. The look on my face was a giveaway that something was wrong, but I knew she was going to misinterpret it.

"What? What's wrong?" she asked, now worried.

"Nothing, it's just..."

Nothing Ashley, I'm just a nervous wreck and I have no idea what I'm doing, or if I'm even doing anything right and I don't know how to tell you that without you thinking I'm a loser, I thought hopelessly.

She quickly backed away and said, "Look, if you're not comfortable with this, we can just stop."

My eyes widened slightly. Panic took hold, "No! No, it's not like that at all! This has been great!"

Something else was taking over. I could see it in her eyes. She was always worried about pushing me to do things I did not want to do, even though neither of us had done anything to overstep each other's boundaries.

"I get it. You don't want to date, fine," she said, her voice a bit shaky as she looked away from me.

I quickly, but gently, grabbed her arm to stop her, "Ashley, it's not like that, I promise."

She still seemed uncertain. I gently pulled her closer.

"Trust me, it's not anything to do with you."

"Oh great. The 'it's not you, it's me' speech."

I huffed in frustration before saying, "Just listen for a second."

I let go of her arm. She watched me carefully.

"This is wonderful. I really do like being with you. I just have...some issues with my nerves."

"Why though? I thought everything was fine with us. And last night...I thought..."

She was racking her brain trying to figure out what she had done wrong, which only made her more stressed and confused. I pulled her against me, rocking her slightly.

Are you really going to out yourself right now? I thought, *You might screw this up if you do.*

I knew keeping my secret was not worth her being so worried all the time, but a part of me was still afraid of her making fun of me for it.

I took a deep breath and murmured, "Last night was one of the best nights of my life. And I know it was our first kiss, but...it was also my first kiss."

She pulled away and gave me a perplexed look, "Really?"

I nodded, feeling embarrassed.

"That's what you were so worried about?" she asked.

"Well," I stammered, "I...I haven't really dated before and I didn't want you to think less of me."

"Why would I think less of you?"

"I don't know. I just didn't want to risk anything."

She gave me a small smile and kissed my cheek lightly.

"Well, you have nothing to worry about," she

said, "It's kind of nice to be with someone who hasn't really dated before."

"That's hard to believe. I have literally no idea if I'm doing anything right."

"Let me be the judge of that."

She kissed me again, but quickly pulled away.

"Oh, now that's just mean," I said as she reached for the door.

She grinned, "You started it."

Her door opened and she got out of the car.

"That's even worse."

I hurried out of the car and quickly ran to pick her up. She squealed in surprise. I laughed.

"You don't have to catch me to hug me," she said as I set her back on the ground.

"That sound you made was totally worth it," I teased.

"Shut up!"

"No, I like messing with you."

"You're such a pain."

"Aw, look, something else we have in common."

She glared at me, but I chuckled and kissed her forehead. She snuggled up to my chest, arms wrapped around me.

"I still like being with you though," I said.

"Look, something else in common."

I kissed her head one last time before we let each other go. We turned to see what looked like a small grocery store. Just in front of it sat a large metal sign with an arrow pointing toward the store that said, "Come on in!"

We glanced at one another before cautiously walking toward the building. The front doors opened automatically, a gust of icy air hitting us as we stepped inside. Aisles of groceries were laid out in front of us throughout the building, along with some registers to the right. I saw produce neatly displayed on refrigerated shelves in various bins to our left. Further to the left sat a deli station with various meats and cheeses wrapped and prepared for purchase, along with wrapped sandwiches displaying labels claiming that they were fresh and used all natural ingredients. Behind the produce section were several rows of freezers and refrigerators filled with packaged foods and bottled drinks. Past those were dry storage shelves of prepackaged snacks and individual ingredients such as various grains and spices. To the right of them, at the middle of the store, there was a gap for people to walk down the aisles, then more shelves with rows of various dry and canned goods. We did not see any other people inside.

I looked down one of the aisles and found the little flying robot from the other levels. It floated toward us, stopping about a foot away.

"Hello players. Welcome to the final level of your tutorial," it said happily, "This level allows you to experience search levels that you will encounter in the future. In search levels you will have to look for characters, teammates, or items. In this level, you will have to find everything on the shopping list provided. Your group is split into teams of two, all but one which is a group of three. Are there any questions?"

"Yeah, what list are you talking about?" Ashley asked.

"Please check your pockets."

She reached into the pocket of her jeans and

pulled out a folded piece of paper. She unfolded it. I looked over her shoulder. It was a short grocery list with ten items neatly written on it.

I turned back to the robot, "And our friends?"

"They have either already started or will be arriving shortly for their debriefing. Any other questions?"

We shook our heads.

"Well, if that's the case, good luck and have fun," the robot said, then floated past us through the automatic doors, which still opened despite the fact that it did not have any feet to activate the sensors.

I turned back to her and said, "Well this is an interesting change of pace."

"Considering we keep having to run from or fight everything, I'll take any break we can get," she replied as her eyes skimmed over the list.

I looked behind us and saw a line of four shopping carts with green handlebars.

"Well, we better get started then," I said as I grabbed a cart.

Ashley walked beside the buggy as we searched the fridges for the first three items. Eggs, milk, and yogurt. I grabbed the dairy items while Ashley got the eggs from a few fridges down.

"What next?" I asked.

She looked it over and said, "Apples, broccoli, and peaches."

We strolled back to the produce section and Ashley grabbed the broccoli, looking at it carefully before picking up a stalk to examine it closer. I walked to one of the produce bins and looked until I found the apples.

"How many do I need?" I asked.

She checked the list and said, "It says five."

I grabbed one of the produce bags and started grabbing random apples. When I grabbed the third one, Ashley lightly placed a hand on my wrist. I looked up at her and raised an eyebrow.

"What are you doing?" she asked.

"Getting the apples?" I said, slightly confused.

She turned my wrist slowly and showed me the other side of the apple, which had several bruises.

"It's not like we're going to eat them," I said.

"If we have to do this, we might as well do it right," she pointed out.

She let me go. I put the apple back down.

"Let me see your bag," she said.

She held her hand out and I set the bag down. She pulled one of them out of the bag and squeezed it slightly.

"This one's good," she said, handing it to me.

When she squeezed the second one, she made a weird face.

"Feel this one."

I lightly squeezed it. A slight indentation from my fingers remained in the skin.

"So, this one's bad?" I asked.

"Not necessarily, but it's probably mushy. Unless you want to make a smoothie or something, you don't want it."

"You're such a perfectionist," I teased as I set the squishy apple back in the bin.

"Like I said, we might as well do it right."

I looked through the apples more carefully, showing them to her for approval. When we had five, I set the produce bag in the cart, which already had three broccoli stalks as well.

As we walked toward the peaches, I asked, "How do you know all this?"

"Dad works a lot. Mel and I take turns getting groceries since he doesn't always have time to."

"So, you guys cook and get groceries?"

"Not always, but sometimes I think dad uses work so he doesn't have to think about everything."

I nodded and watched as she searched through the peaches, trying to pay attention.

"Good thing you already know all this stuff. I will probably be asking a lot when I have to feed myself."

She smiled, "Well, I'd rather you ask me than make yourself sick."

I started pushing the cart again. She set the bag of peaches in the basket while we walked.

"Now we need to get trail mix, jerky, and bread."

She grabbed a random loaf of bread from the aisle and threw it in.

"What happened to 'we might as well do it right?'" I asked.

"That's the same bread I normally grab. Same package and everything, so I only needed to look at it."

I looked at the package and said, "Dang. Whoever was in charge didn't even take the time to come up with cheesy fake labels. I'm a little disappointed."

She grinned and said, "We're in a game where we are fighting robots and can literally feel pain, but that's all it takes to disappoint you?"

"It's all about the little details."

She lightly nudged me with her elbow and I

chuckled. We turned down a snack aisle to look for the trail mix. Ashley's hand slowly rested on mine as I pushed the cart. I turned my head to look at her and smiled. She smiled back, then leaned against my shoulder. About halfway down the aisle, she tugged on the handle to stop.

"What's up? Did you find it?" I asked.

She shook her head, "We're okay, right? I know I freaked out a little back there."

She looked as if she felt guilty. I turned and took both her hands in mine.

"It's like I said before, I'm not going anywhere. I just have to get over my nerves."

She nodded once more. Before she could turn away I gave her another kiss. It was much longer than the one in the car. When I pulled away, she tried to pull me back.

"Oh no," I teased, "it's your turn to wait now."

She narrowed her eyes and said, "You're such a pain."

"Takes one to know one."

She rolled her eyes.

"What's gotten into you today?" she asked curiously.

"What do you mean?"

"Really? You said you're nervous, but you keep wanting to cuddle and kiss every chance you get."

"Well, we kissed last night. I think I should consider that to be the green light."

I nuzzled her nose. She giggled and did the same to mine.

"Eww! Come on! Give a guy a warnin' if you two are goin' to get all lovey dovey on us!" a voice shouted.

We both turned to see Ulysseus and Peyton standing at the end of the aisle. He had a look of disgust on his face. Meanwhile Peyton laughed at his reaction.

"Oh, leave them alone," she said while nudging his arm, "I think it's adorable."

He crossed his arms and turned to her, "Yeah, *you* think it's adorable. *I* think it's gross!"

She raised an eyebrow, "Really? Then why is it that you keep looking at Ellie Martins like you have hearts in your eyes?"

"What does that even mean?" he growled, seeming stunned by the remark. His face started to turn red and his voice got a little higher.

"Judging by the look on your face, I think you know," Ashley chimed in.

He glared at her and shouted, "You're all so weird!"

He hurried off to another aisle, Peyton laughing as she followed close behind. Ashley and I laughed.

"He'll learn eventually," I murmured.

"What does that mean exactly?"

I turned back to her, "Did I say that out loud?"

"Well, unless I just imagined it. Yeah, you did."

I nuzzled her again, hoping to change the subject.

"Don't try to distract me," she said, "What do you mean?"

"You'll probably laugh and call me a dork."

"I'll probably do that in five minutes anyway. You might as well get it out of the way."

I grinned, "You're probably right."

"I think by now we both know I'm right about

that. So, what did you mean?"

"I just meant that us being this close is one of the greatest feelings in the world."

"Wow, that kiss really messed with your hormones, huh slick?"

I chuckled, "Maybe, but I'm okay with it."

I kissed her forehead and squeezed her tightly.

After another minute of hugging, she cleared her throat and said, "Don't get me wrong, I'm really enjoying this, but we need to get this list done."

"Okay," I said.

I let her go. She took my hand as she said, "But maybe we can convince the others to take a break so we can do this in the real world."

I grinned, quickly grabbing the cart and charging down the aisle.

"Let's go!" I shouted.

She laughed, "You didn't even make it to five minutes you dork."

"Just remember that you're the one who said yes when I asked you out."

"One has nothing to do with the other."

She caught up with me and rested her hand on mine as we walked. Moments later we heard Ulysseus shouting again.

"What is wrong with you people?!" he screeched.

Ashley raised an eyebrow. I shrugged in response. We left the buggy on our aisle to check on him. A few aisles down he stood covering his eyes. Peyton was too busy laughing to tell us what was wrong. I glanced down the aisle and laughed when I saw Adrian and Vivian making out a few feet away.

Adrian paused to ask, "Hey General, do ya

mind?"

"Stop callin' me that!"

He turned around, grumbling under his breath while marching away. Then stopped when he saw me and Ashley.

"Oh, no! Don't you two start again!"

He quickly ran off, desperate to get away from the rest of us.

"James, Brandie, if I find you two makin' out somewhere in this store, I'm leavin'!" he shouted, his voice much higher than normal both in volume and pitch.

Peyton rolled her eyes but she was still grinning. She walked toward us to give Adrian and Vivian some space.

"Sorry about him. He's a little overdramatic, and he still isn't very comfortable with the idea of dating yet," she explained.

Ashley raised an eyebrow, "Isn't he fifteen now?"

Peyton nodded, "Yeah. I know, it surprises me too. I think it's more that he's nervous though, not that he's disinterested."

I shrugged, "Everybody matures at their own pace. He'll get there."

"And guys mature slower anyway," Ashley added, looking pointedly at me.

"What's that look mean?" I asked.

"It means that while I enjoy being with you, you are still very immature."

"I can be mature when I want to be," I defended.

She crossed her arms as she said, "Prove it."

"I would, but you see, I don't really feel like it

right now."

She turned to Peyton and pointed at me with her thumb as she said, "See what I mean?"

I quickly pulled her against me before ruffling her hair, keeping a tight grip so she could not get away until I was done.

"You do realize that you're just continuing to prove my point," she said as she tried to rearrange her hair.

"Happy to help," I replied.

Peyton was grinning as she watched the two of us.

"Alright," she said, grabbing her cart, "I've had enough cute bickering for today. Besides, I better grab my brother before he has another freak out."

"Good luck with that," I replied.

She pushed the cart forward and searched for Ulysseus. Ashley and I walked back to our cart hand in hand. We searched through the snack aisle until we found bags of trail mix, all in green packages with a clear front to see the contents inside.

I picked up a bag and looked through the clear front. She grabbed another one nearby and turned it over.

"Wonder if this one's any good," she murmured.

"What's in it?"

"Pretzels, dark chocolate, almonds, cashews. A few other things."

I took a small instinctual step away. Her brow furrowed.

"Something wrong?" she asked.

"Sorry, natural reaction."

"Okay, but that still doesn't explain what's

wrong."

"I'm just allergic to cashews, that's all."

"Why didn't you tell me?"

I shrugged, "I didn't think it was a big deal."

She put the bag down and rubbed her forehead with irritation.

"What?" I asked.

She punched me hard in the shoulder.

"Ow! What was that for?!" I yelped.

"Logan, I eat cashews all the time. You can't just keep allergies like that a secret!"

My eyes widened in surprise, "How did I not get sick at your house then?"

"Because, lucky for both of us, I usually eat them after dinner and you're usually at home by then. On top of that, we've been out for two weeks, and Mel keeps forgetting to get more when he gets groceries, so I was waiting until the next time I went."

She rubbed her forehead again.

"I'm sorry," I said, "Like I said, I didn't think it was a big deal."

She thought for a moment, then put her hands down and asked, "So what happens if you eat one, or touch one?"

"I...I get anaphylaxis."

"Which means?"

"My skin reacts, then I have trouble breathing and I get nauseous. The doctor told me if my blood pressure drops low enough, I pass out."

"Is it just cashews, or other tree nuts too?"

"Just cashews, I've never reacted to the others."

"Are you allergic to anything else?"

"Nothing that I know of."

"Okay."

She started walking again, but I heard her mutter, "Dating is like a freaking rollercoaster."

I dropped the bag of trail mix I had been holding into the basket, then grabbed a bag of random jerky from the shelf as I hurried after her.

"Hey, I'm sorry. I'm not trying to freak you out. I wasn't trying to hide it, I just didn't think about it," I explained.

She shook her head, "I know. It's just...Logan, I could've killed you."

I held her hand again and said, "But you haven't. I'm fine."

She nodded, then rested her head on my shoulder again as we walked.

"So, since we're having the conversation, are you allergic to anything?" I asked.

"Not that I know of, no."

"Okay."

We walked aimlessly a little longer before she pulled the list back out of her pocket. As she looked at the last few items, my stomach growled. She flinched, then laughed when she realized what it was.

"Is that the virtual you or the real you that's hungry?"

"I don't know, but I'm going to say it's probably both."

We started walking past the deli. She grabbed a package of sharp cheddar and put it in the basket. Then she looked at the pre-wrapped sandwiches and read the labels.

"Close your eyes," she said.

"What?"

"Just do it. I want to see if I can remember what

you like."

"Why?"

"Because I just want to. Now close them."

"Okay. We're doing a big trust exercise here."

I closed my eyes and waited. I heard her pick up a sandwich and unwrap it.

"Take this one and eat it."

I took a bite of the sandwich, then opened my eyes.

"Turkey and cheddar?" I asked.

She nodded.

"Good guess. That's my favorite."

"Yes!"

I grinned at her excitement, then said, "Alright, my turn. Close your eyes."

She did and I looked through the options as I continued to eat.

Okay, I know for a fact that she likes Swiss, but I don't remember what deli meat she likes.

I tried to remember what lunch meat she ate the few times she had brought a sandwich to school.

I know it wasn't ham. It was either chicken or turkey.

I took a guess and grabbed the chicken with swiss, then unwrapped it and handed it to her. She took a bite and opened her eyes, saying nothing.

"Well don't leave me in suspense," I said.

She shook her head, "Tsk tsk, not the right meat."

"You like turkey, don't you?"

She nodded.

"Dang it."

She smiled, "It's okay, I eat chicken too."

I squeezed my eyes shut and made a weird

face.

"What are you doing?" she asked.

"Drilling it in my brain so I remember."

"Sometimes I wonder if you're trying to get me to call you a dork."

I opened my eyes and grinned, then started eating my sandwich again.

"How did you know we would be able to eat in this?" I asked between bites.

"I wasn't sure but considering this is supposed to be super realistic and you were hungry, I figured we could at least try."

"I'm glad we did. I feel a million times better."

I finished eating and took the list to look it over.

"We just have to get the last three items, right?"

She nodded.

The only items left were cereal, jelly, and peanut butter. I looked at the front shelves across the center gap and saw the cereal.

"I see the cereal aisle. I'll grab it while you finish up."

She nodded again and took another bite. I looked over the shelves full of cereal, grabbing a random box. I looked at the name on the package, which said "Oat-Rings."

Wow, even the made up names are a little disappointing.

I walked back to the cart, but heard Melvin shouting, "Almost done y'all! We're gonna win!"

"It's not a race Melvin!" Diego shouted back.

I chuckled and dropped the box in our cart, but Ashley was gone. Moments later, she returned with a jar in each hand.

"Got the last of it," she said.

She set them down in the basket.

"So, what now?" I asked.

Objective Complete
Please wait for other players to continue.

Ashley blinked a couple of times.

"I guess we just wait at the front of the store," she said.

We walked past the front registers and realized we were the second team to finish, only after the youngest members of our group.

Ulysseus raised his hands as we approached them, "Nope. Nope, not doing it. I'm going outside."

Ashley and I grinned as he walked out of the automatic doors and sat on a nearby bench.

She turned to me and said, "I'm going outside for a minute too. I need to just sit down for a while before things start getting crazy again."

I nodded and gave her a light kiss on the forehead before she walked off. She sat outside on the bench with Ulysseus. I took a few steps forward and stood next to Peyton. She was nervously tapping the screen of her watch with a look similar to the one Ulysseus had in the sewers.

"Everything okay Peyton?" I asked.

She flinched and put her arms down before nodding. I raised an eyebrow.

"Are you sure?"

She ran her fingers through her hair while responding, "I'm fine. Just a lot on my mind."

"Do you want to talk about it?"

She turned to me, "It's not something I really

talk about."

"Does it have anything to do with your grand-father?" I asked cautiously.

Her brow furrowed. She eyed me carefully, "How do you know about that?"

"Ulysseus," I said, "He told me about your grandfather hurting both of you."

She turned to look at her brother through the glass, "Is that why he was upset?"

"Yeah. He nearly had a breakdown when it was just us, so I told him he could talk it out if he wanted to."

"Well, thank you for being there for him. He doesn't talk about that very often, even with me."

I waited a moment before saying, "He told me you got cut really bad when you were kids."

She nodded, "Yeah. Right above my hip. There's still a scar from it."

"For what it's worth, I'm sorry about what you're going through. Both of you."

"Thanks."

I quietly waited to see if she would say more. After a long silence she said, "He always has me worried. I know that the punishments hurt more than he lets on."

I rubbed her shoulder comfortingly and said, "He also told me you guys won't tell anyone."

"Besides Mel and Ash, you're the only one in the group that knows. We've been trying to hide it so we don't stir up trouble, but it's getting harder."

I let her go, "How so?"

She took a deep breath, "Ulysseus almost had to go to the hospital, maybe a month ago. If I hadn't gotten home when I did, I don't know what would've happened."

My eyes widened in surprise, "He didn't tell me that."

"We didn't even tell Melvin and Ashley," she said, pausing before she continued, "When I got home from work, Ulysseus was standing in the driveway slamming his hands on grandpa's car. He was cursing and driving grandpa crazy. When I got close, I heard the car start and I had to push Ulysseus out of the way or...he would've been hit. Grandpa just took off down the street. I scolded Ulysseus for making him angry, but he apparently deserved it."

"Why?"

"From what I was told, he threatened Ulysseus and said that he would kill us. He beat Ulysseus, then decided to get drunk down the street instead of at the house. Ulysseus thought he was going to go to where I work and hurt me."

She did not say anything for a moment, but she did not cry either.

"I keep checking the time because we don't have much longer before curfew. I'm trying to lay low and get him to do the same, so I've been trying to keep track."

My heart ached as I watched her, knowing more was going on inside her head. I gave her a quick side hug to comfort her. For a moment, it pulled her away from her thoughts.

"The only problem right now is that I can't find any kind of pause or exit menu on this watch," she added.

"Maybe it's just in a weird spot?"

I looked at my own watch and scrolled through

the various menus, but I could not find it either.

"That's weird," I said.

She nodded, "It's almost five, so we'll have to figure it out soon."

"Five already?"

"Yeah. You know what they say, time flies."

We stopped as other teams started to join us. Ashley and Ulysseus walked back inside to join us. When everyone had finished, we all waited to pass out and move on to the next level. But nothing happened.

I heard the familiar buzzing from the robot as the automatic doors opened once more.

"Congratulations players!" it exclaimed, "You have completed the tutorial levels for Seventy Five Lives! You now have experience in the four basic types of levels and have explored some of your abilities. Please be aware, there are other types of levels and the first four are meant to allow you to get used to your virtual experience. From this point forward, you will be primarily on your own, and I will only be able to help if any of you come across new game features. Allow me to formally introduce myself. My name is GuideBot, and I have been your faithful companion up to this point. Please enjoy the remainder of your virtual experience."

Before anyone could say anything, the world went dark.

Love and Undeath

I awoke in pure darkness. My nose wrinkled as the smell of mold and rotten wood filled the air. I felt along the floor until I found a wall, then pushed myself to my feet. My hand felt along the old timber as I walked. I flinched when my hand bumped something sticking out of the wall. When nothing attacked me, I reached out again and realized it was a doorknob. I started to turn it but froze at the sound of moans and rasps.

What is that? I thought.

I pushed the door slightly, making sure it was completely closed. My ear pressed lightly against the door. Suddenly, whatever was on the other side slammed against it, startling me. I jumped back and took a few steps away.

I'm definitely not going that way.

I turned around and put my hand on the wall again, searching for another exit. A long walk later, I found another handle. I pressed my ear against the door and waited.

Nothing here. Hopefully this isn't some stupid trick.

I turned the cold, metal knob and pushed against the door. It squealed as if in agony until it opened. My feet hit the grass and took a few steps away from the little cabin I awoke in. The cabin sat at the top of a hill overlooking a massive gathering of pines from all sides. Beyond the trees, the sun slowly rose above the horizon as a new morning began.

I looked down at my clothes; an old dark grey shirt and an army green jacket, hooded and lined with fleece, with a breast pocket on each side. Below were tattered denim jeans and brown hiking boots caked in mud and another dark substance I couldn't identify. My hands were covered with a set of fingerless leather gloves, which seemed dingy and worn. A handgun holster sat at my right hip holding a pistol. A small axe rested in a belt loop next to the pistol. To my right sat a scabbard with some kind of sword inside. I reached behind me to find a backpack, which I thought must have been empty, or at least close to it, because it was so light.

I froze when I heard the moaning again and turned.

You have got to be kidding me.

The corpse let out a choked growl as it staggered toward me, dragging a leg behind the rest of its body. Its ankle and calf were bent at unnatural angles and a bone jutted from the decomposing flesh. From what I could tell, the figure may have been a man at one point or another, or at least it was programmed to look that way. Tattered clothes draped over the figure as it limped forward, its glazed eyes fixed on me.

Well, good thing I watch too many zombie movies.

I grabbed my axe and took a step forward. The corpse's hands reached out to grab me. I swung the axe above my head and drove the blade down with all of my strength. The rasping stopped. I removed the axe, grimacing as blood splattered onto my face and clothes.

Delightful, I thought sarcastically.

I shoved the figure to the ground and looked at the axe. A stream of red ran along the edge of the blade before slowly dripping to paint the grass.

My eyes scanned my surroundings, landing on something shiny in the corpse's coat pocket.

I crouched down, hoping for some kind of weapon or clue to the mission. When I reached inside the pocket, all I got was a small key attached to a keychain. The key was silver with a worn label attached to it. Only the letter "S" in black ink could be made out. At the end of the keychain, there was a fake wedge of cheese with the consistency of a stress ball.

I thought about leaving the key behind, but as I set it down, something beeped. I looked for the sound until I found a watch on my wrist, the representation of the watch I wore in the real world. It continued making noise until I picked the key up again.

Weird.

I slipped the keychain in the pocket of my jeans before standing. I then turned and started down the hill, axe ready to strike. As I reached the tree line, a new line of text appeared before me, now a bright shade of blue.

Objective: Reach the Safe Zone

I looked up as a blue beacon appeared in the sky, miles away from me.

Looks like I'm on my own, I thought.

I marched forward, alert and waiting for another zombie. Sunlight peeked through the leaves, allowing me to see in the otherwise dark forest.

Humming a song softly, I walked through the abandoned twigs and pebbles spread across the dirt, my footsteps matching the beat.

I wonder where everyone else is.

I flinched due to the sound of gunshots to my left.

I just had to ask.

I trotted toward the sound, careful to rest my hand just below the axe blade rather than flailing the weapon.

Another loud boom came from the path ahead of me. I quickened my pace until I reached a small clearing in the trees. I raised my hands in surrender as Brandie aimed a gun at me.

"Whoa, whoa, truce!" I shouted.

"Logan?" she asked, one eyebrow raised.

She lowered the hunting rifle.

"Sorry," she said timidly.

I looked at the fallen corpses littering the field, four in total.

"It's okay. Looks like you were a little shook up."

She put the rifle sling over her shoulder and stepped closer. Her blond hair was braided. She wore a plain black shirt and jeans, along with boots similar to mine. A leather satchel was strapped across her torso. Her clothes were covered in mud and zombie blood.

"What happened to you?" she asked, pointing at my face.

I wiped some of the blood off and said, "Same

thing as you."

"You alright?"

I nodded, "Yeah, I'm fine. You?"

"I'm good."

"Have you run into anyone else?"

"No. Honestly I thought I was alone for this one."

"Hopefully we'll run into some of the others."

She nodded and started in the direction of the safe zone. I followed close behind her.

The farther we walked, the harder it was to stay on course. The forest floor was littered with fallen trees and large jagged rocks. We kept turning and changing directions.

"I don't even know where we're going anymore," I growled.

"Me neither."

I looked up at the trees, which had become bare in the patch of forest we walked into.

We froze at the sound of ragged growls ahead. She started trembling. Directly ahead of us stood three of the undead, none of which had spotted us yet. I readied my axe and took a silent step forward, but she quickly grabbed me by the arm and shook her head, eyes wide with fear. My brow furrowed.

Does she know something I don't? I wondered.

She pulled me to the side and we crouched down behind a cluster of bushes.

"What is it?" I whispered.

She put a finger to her lips, then looked through the leaves.

"Brandie–"

She pressed her hand over my mouth, trying to shut me up. I looked over the brambles at the zombies, which were now looking around as if they heard us.

How?

I ducked back down, pulling her hand away from my mouth. She readied her rifle, in case she had to fire, then pointed at my pistol. I shook my head, wanting to attack quietly. Her jaw tightened and her eyes lit with silent irritation. The growls grew closer. Her irritation was doused by fear.

I glanced over the bushes again and saw one less than a foot away. It started walking off to our right. My knuckles turned slightly pale as I crawled after it. Brandie grabbed my jacket to stop me, but I pulled away and hid in the next cluster. The zombie stopped and moaned just next to the leaves.

I quickly rose to chop into its decrepit skull. When the growling stopped, I pulled my axe back and kicked it away. Brandie fired her rifle to take out another.

What is she doing? She's just going to attract more of them.

I fell on my back as the third one slammed into me with the force of a bull. The hatchet flew from my hand. I managed to react just in time to grab the zombie's shoulder before it bit into my nose.

"What the heck?!" I shouted.

The zombie rapidly writhed and snapped at me. I could hardly fend it off. Then it was gone when Brandie heaved it off of me. She screamed as it turned to her before she could raise her weapon. She gripped its shoulders and pushed it back, but her hands started to sink into the decaying flesh. Her eyes were wild, repeatedly glancing at the axe as she tried to figure out a way to get it.

I jumped up and drew the sword, quickly thrusting the blade through its skull. The sickening sound of bones crunching came from the monster before it fell to the ground. When the corpse collapsed, Brandie turned on me.

"What were you thinking?!" she shouted.

I raised my hands in surrender, "Truce, remember?"

She shoved me hard. I stumbled back a step.

"Brandie calm down."

"Calm down? Are you insane?!"

I reached out and gently held her shoulders. She was shaking with rage and adrenaline.

"Brandie, I didn't know they moved that fast."

"How could you not know? You said you already fought one!"

"The one I saw before had a broken leg. It couldn't have run if it wanted to."

Her expression changed as we heard more groaning. We turned to see two more corpses racing toward us. These were different from the others I had seen. They looked fresh, the only difference between them and the living were pale skin and gaping wounds. On the one directly in front of me, there was a wound in its abdomen. As it ran, various intestines fell from the gash. My stomach felt ill at the sight of it.

I grabbed the melee weapons, giving Brandie the axe.

"What about the guns?" she asked.

"We don't need to attract any more of these things."

She nodded and turned to the zombies. They were less than a foot away from us, a horrific screech escaping their throats. I swung the sword, completely removing the head of the monster in front of me. Due to the force of motion, the rest of its body slammed into me. I staggered back as the body crumpled in a heap. I turned to check on Brandie. She had killed the zombie, but the axe was stuck in its head.

"Need help?" I asked.

"I can do it," she insisted.

She kept yanking at the axe but couldn't get it loose.

"I can show you," I offered.

She huffed, then let me step in. I showed her how to remove the axe, then handed it back to her.

"Are you sure?" she asked.

I nodded, "You need a quieter weapon. Besides, we should save the bullets."

She nodded and slipped the axe in her belt. I put my sword back in its scabbard while she grabbed her rifle, securing it to her shoulder. She was still shaking, high on adrenaline.

"Are you okay?" I asked cautiously.

She shook her head, "I think this is all starting to mess with my head."

"How so?"

"I don't know, something just doesn't feel right."

I put a comforting hand on her shoulder. She looked up at me.

"I probably sound crazy," she said.

I shook my head, "No, I'm with you actually. Ashley and I are getting wary about all of this too."

"Did something happen?"

"We both got hurt at some point or another,

which isn't something we expected."

"It happened to me and James too."

I was surprised I had not noticed them getting hurt.

"What happened?" I asked.

"James sprained his ankle during the robot battle, then when we were in the sewers I got hurt when I fell."

"You mean when I helped you up?"

She nodded, "Yeah, my hands were scraped up and my knees were bruised. James completely freaked when he found out."

I gave her a small smile, "Well, it's not hard to see how much he loves you."

"Plus, he's a total spaz," she replied.

"Well, we all know that. He says it all the time."

She returned my smile for a moment, then checked our surroundings for more zombies.

"We should go before more of them find us," she suggested.

I nodded and let my hand fall. As we walked, I took the backpack off to see what was inside.

"Do you have any supplies in that bag?" I asked.

"I haven't had time to check," she replied.

I clumsily unzipped my bag as we walked. Inside there was a tattered blanket, a couple of cans, and a half-filled water bottle.

"I've got some jerky, bandages, and a map," Brandie said, "What about you?"

I reached into my bag and looked at the cans.

"Looks like beans, a blanket, and some water."

"That's something at least, but we'll probably need to find more water."

"Maybe there's a town or something on this

level. Hopefully we're not just thrown in the middle of nowhere for the apocalypse."

She peeked inside my bag and replied, "I hope so, because what we have won't last long, and the safe zone is really far away."

"We need to find shelter too. I don't like the idea of hanging out with those things after dark."

She shuddered, "Agreed."

I closed my bag and slung it back across my shoulders. My hand rested on the hilt of my sword as we walked.

I looked up at the trees, their branches bare or close to it. Crinkled brown leaves and frail twigs littered the forest floor. The trees ahead of us seemed to never end.

The sun started setting and the wind began to blow, sending a chill through the air. Brandie shivered slightly. I stopped walking and took off my bag, then my jacket.

"Here, take this," I said, holding it out to her.

She shook her head, "I'm fine."

"Brandie, just take it."

"Why?"

"Because you're my friend and you're cold. Besides, James will literally kill me if I just let you freeze."

She grinned.

"I hope you don't like that idea," I said smiling back.

"Not necessarily. I just like knowing he cares."

"Trust me, you have him wrapped around your finger."

She hesitated a moment longer, then put on the jacket.

"What about you?" she asked, "Won't you get cold? I really don't need Ashley coming after me later."

I chuckled, "I'll be fine. We can find shelter and I'll use the blanket if I need to."

We looked up when the sky rumbled. Dark clouds rolled across the sky.

"We better hurry," she said nervously.

We jogged between the trees, trying to find anything for shelter. A drizzle of droplets poured from the sky.

"Look, the trees end there," Brandie said, pointing straight ahead.

"Careful, we don't know if there are more in the clearing," I warned.

We slowed our pace as we reached the tree line, finding a small field with a town just beyond it. We checked our surroundings before going out in the open.

"I don't like this," Brandie said nervously.

"Me neither. Let's just clear out a house to stay in tonight."

I drew my sword and marched forward. Brandie raised her axe to cover me. We stayed close to the houses at the edge of town just in case we needed an escape.

Settling on a small two story house, I leaned close to the front door to listen for monsters. Something bumped into the door and I flinched away. Brandie peeked through one of the dingy windows. She turned to me and held up two fingers, then waved for me to follow her. We ducked low and hurried through a gate to the backyard, finding a body on the ground. Brandie prepared to swing while I locked the gate, but she stopped.

"What is it?" I asked, my voice low to avoid unwanted attention.

"It's already dead."

"I think all zombies are already dead."

"Now is not the time to be a smartass," she growled, "Look."

I stood next to her and looked down. The zombie's head had a hole between its eyes.

"Do you think it could've been from someone in the group?" I asked.

"Maybe, but we don't know if they're still here."

I looked at the house and said, "Maybe they got trapped inside."

We flinched at the sound of a gunshot. I looked in the window and saw a body tumbling down the stairs. The two zombies on the main floor charged upstairs.

"Somebody help me!" a voice shouted.

I swung the door open and followed them. Brandie closed the door behind us, staying close to my heels. As I reached the top of the stairs, the two corpses repeatedly slammed into a door. Someone was trying to push the door closed from the other side, but the monsters kept pushing back before the door completely closed. Three more were coming from the other end of the hall, glazed eyes set on the two of us.

I grabbed my pistol and shot the closest one. It collapsed, catching the attention of its friend. The second corpse stopped pushing on the door and whoever was on the other side got it closed.

Brandie raised her rifle and fired before it could run to us. I shot the next one, but it was followed closely by the last two. One shoved Brandie into the wall to the right. She managed to raise her rifle as a guard, holding the zombie back by mere inches. The other barreled into me. Before I could catch myself, my weapons fell from my hands and we rolled down the stairs.

"Logan!" Brandie shouted.

She tried to get away from the zombie, but it was too strong. My head felt dizzy as I raised it. A hissing sound came from my right and I turned in time to see the zombie lunge. My arms reached forward and caught it, but my strength was waning. It did not help that my hand felt as if it were on fire and my head was spinning.

After several long minutes, there were two more loud booms. The corpse went limp and I shoved it off.

My head hit the floorboards. I was too dizzy to sit up. The fire in my hand felt worse and I rolled onto my side, cradling it against my chest. A hand gently touched my shoulder.

"Logan? Can you hear me?" Brandie asked.

I did not reply. I was too tired and in too much pain.

Someone sat down in front of me.

"Easy buddy, I've got ya," Melvin said.

He reached for my wounded hand. My vision blurred. Brandie rubbed my shoulder. I lifted my head, then tried to sit up. Melvin let go of my hand and they both pushed me back down.

"Lay still," another voice said, the one that had been shouting before.

I blinked and squinted, "Ash?"

She shushed me, "I'm right here baby."

Melvin turned to her, "Wanna trade?"

He moved over so she could sit near my head. Her fingers delicately brushed through my hair. I flinched when Melvin's hand touched my ankle. The girls held my weak body still so I could not jerk away.

"Ash?" I said again, unable to get more out.

"You're going to be fine," she said softly.

Drowsiness took over and my eyes closed, my mind slipping into darkness.

I slowly awoke in a dark room.

Did I lose? I thought.

A small circle of light appeared on the wall ahead of me. It danced along the partition, drawing closer to me. As it moved, I saw shelves with books scattered across them, along with a broken window next to the shelf. It had what looked like a bullet hole near the middle. As it continued, I realized I was lying in a bed covered with a familiar, ragged blanket. I heard footsteps creep closer to me and the light stopped, showing my left hand wrapped in bandages.

"Logan?" Ashley whispered.

She stepped closer and set the flashlight on a small bedside table, careful not to shine the beam on my face. She sat on the bed next to me and took my unwrapped hand.

"Are you awake?" she asked.

I realized she could not see my face, and the flashlight was too weak to give off enough light. I squeezed her hand slightly. She lifted her head.

"I'm here," I murmured.

She gave me a small smile while rubbing the back of my hand with her thumb.

"What happened?" I asked.

She scooted closer to me and stroked my hair again.

"You got a concussion when you fell. You broke your hand too."

"Is that why I'm so tired?"

"Yeah, Mel said you would be like that for a little while."

"How long was I asleep?"

"A couple hours. I actually came to wake you up."

"Why?"

"To check on you. You had me worried."

She kissed my forehead softly. I squeezed her hand again.

"I'm so tired," I muttered.

"Yeah, I know. Go back to sleep, I'll wake you up again in a bit."

"But I don't want to. I have more questions."

"Like what?"

"How did you and Melvin get here? Kind of convenient."

"I was trapped in here when I woke up. I tried to get out and when I finally broke the lock I got swarmed. Luckily, you and Brandie got here in time."

"And Melvin?"

"He said he heard the gunshots and the screaming, so he ran over."

I had to catch my breath before asking, "Is Brandie okay?"

She nodded, "She's fine. I got that thing off of her and Melvin got the other one."

Still holding my hand, she ran the other along my forearm as if for comfort. I was not sure if it was more for me or for her.

"Are you okay?" I asked.

"Better now. I'm just glad you're awake."

"Ashley."

"Yeah?"

I hesitated. I did not want to scare her, but the question started spinning around in my brain.

"What do you think happens if one of us dies?"

She leaned closer to me, "What do you mean?"

"In game. If we die here, what happens?"

"The instructions say that we just start over."

"I know, but I got a concussion. And you got hurt. Brandie said that she and James did too."

"They did?"

I nodded slightly, "She told me when we found each other."

She was shaking slightly. A sort of instinct took over, one I had never experienced. I let go of her hand and wrapped my arm around her.

"Careful. Don't hurt yourself," she warned.

"I'm fine."

I pulled her close. She did not resist, worried that she might hurt me.

"Let's not find out what happens, okay?" I whispered.

"Agreed."

She lightly rested her forehead against mine. She was still trembling.

"I'm not going to let anything happen to you, I promise."

"Logan, don't worry about me right now. Just rest."

She slowly pulled away and sat up straight.

"I'll be right back," she said.

Ashley took the flashlight and walked out of the room, leaving me in the darkness. I had already fallen asleep before she got back.

The next time I woke up, she was there again, sitting in a wooden chair. This time the sun was peeking through the window across the room. Her head rested on the bed next to me, eyes open slightly as if she were falling asleep. In the light I could see her better. She wore a pair of tattered jeans and a black shirt. I saw that she was also wearing the jacket I had given to Brandie, who must have given it to Ashley at some point in the night.

I gave her a small smile and covered her hand with mine. She raised her head slightly to look at me. With the slight amount of sunlight, I could see the dark marks under her eyes. My smile fell.

"Ash, did you sleep any?" I asked.

"I'm fine," she replied, moving the chair closer to me.

"You sure?"

She nodded and rested her head on my chest.

"What kept you up?"

"Mel said I should wake you up every few hours to make sure you're okay."

"Why?"

"He takes first aid classes outside of school. He said that's what I should do since you have a concussion."

"Specifically, you?"

She looked away, seeming embarrassed. I rubbed her shoulder gently.

"Well, I'm awake now. You should sleep."

"I'm fine Logan."

"Ashley. Trust me, you need your strength. I'll already be slowing us down."

She studied my face, a worried look in her eye.

"What's wrong?" I asked.

She bit her lip, but before she spoke, the door opened. She sat up suddenly. Melvin peeked through the ajar door.

"Sorry to interrupt," he said nervously, "Just came to check on you guys."

He stepped into the room.

"How's your head?" he asked.

"Better. I can think a little bit now."

He grinned and held his fist out toward me. I gave him a light fist bump. He turned to Ashley.

"See, told you he was tough. No need to worry," he stated.

She glared at him. I grinned.

"Aw, you were that worried?" I teased.

"Shut up Logan," she growled.

I tried to sit up and flinched from a shock of pain. Her features softened before she gently pushed me back down.

"Don't. You need to rest," she said, a stern tone to her voice.

I nodded and laid back.

"Dang man, she's already got you whipped," Melvin teased.

Ashley turned and glared again.

I chuckled, "Maybe, but it's not my ass she'll be kicking later."

He grinned at his sister, then started back toward the door.

"I'm going. You just rest for now man."

He grabbed the doorknob and paused to say,

"But remember, I'll be checking on y'all, so don't be getting any ideas, simulation or not."

"Melvin!" Ashley shouted.

He quickly closed the door. The sound of his boots hitting the floor quickly faded. I laughed while Ashley ran a hand through her hair, her cheeks bright red.

"It's like he wants me to kill him," she grumbled.

I rubbed her hand gently, "You know he means well."

"That doesn't make it any less embarrassing."

"If it's any consolation, you're cute when you're embarrassed."

Her eyes narrowed at me.

"Well, it's less cute when you look like you're gonna punch me," I pointed out.

She shook her head, then yawned.

"Ashley, go to sleep," I said softly, "I'll be alright."

The look of uncertainty crossed her face again. I scooted to the side.

"Baby, don't," she said, her voice filled with concern.

I moved over despite her complaints, then patted the empty space next to me. She hesitated.

"Come on," I said, "This way you can sleep and keep an eye on me."

"How?"

I did not have an answer for her. She seemed to know that and raised an eyebrow.

"Okay fine, I just want to snuggle with my girl-friend. Is that so wrong?"

A small smile appeared on her face, "I guess

not."

She crawled into the bed and we cuddled under the blanket. I wrapped my good arm around her shoulders. Her head rested on my shoulder and her hand rested over the fingers on my left hand, careful to avoid my wounds. Soon she dozed off. Her muscles relaxed against me. I lifted my head a little, just enough to see her face. I had only seen her sleeping once, despite the fact we always ended up falling asleep while watching movies together. I was always the first one to doze off.

She shifted slightly. I kissed her hair softly before laying back down. She nuzzled me slightly before settling again. I grinned, squeezing her lightly. As I started to drift, my eyes widened slightly at a strange sound. I lifted my head again and looked around the room. It was a soft sound, almost nonexistent. It seemed to disappear as I looked around.

Guess I just imagined it.

As I rested my head, the sound returned. I looked around once more, but we were alone in the room. I turned to Ashley. Her eyes were closed. Her breathing had become slower and much deeper. I leaned my head closer to hers, the sound growing slightly louder.

Is that a snore? I thought, *That's the quietest one I've ever heard.*

It was almost like humming more than snoring. There was something odd about the sound. It was just so soft, even relaxing in a weird way.

I smiled slightly and laid back, listening to the sound as I fell asleep.

"Logan. Logan wake up."

I grumbled incoherently. Someone giggled and shook my shoulder lightly.

"Come on baby, wake up."

My eyes opened to see Ashley still huddled against me, now propped up on her elbows.

"What?" I murmured.

"Mel said we have to go soon. Brandie found a van with some fuel we can take so you don't have to walk."

"When are we going?"

"It won't be long. Mel and Brandie are looking for supplies in the nearby houses. We'll load up and leave when they get back."

"Then why did you wake me up now?" I whined.

She kissed my forehead softly and said, "Because I was lonely, and I can't go back to sleep yet."

"Why not?"

"Because I really don't want to get attacked by zombies. Do you?"

"Fair point."

She shivered slightly.

"Come here," I said.

"No, I'll fall asleep."

"If you don't, you'll freeze."

"I'm fine."

"Alright, your loss. No cuddling for you."

I rolled over and closed my eyes, pretending to go back to sleep. After a moment, she wrapped an arm around my waist. I held her hand. Our fingers intertwined.

"No cuddling, huh?"

"I can let go if you want."

She squeezed my hand and snuggled with my shoulder, "I'm good."

The sun rose a little higher. I groaned and squeezed my eyes shut as sunlight filled the room.

"Does something hurt?" she asked, her voice filled with worry.

I shook my head while covering it with the blanket.

"Too bright," I grumbled.

She pulled the blanket back a little and grinned.

"Does your head hurt?"

"No, but my eyes are burning."

She kissed my cheek.

"Any better?" she asked.

"A little," I replied.

We both flinched as a door slammed downstairs. She quickly stood, reaching for one of the handguns on her waist. I rolled over to follow her. She put a hand on my shoulder to stop me.

"Just rest Logan."

"You must be crazy as hell to think I'm letting you go alone."

We locked eyes, a moment passing between us that said neither was willing to back down. After it passed, she huffed and handed over a pistol.

I rose slowly and quietly as we listened to someone stomping frantically downstairs. The sound of furniture being dragged across the floor echoed through the empty halls.

Ashley grabbed a rifle from behind the bedroom door and slowly stepped out of the room.

"Hurry up!" a voice growled.

"You know, this would go faster if ya'd help."

"I'm checking the house. Just keep those things outside."

We reached the end of the hall at the top of

the stairwell. I raised the pistol with my good hand, hoping that all my time playing video games in the past would help. I had never really shot a gun before, and the idea of learning in the moment was not appealing.

Ashley raised the rifle, seeming much more confident with the weapon in her hands. She remained two paces ahead of me as we started down the stairs.

"I'll go make sure nothin's upstairs," one voice said.

Ashley glanced at me over her shoulder, looking forward just in time for someone to round the corner. He yelped and jumped back in surprise at the barrel of a rifle being mere inches from him. Ashley and I lowered our weapons.

"You scared the crap out of me!" he shouted.

I grinned, "How's it going General?"

"Oh no. Not you too," Ulysseus groaned.

Ashley smiled and wrapped him in a hug. He gave me a nervous look. I just kept grinning, highly entertained by his freakout. After a moment of hesitation, he hugged her back.

"What? No hug for your best friend?" the second voice asked.

We turned as Vivian rounded the corner. Ashley walked up to her and gave her a tight hug. As they pulled apart, Ulysseus looked over me.

"Jeepers Logan, what happened to ya?" he asked.

I tried to reply, but dizziness washed over me. I moaned and fell forward after a spike of pain drove through my skull. He and Ashley quickly dove forward to catch me.

"Easy baby, I've got you," Ashley whispered as they set me down.

When I was on the floor, she took my face in her hands.

"Can you hear me?" she asked.

I nodded slightly. She let me lay my head down and rubbed my shoulder softly.

"What happened to him?" Vivian asked.

"He ran in here with Brandie to save me from those things," she motioned toward the front door as she spoke, ragged snarls and groans coming from it, "When they were fighting, he fell down the stairs and hit his head."

"Guessin' he broke his wrist in the fall too?" Ulysseus asked.

Ashley nodded, "And sprained his ankle."

She kissed my cheek.

"I told you to stay in bed," she murmured.

Something slammed into the door, making us all flinch.

"I don't know if that's goin' to hold them long," Ulysseus said nervously.

"You said Brandie was with him. Is she still here?" Vivian asked.

Ashley looked up and shook her head, "Melvin was here too. They're looking in some of the other houses for supplies."

She turned to look at the door. I knew that she was thinking about her brother. I squeezed her hand.

"How long until they get back?" Vivian asked.

"I don't know. Any time now," Ashley replied.

Another corpse slammed into the door. The furniture shifted slightly.

"Let's get 'em upstairs. Get another barrier between us and them," Ulysseus suggested.

Ashley wrapped my arm around her shoulders and pulled me up, struggling to get me in a seated position. Ulysseus quickly followed her lead and they pulled me to my feet. Vivian raised her rifle, aiming for the front door while the others helped me hobble up the stairs.

"Let's get him back to the bedroom. There's plenty of stuff to barricade the door," Ashley said.

Ulysseus nodded.

"Stay off that foot bud, we're almost there," he said.

I nodded slightly, trying to focus. My blurry vision made it more difficult to walk straight.

Once we were in the room, Ashley let me go to start pushing furniture. Ulysseus helped me sit on the bed while Vivian closed and locked the door.

"Just rest, bud," Ulysseus said.

I tried to stand to help, but he gently pushed me back.

"I mean it Logan. Rest," he commanded.

My jaw tightened. I did not like the idea of sitting out while they worked, nor did I like the idea of him telling me to do so. But I knew I would not be any help as another wave of exhaustion hit me. I nodded again.

He hurried to the dresser to help Ashley push. Vivian grabbed a desk chair and propped it against the doorknob. It wasn't long before they had the dresser, desk, and a bookshelf blocking the door. When they finished, Ashley sat beside me and took my chin in her hand.

"Are you feeling okay?" she asked.

"Yeah. Yeah, I'm okay."

She kissed my forehead lightly. I gave her a small smile in return.

"Hate to break up the love fest, but we should probably figure out how to get out of 'ere," Ulysseus said.

"Could we wait until Mel and Brandie are back with the van?" Ashley asked.

Vivian yelped at a crashing sound from downstairs. Moments later a zombie rammed into our door, attracted by the sound.

"Not likely," she growled between clenched teeth.

I looked around the room. My eyes landed on the window and I pointed.

"Could get out there," I suggested, "maybe make a run for it."

"Are ya kiddin'? Ya can barely walk!"

"I didn't say I was going."

Ashley glared at me.

"I'm not going if you're not," she said.

"Yes, you are. You can find Melvin and Brandie, then bring them back with the van to get me."

She squeezed my hand tightly.

"You must be crazy as hell if you think I'm leaving you here alone with those things," she growled.

We all flinched as we heard the sound of a car horn.

"I don't think we'll have to do that," Vivian said.

Ashley stood and looked out the window. She wrenched it open after a few tugs. Ulysseus slipped past her to crawl out. His head poked back into the room a moment later.

"There's a hatch on top of the van. We can get in through there," he stated.

He hopped down from the window frame to help me walk. I held a hand up as I slowly rose on my own. He put a hand on my shoulder and leaned close to my ear.

"It's okay to ask for help, bud," he whispered, "You don't have to prove anythin' to yer friends."

I nodded in response. He noticed me watching Ashley as she slipped the rifles out the window.

"Ya don't have to prove anythin' to her either. She's crazy about you."

I turned to him, resting a hand on his shoulder in turn as I said, "Thanks bud."

He gave me a small smile, then helped me stay off of my bad foot as we walked.

Vivian hurried out the window, but Ashley waited for me. She and Ulysseus helped me maneuver out so I would not hurt my leg or put weight on my broken hand.

The outside air was flooded with the sound of raspy growls. I wrinkled my nose at the stench of death. I looked over the edge of the roof to see Melvin standing next to an opening on top of a dingy grey van.

"Vivian? When did you get here?" he asked.

"Right before you slowpoke," she replied.

"Don't be mean or I'm not sharing my food," he joked.

Brandie poked her head out of the opening and growled, "Can you two quit joking around? Those things are going to break the van if we don't hurry."

She disappeared a moment later. Melvin crouched down as the van pulled closer to the house. Once it was alongside the building, Vivian hopped down next to him. Ashley and I scooted to the edge of the roof. Melvin reached out a hand for me to take.

"Don't jump," he warned, "You'll make that ankle worse."

I clasped his hand as he helped me step on the dilapidated metal. Vivian reached for my arm as I limped toward the trapdoor. I paused to look up at the sky, which started to turn dark as angry grey clouds filled the sky. Ashley crawled down onto the van as cool raindrops started to fall. The growls of the undead mixed with the grumbling thunder as they started to wander outside. One realized what was happening and slammed full force into the side of the van.

"Hurry up!" Brandie said, "I don't feel like being something's dinner today!"

"How about tomorrow?" Melvin asked, a goofy grin on his face.

"Melvin!"

"Relax. We're fine."

Ulysseus shouted in terror at that very moment. We turned to see the light rain caused him to slip, leaving him clawing at the steel top to stay on. Melvin grabbed his arms to pull him up. It helped that Ulysseus had managed to plant his foot against the rearview mirror to push himself. As he climbed, the zombie clawed at his legs, barely missing simply because his feet flailed wildly.

"Hurry!" Ulysseus yelled.

Melvin lifted him up. Ulysseus steadied himself on the roof before glaring at Melvin.

"Could ya've gone any slower!" he shouted, "It 'bout took my leg off!"

Melvin held his arms up in surrender, "You guys need to chill. It's a video game."

"That doesn't mean I want to lose a leg! Real or not!"

"Guys, can we go? The van's going to be surrounded if you two keep shouting," Brandie growled.

Ulysseus turned to see the undead starting to wander out of the house. He huffed and nodded.

I crouched down to drop through the opening, clinging to the rim to slow the fall. Landing carefully on one foot, I limped away to let the others inside. Melvin landed beside me and helped the girls down, with Ulysseus following close behind. Melvin hurried to the passenger's seat at the front of the van while Ulysseus reached up to close the hatch.

"How do you feel?"

I turned to see Ashley beside me, a worried look in her eye. I gave her a small smile.

"I'm fine. You worry too much."

"I can't believe you didn't figure that out before," Vivian said.

Ashley glared at her, but she just grinned in return. Brandie started the vehicle's engine and hit the gas pedal, giving us just enough time to sit and avoid being thrown across the back. Ashley and I sat next to a pile of stacked cans filled with beans, vegetables, and various types of soup. Vivian and Ulysseus sat at the opposite end of the van with a pile of blankets to their left and several gallons of water to their right.

"Where did you guys find all this stuff?" I asked.

"These houses are full of supplies. We figured we should grab it while we can in case houses by the beacon are empty," Brandie said.

Ulysseus's brow furrowed.

"What's wrong with you?" Vivian asked.

"Nothin'. Just thinkin'."

She just nodded in response.

Wait, so he doesn't get asked the "about what" question? Seriously?

"We'll have to watch our ammo. I only found a small box of bullets, and I honestly don't know if it'll work with any of our guns," Melvin said.

Ashley rolled her eyes, "Did you not pay any attention when dad taught us about this stuff?"

"I did. I just only paid attention to the parts that involved actually shooting things."

She shook her head, seeming disappointed but not surprised.

"When did your dad teach you that?" I asked.

She thought for a moment, then said, "I think we got BB guns when we were, maybe eleven? He didn't let me try the real thing until about a year ago."

"That's cool."

"What about you?"

I shook my head, "Mom and dad didn't like guns, and it's harder to get them in the north anyway."

"Did you ever want to?"

"I thought it would be cool, but I never got the chance to try it out."

"Maybe I can show you sometime."

I smiled, "Are you really qualified for that?"

"More than you."

"I guess that's true."

I turned to look out the windshield. The sun was already setting in the distance.

"How long did I sleep?" I asked.

"Most of the day."

"I don't like this sleeping all day thing."

"You're hurt. I think you can stand to get some extra rest."

I sat back against the metal.

"So, what's happened to you guys in this level so far?" I asked, directing the question to our friends in front of us.

They glanced at each other before Vivian said, "Well, I woke up in a tree with a bunch of undead lunatics surrounding it. So, I slept in the tree and hoped I wouldn't starve until Ulysseus found me this morning."

I turned to look at him.

"I woke up on a roof. When I realized what was happenin', I climbed down to look for y'all. One of them cornered me in the house and I had to stab the lout in the brain to get it off me. Then I barricaded the place so I could sleep and got up early to keep searchin'. When I found Viv, I climbed a tree and threw rocks at the decayin' dolts until I led them away."

"Then we met at a gas station down the road and kept running."

"Aye, we had to stop a few times to rest, then thought we'd hide in the house we found the two of you in."

"What about you guys?"

Ashley and I explained what had happened to us, with Melvin chiming in to share his own story. He had woken up in the woods lying against a tree, and apparently had been the one to shoot the zombie Brandie and I had found in the yard. After shooting it, he searched some of the other houses for food before Ashley had cried out for help. By the time we had finished telling our stories, it was nearly dark.

"Someone should go ahead and get some sleep. We shouldn't stop unless we have to, and I can't drive forever," Brandie said, a drowsy look in her eyes.

I yawned in response. Ashley smiled a little.

"What are you grinning at?" I asked.

"Just you. That's all."

"Alright lovebirds, break it up," Vivian teased.

Ashley turned to her, "Look who's talking."

Ulysseus chuckled, "She's got a point Viv."

She rolled her eyes, then laid down to sleep. Ulysseus grabbed one of the blankets next to him for Vivian before tossing a couple over to us.

As the night drew on Brandie started to slowly drift off despite the cold keeping the rest of us awake. Melvin rested a hand on her shoulder.

"Hey, stop the van."

She nodded slightly. The brakes squealed despite the slow stop, probably because the vehicle was so old. Melvin checked outside for a moment before stepping out of the van. Brandie crawled to the passenger's seat. Ulysseus sat up to toss her a blanket, but she was too tired to adjust the folded bundle.

Melvin hurried around the front of the van, trying to get out of the downpour as soon as possible. He climbed into the driver's seat and closed the door.

"Are you sure you can drive okay?" Brandie asked sleepily.

He grinned, "Yeah, I'll be fine. I'm not tired yet."

He unfolded the blanket to cover her. She snuggled with the cloth as her muscles relaxed. Her breathing slowed almost instantly.

Melvin put the van in drive and started forward again. Vivian shivered across from me, her eyes still slightly open. She grumbled something under her breath before shifting to find a more comfortable position.

Ashley sat back against the wall of the van, shivering a little. I held my hand out to her.

"You know, we can cuddle if you're cold," I suggested.

"I'm not ready to go to sleep yet," she replied.

I nodded and huddled under my blanket, very much aware of the suspicious glare Vivian was giving me at that moment. Ulysseus snickered before closing his eyes, leaning against what was left of the blankets.

My mind started to drift. The sound of Ashley and Melvin's voices turned into simply background noise while my eyes closed. At some point, I heard Ashley scoot closer to my head. Her fingers gently tousled my hair as I slipped into unconsciousness.

River of Repulse

I groaned as my head slammed against the floor of the van. I reached for the throbbing bump on my head.

"Are you okay?"

I opened my eyes and turned to see Brandie sitting next to me. I nodded slightly and laid my head back down on the floor.

"Anything happen while I was out?" I asked.

"Nothing really. Ulysseus is driving and the others are asleep."

"Where's Ash?"

She turned and pointed. Ashley had curled up under a blanket about a foot away. A small smile crossed my face.

"How far are we from the beacon?" I asked.

"Another day or two. Longer if we have to stop for gas."

"There's no if," Ulysseus grumbled, "We're runnin' on fumes 'ere."

Brandie stood, "Is there a gas station nearby?"

"How should I know? Viv's got the map," he snapped.

"What's wrong with you?" Brandie asked.

He rubbed the side of his neck, "I slept funny.

I've got a bad crick in my neck now and it's drivin' me crazy."

"Well, you'll just have to tough it out grouchy."

He rolled his eyes before refocusing on the road.

"Just tell me where I can get gas," he grumbled.

Brandie turned and searched near Vivian for the map, careful not to wake her.

I asked Ulysseus, "Since when can you drive?"

"Harold's been teachin' me," he replied, "My grandfather won't, and I need to be able to drive if I'm gonna start workin' after I turn sixteen."

"I can't read this stupid thing," Brandie griped.

"Well then wake Viv up," he replied.

"No way!"

"Why not?"

"Because I actually value living to see tomorrow."

"Well, she's the only one of us who can read a map, so someone needs to get her up."

"Why don't you do it?"

"Oh, sorry. You see, I would, but I'd like to turn sixteen so I can drive like this for real."

"You're just as scared as I am."

"Aye, but I'm the driver so I have an excuse not to get up and get her."

Brandie rolled her eyes, then crouched down next to Vivian, cautiously resting a hand on her shoulder.

"Viv. Viv, wake up," Brandie murmured.

Vivian shifted slightly but did not wake up. Brandie shook her arm a little more. Vivian grumbled something under her breath and rolled over. I chuckled.

Brandie rolled her eyes, "Viv, I need your help. Wake up."

"Five more minutes," Vivian mumbled.

"I don't think we have that sort of time Viv," Ulysseus said.

"You guys talk too much," another voice said.

I turned to see Ashley stretching.

"I agree. Now goodnight," Vivian said.

"Oh no you don't," Brandie replied.

She grabbed Vivian's blanket and quickly jumped away, trying to get the blanket off while also avoiding our friend's oncoming wrath. Surprisingly, she just grumbled and sat up while trying to rub the sleepiness out of her eyes.

"What is it now?" she asked.

Brandie handed her the map, "Is there a gas station near us?"

"Well, it would be a lot easier to tell you if I knew where we were," she replied sarcastically.

"On some road called Whizzer Drive. About to reach an intersection with Fartwood Lane."

"These developers are not very good at naming things," I said.

Ashley scooted closer, "They're techies, not street developers."

"I dunno, I thought it was pretty funny," Ulysseus said.

I grinned. Vivian looked over the map, seeming in a bit of a haze.

"There's a gas station a few miles west," Vivian said, "Turn right on Fartwood."

Ulysseus and I both laughed in response.

"Oh, shut up you children," Vivian said.

"Relax Viv," Ashley said, "Go back to sleep."

"Gladly."

She gave the map back to Brandie and told her how to get to the gas station, then nestled herself under the blanket again.

"Does anyone else think it's hilarious we have to drive down a road called Fartwood to get gasoline?" Melvin said lazily.

I turned to see him sit a little straighter in the passenger seat.

Ulysseus laughed even more, "I hadn't even thought about that yet."

I laughed again, then turned as Ashley laid down beside me. I kissed her forehead softly and pulled her closer.

"Hey, hey, hey," Melvin said, "I get it y'all like being all cuddly and kissey, but can't ya at least wait until we're not all trapped in a van together?"

"I concur," Ulysseus said, "I don't want that turnin' into somethin' else with me around."

"Shut up!" Ashley yelped, her face turning bright red.

I roared with laughter as she flicked them both on the back of the head, then curled up on the floor in embarrassment. I hugged her tightly.

"Don't worry," I murmured, "They're just jealous you're dating someone and they're not."

"No, I just don't want to taste my breakfast again. I don't think it'll be as good the second time around," Ulysseus proclaimed.

"Gross!" Ashley said.

"Exactly. Now you know how I feel."

"Whatever bro," Melvin said.

Ulysseus raised an eyebrow, "What's that supposed to mean?"

"As if you wouldn't date a girl if she said yes when you asked."

"Well, we don't have to worry about that because I ain't askin' anyone."

"Not even Ellie Martins?" Brandie teased.

"How did you know about that?" Ulysseus asked. He thought for a moment and then added, "Oh no, Peyton told you, didn't she?"

Brandie nodded.

"Who's that again?" Melvin asked.

"That new head junior varsity cheerleader. The Sophomore with the brown hair. She was at that bonfire at Daniel's house last year."

Melvin thought for a moment. Then his eyes widened with realization, "That's who you like?"

Ulysseus groaned.

"I wonder if she's a cougar. You might have a chance then," Melvin joked.

"How did this get turned around on me! Besides, we're almost the same age!" Ulysseus shouted helplessly.

Melvin and Brandie continued to tease Ulysseus, asking him all sorts of questions about why he liked her, when they met, and so on.

"I'm gonna kill Peyton when we get home," Ulysseus grumbled.

Ashley tapped me on the shoulder. I turned to her.

"How do you feel?" she asked.

"Tired, but a lot better actually. My head doesn't hurt much anymore."

I stretched my legs and felt no pain. When I moved my wrist, it felt as if it had been stabbed with a knife. Of course, that was still better than how it felt before.

"I think my ankle is healed too," I said.

Her brow furrowed in confusion. She sat up and touched it. No pain.

"Can you stretch it?" she asked.

"Yeah, it's just a little stiff, but it doesn't hurt."

"What are you guys talking about?" Melvin asked suspiciously.

"I think his ankle has already healed," Ashley replied.

Melvin crawled to the back of the van to check on me. He held my foot and had me move it around in multiple directions, then nodded approvingly.

"Your leg will probably still be tired, but it looks like we can heal pretty quick in this game. I was wondering how that would work since we haven't seen any health boosters yet," Melvin said to no one in particular.

He leaned over and whispered something to Ashley. Her eyes widened. She audibly smacked his arm, seeming angry. He laughed as he stood to get away before she could hit him again.

"What did he say?" I asked.

"Trust me, you don't want to know," Ashley replied.

Suddenly, Ulysseus smacked his palm against the steering wheel in frustration.

"Dang it," Ulysseus growled.

"What?" I asked.

The van sputtered to a halt. Ulysseus put it in park and removed the key.

"That. Gas is gone," he grumbled.

"How far are we from the station?" Melvin asked.

Brandie looked at the map.

"Still a couple more miles," she said.

"We can walk that easy," he said.

"And how exactly are we going to carry that gas back here Mr. Genius?"

"I'm sure they probably have some gas cans sitting around somewhere. We'll find as many as we can, fill them up, and bring them back here."

"And where will we put the spares? They're not going in here. I'm not getting sick on gas fumes."

"Maybe we can find a truck or something to put them in," he suggested.

Vivian sat up abruptly, "What are we waiting for then? Let's go."

"I thought you were sleeping," Ulysseus said.

"Like Ashley said, you all talk too much."

She stood and opened the back of the van. She hopped out with Brandie following close behind. They both turned to get a weapon each for the road. Vivian grabbed her rifle while Brandie grabbed the hatchet I gave her. Ulysseus started to get out of the van, but Melvin grabbed his shoulder.

"You stay here man," Melvin said.

"Why?" Ulysseus asked.

"We need somebody watching the van. Logan's still hurt and Ashley's not going to leave him alone, so she won't be paying attention.

"I can hear you!" she snapped.

"Well, why don't you stay then?" Ulysseus asked.

"No offense Ulysseus," Vivian chimed in, "but if we find any supplies, Melvin's going to be able to carry a lot more."

Ulysseus tried to stare down Melvin, but gave

up a moment later. He huffed and sat back in the driver's seat.

"Next run buddy," Melvin said, "When Logan's better and Ashley's not bothering him."

Ashley glared. Melvin hugged his sister tightly.

"I'm only teasing," he said.

"Yeah, I know," she replied.

She hugged him back, then Melvin grabbed a knife and his rifle before hopping out of the van. Brandie grabbed some water and canned goods to put in her bag for the road. Then the three of them took off.

I sat up soon after they left. Ashley sat beside me, snuggled against my shoulder as she drifted off to sleep.

Ulysseus reached for the glove compartment and started digging through it.

"What are you doing?" I asked.

"I don't know. I'm just bored," he said, "I'm hopin' the developers didn't just leave us with nothin' to do."

"So, fighting robots and running from British soldiers isn't good enough for you?"

"You know what I mean."

He continued to dig through the glove box until he found a deck of cards held together by a rubber band.

"Go fish?" Ulysseus asked.

I smiled, "Sure, but you'll have to come back here. It seems that I am no longer Ashley's boyfriend, but simply her pillow."

He nodded, checking the locks on the doors before crawling over the middle console of the van.

He sat across from me and divvied up the cards for the game.

After a long silence, Ulysseus spoke up, "So, what was growin' up like for you?"

"What do you mean?"

"It's not that complicated of a question Logan," he replied sarcastically.

I chuckled, "Good thing I have a good sense of humor."

"Aye, good for you. I'm not even teasin' ya yet."

I thought about how to answer his question for a moment, then said, "It wasn't that exciting. We moved around a lot, mostly to big cities. My dad was always trying to get new investors for a project he was working on."

"What kind of project?"

"Some kind of new medical device. He was a programmer, but he got together with some friends to try to help him work out the medical side of the project. He was convinced that if the machine worked, they could potentially find a cure for a lot of different diseases. The plan was for the first device to end things like Parkinson's and Alzheimer's, but he always talked about taking it a step further."

"Further?"

"Yeah. He wanted to find a cure for cancer. Be it through that device or using the profits from it for more research."

"That's cool."

"Yeah. It would've been if he'd ever finished it."

"Why didn't he?"

"Not enough money. My mom told me that the treatment had the potential to be dangerous. One coding error. One split wire. If anything went wrong at all, it could kill the patient."

His eyes widened slightly.

"It turns out most investors don't want to give money to a project like that. Even if they aren't held liable, it could ruin them. Their lives, their businesses," I continued, "Soon his partners started leaving one by one. My dad got a little crazy and told them they had to work more to finish it. More hours. More money. More resources they didn't have. He ended up driving all of his friends away for nothing."

Ulysseus sat silently for a moment, then said, "It's too bad. It would've been something cool that could've helped a lot of people."

I nodded.

"What was he like at home?" Ulysseus asked cautiously.

I rolled my eyes, "Kind of crazed."

"How so?"

"He was always talking about work, usually complaining, which wasn't terrible at first. Sometimes he would get angry about how someone didn't do their job or wasn't pulling their weight. Then when everyone left and the investment money dried up, he got my mom involved in the project and never wanted to talk to either of us about anything else. Every time we moved it was to help him. And to a degree, I get it, but," I paused for a moment and thought before finishing, "it was like mom and I didn't matter to him anymore."

Ulysseus raised an eyebrow, "That's a bit harsh, don't you think?"

I shook my head, "If you weren't there to praise him for his work or help him when he needed it, he had no interest in you."

"Really?"

"Yeah, really. The guy was at home all the time and wouldn't even look at me most days, and when he did it was usually just to yell about something I did wrong. And he would only talk to my mom when they were working. He did a few freelance jobs so we could live and keep the lights on, which I appreciate, but it seemed like I lost my dad and there was some stranger living in the next room."

Ulysseus gave me a sympathetic look, "I'm sorry bud."

I shrugged, "Could've been worse."

He shrugged in return, then asked, "What happened to them? Your parents?"

My brow furrowed slightly, "I don't really know. They went on a trip one day and said they would be gone for a while. A couple weeks later I got picked up by the police and told I'd be given a new guardian."

"How did you end up with Jared? Don't they usually try to find someone in the family to take you in?"

"Yeah, but most of my family members are either homeless, drug addicts, or just couldn't afford to take me in on their income level. The court opted for the foster care system instead."

"You didn't have anyone at all?"

I thought for a moment, then said, "Maybe one branch of the family, but they didn't want me. They claimed that they didn't have the funds to take me in. Already too many kids, they wouldn't be able to feed them if they added one more, and so on."

"Jeepers, our family didn't do that."

I looked up at him, "Then how did you end up

with your grandpa?"

"Dad's side of the family all live in Ireland. The court thought it would be better to keep us in America since we're citizens here, and my grandfather was the only family we had here after mom and dad died."

"I'm sorry."

He shrugged, "Everyone gets a bad deal in some way, right?"

"I guess so."

Ashley shifted. I had moved her shoulder pillow a bit too much, accidentally forcing her to readjust. I smiled slightly and lightly kissed her hair.

"I think it turned out alright for me in the end though," I said, turning back to Ulysseus, "Good friends. Sweet girlfriend."

"Sweet? Jeepers Melvin was right, you are whipped."

I grinned, "What do you mean?"

"Have you ever seen her actually angry before? Hell's not as scary as that!"

I could not hold back my laughter because I was not sure if he was joking or serious. Ashley rubbed her eyes a little.

"What are you guys doing?" she grumbled.

"Nothing. Just go back to sleep. I'll wake you when we eat lunch," I whispered.

She stretched her neck a little and rolled her shoulders, then laid on the floor of the van. I rubbed her arm. She shifted a little, then drifted off into a deep sleep.

"How is she so tired?" Ulysseus asked, then after a moment said, "Never mind. I don't want to know."

I rolled my eyes, "It's nothing like that you weirdo. She just didn't sleep very well after I got hurt."

He looked at her for a moment, then said, "Well, I'm glad she's catchin' up on some rest. These undead buggers run like their arses are on fire."

"I think that's putting it mildly."

He looked down at his cards and asked, "Got any threes?"

"Go fish."

Ulysseus and I continued playing card games for a while longer, but soon our stomachs started growling. He started searching through our supply of canned goods while I woke Ashley.

I shook her shoulder. She grumbled something inaudible.

"Ashley, come on. You need to eat something," I said.

"Five more minutes," she mumbled.

"I already gave you thirty."

"So, what's five more?"

"Come on."

She opened her eyes and looked up at me as she said, "Fine."

She sat up to stretch her stiff muscles. Then she let out a yawn.

"Alright, what'll it be?" Ulysseus asked, "Green beans, chicken noodle soup, or cooked carrots?"

"Is that really all they got?" I asked.

"No, I just don't think I can get to anythin' else without knockin' the whole pile down."

We each took a can of soup and decided to split a can of each of the two vegetables between the three of us. Ulysseus rummaged through some of the remaining supplies until he found an open package of plastic spoons. He took one for himself before handing us the package. He then searched until he found a can opener and started breaking into the cans of food.

We ate in silence, wolfing down our meal. When we finished Ashley seemed a little embarrassed.

"You alright?" I asked.

"I just didn't realize I was that hungry," she replied, smiling slightly.

Ulysseus grinned, "Who'd of thought you could feel hungrier in virtual reality than you do in real life."

"I probably looked like a slob while I was eating."

I shook my head in disagreement.

"Nah," Ulysseus said, "You just looked like you were eating fast. Trust me, I've seen much worse in the cafeteria at school."

I chuckled, thinking of a few of the football guys challenging each other to eating competitions at lunch. The worst ones were when spaghetti had been offered at lunch, not only for us to watch but also for the janitors to clean up afterwards.

The rest of the day crawled by. That night the three of us took shifts guarding the van and looking for our friends. I offered to take the first shift considering I had already slept so much since I fell.

I carefully crawled into the passenger seat at the front of the van. Ulysseus sat in the driver's seat to sleep, while Ashley snuggled under a blanket in the back.

I looked out of the windows, keeping an eye on the road our friends had taken to find gas. Sadly, the only thing I saw happened to be sporadic occurrences of walking corpses passing by. Luckily, they didn't notice us inside the vehicle as they staggered along.

I flinched when I heard Ashley's voice say, "Logan?"

I looked at her over my shoulder. She was sitting up, leaned back against the wall of the van. The blanket laid sprawled across her lap. Her hair was a bit messy from sleep.

"Yeah?" I whispered, trying not to wake the snoring beast that was Ulysseus.

"Do you think they're okay?" she asked.

I nodded, "I'm sure they're fine."

She stared off into space a little, seeming uncertain.

"Hey," I said.

She looked up at me. I held a hand out to her. She took it, her grip slowly tightening.

"Everything's going to be fine. I promise," I said.

She nodded slightly. I squeezed her hand.

I knew what she was thinking. She was thinking about how some of us had gotten hurt. She was probably reflecting on our conversation in the house too. About what would happen if we died there.

We held hands in silence for a long while, then Ashley said, "Go ahead and get some sleep. I can take the next shift."

"I'm fine."

We both stayed awake until it was time to wake

Ulysseus. I let go of her hand and shook him.

"Come on bud, your turn," I said.

He grumbled and turned away from me, eyes still closed.

"Ulysseus, please?" Ashley asked sleepily.

"Why are you both up?" he asked hazily.

"I can't sleep," she replied.

He laid still for a moment longer, then said, "My neck's startin' to ache anyhow."

He sat up, rubbing the back of his neck and stretching his limbs. I crawled into the back of the van and sat by Ashley. I gently took her hand as I kissed her cheek. We sat quietly for another moment, then she let out a big yawn. I grinned.

"Come on. Let's go to sleep."

"But what if-"

I shushed her softly and nuzzled her, "Everything's going to be just fine. You need to keep your strength up."

She hesitated a moment longer, then nodded. I reached for another blanket and covered up as I laid down. She cautiously snuggled with me, laying her head on my shoulder. I smiled.

"What?" she asked.

"Nothing."

"What?" she repeated.

I nuzzled her nose. She giggled.

"Hey, remember. You two are not alone in this van," Ulysseus grumbled.

"Mind your own business, General," Ashley said.

He groaned at the sound of the nickname.

"I'm goin' to kill Peyton for startin' that," he growled.

The two of us laughed, then she turned back to me.

"Now tell me," she said.

I wrapped an arm around her shoulders and gave her a tight squeeze, "Nothing, really."

She gave me a very unconvinced glare. I kissed her nose.

"You're just pretty," I said.

She raised an eyebrow, "We're in the apocalypse. I look like a disaster."

"No, you don't. And you are terrible at taking compliments."

She stuck her tongue out at me. I chuckled in response.

"Come on. Let's go to sleep," I said.

"Yes. Please. For goodness sake, go to sleep so I don't have to listen to this anymore," Ulysseus whined.

Ashley rolled her eyes as she laid back down and said, "You're such a drama queen,"

"Whatever," he replied.

She smiled a little, reaching for my good hand. I held hers and squeezed lightly. A few minutes later, I grinned at the sound of a soft humming, telling me that she had fallen asleep. I checked her blanket to make sure it was tucked around her for warmth, then closed my eyes to sleep.

My eyelids opened slowly the next day. They blinked a few times, trying to clear the goop from my eyes that had formed while I slept. I raised my hand to wipe it away, then flinched when something shifted against me. I removed the eye boogers and turned to see Ashley still laying against me. My hand had been resting on hers when I woke up. When I rested my hand once again, I found that hers had quickly become cold.

She shifted again, shivering rapidly. I gently rubbed her forearm, trying to use the friction to warm her up.

"Ulysseus?" I whispered.

There was no response. I looked up to find that both the driver and passenger seats were empty. I glanced around the van. The remaining rifle was gone, leaving only one more gun in the van.

Where did he go? I thought.

I listened, wondering why he would have left the van by himself. My body then jerked at the sound of a gunshot. Ashley awoke, momentarily in a state of terror. She shot straight up and looked around wildly.

I sat up and touched her shoulder. She whirled around quickly, a fist raised. I managed to catch it just in time.

"Easy," I said, "Easy. Calm down."

After another moment of mind fog, she realized it was me. Her eyes widened as she was suddenly aware of me holding her fist in my palm.

"I'm sorry!" she said frantically, "I didn't...I..."

She seemed unsure of what to say, her brain frantically searching for some way to explain it. But she was still too tired, and adrenaline was running rampant through her veins. I hugged her shaking body.

"It's okay," I said, "It's okay. I'm not mad."

She seemed to relax for a moment, then pulled away from me.

"You heard that too, right?" she asked.

I nodded. We both instinctually ducked at the sound of another shot, much closer than the first.

"What is it?" she asked.

"I don't know."

I stood and grabbed the last firearm we had, just a small handgun. I fumbled to open the chamber to see how many shots were left. Only one. I huffed.

I slowly leaned into the front of the van to look out the window, then jumped back as the door suddenly opened.

"Oh, hey Logan," Ulysseus said nonchalantly.

He sat down in the driver's seat and closed the door.

"Dude, where were you?" I asked.

"I had to take a leak. Want to hold my hand next time?" he asked sarcastically.

"Where did the gunshots come from?" Ashley asked.

He raised the rifle in his hand.

"Why did you fire the gun?" I asked, "We need to stay quiet until the others get back with gas."

"Well Logan, to be frank with ya, I'm not too worried about bein' quiet when I've got a couple of dead freaks on my heels. I thought I could get back here in time and they got too close."

I huffed, then said, "We just need to be careful, okay?"

"Hey, don't get mad at me, I brought my knife too so I could stay quiet. Those things are just too fast to take on more than one at a time."

Since I didn't have a holster, I put the gun in the waistband of my jeans and sat down next to Ashley again.

"Are there any more nearby?" Ashley asked.

"Not that I saw. Why?" Ulysseus replied.

"I need to go too."

Ulysseus checked the rearview mirrors of the van, then opened his door slightly to check.

"We're clear if you want to go," he said.

Ashley stood, but hesitated to go out the van's rear doors. She turned to me.

"Will you go with me?" she asked timidly.

I nodded.

"I'll keep an eye out from here," Ulysseus said.

I reached for the door handle, but paused to ask her, "Do you have a weapon?"

She nodded, patting the scabbard of a Bowie Knife at her belt. I grabbed my sword and scabbard, clumsily strapping it to my belt, then opened the door and carefully stepped down. I turned and held my hand out for her to take as she followed.

"Look at you being a gentleman," she said with a grin.

I smiled back, "Don't seem so surprised at least."

She held my hand as her feet touched the grass. We walked silently to the woods after closing the van doors, making sure not to go too far into the trees. Ashley stopped me as we walked among the mighty oaks.

"You wait here. And don't look," she said.

"No worries," I said.

I turned around and drew my sword to stand guard while she hid behind a tree. My senses seemed to heighten as I watched between the trees.

I flinched when Ashley tapped my shoulder.

"Ready to go?" she asked.

I shook my head, "Nope. My turn."

Ashley took my spot standing guard while I looked for a nearby spot. When I finished, I rejoined her.

"Ready now," I said.

We slowly walked back to the edge of the forest, just before we emerged from the trees, Ulysseus ran straight into me. We both fell to the ground on impact. He scrambled to stand up, struggling because of the heavy backpack he was wearing.

"What are you doing?" I asked.

"Run!" he shouted.

He hopped up, taking a moment to help me stand before running off.

"Logan," Ashley said.

I turned. My eyes widened as I saw dozens of corpses running straight for us at impossible speeds. We both followed Ulysseus's lead, trying to keep up with him while also avoiding crashing into one of the surrounding trees. The growls and groans only seemed to grow closer. My calves burned, but I refused to stop.

"There's a river up ahead!" Ulysseus shouted.

He ran past the trees and made a sharp left turn.

I tried to speed up, struggling because of my weakened ankle. I glanced over my shoulder to find one of the corpses less than a foot away from me.

"Run Ash! Run!" I shouted.

Ashley and I sprinted toward the clearing in the woods.

I don't understand why anyone ever believes anything on TV, I thought angrily, *Most of those stupid zombie movies never said I would have to deal with The Running Dead.*

Ashley managed to stay a few feet ahead of me for most of the chase but looked over her shoulder. She started trying to match my pace in case I needed help.

"Don't slow down! Keep going!" I hollered.

I looked past her and realized we had just trapped ourselves. The river was only a few yards ahead, and there was no way to know if it was infested with the dead. She seemed to come to the same realization as she came close to the spot where Ulysseus had turned.

"What do we do?" she shouted.

"I don't know, just keep going!" I replied.

When she reached the riverbank, she made the turn and I followed close behind. The tattered moans and groans were getting louder as the dead only seemed to draw closer. My chest heaved as stabbing pains ran through my body. Adrenaline was the only thing pushing me forward.

"Logan! There's a boat!" Ashley shouted.

I looked ahead and saw it. A small pontoon sitting near the shore.

"Come on!" Ulysseus shouted.

He had already reached the boat and raised his rifle, firing a couple of rounds at some of the zombies closest to us.

"We don't even know if it works!" I said.

"It's better than running! Maybe there's an oar on it," Ashley replied.

She reached the boat long before me, hurrying to check the motor and then the control panel.

"The gas tank's full, but I need a key!" she shouted.

Ulysseus seemed to be saying something, but

I could not hear him. It was likely curse words because we were trapped.

My mind raced faster than my body as I tried to find another way out of this mess. My eyes scanned the boat, landing on the words *Sea Raven* painted on the fence paneling, presumably the name of the vessel. Then I remembered something.

Stumbling slightly, I reached into the pocket of my jeans and pulled out the small silver key attached to its cheesy keychain.

"Try this one!" I shouted. I threw the key with all the force I could muster. She hurried to the edge of the boat and managed to catch it by the worn tag. I slowed my pace a bit as I waded in the water to reach them.

Please don't bite my foot. Please don't bite my foot.

I grabbed onto the rusted ladder and heaved myself up with one hand. At the top, I closed the gate and grabbed my sword. Ulysseus reloaded his rifle with rounds from a small box he must have brought with him.

"Where did you get those?" I asked.

"They were in my pocket when we started the level. Is this really the time to be askin' those questions?" he exclaimed.

I turned back to find zombies trying to grab ahold of the boat. I quickly sliced into the heads of several at once, careful not to drop my blade. Ulysseus fired a few more rounds into the horde.

I heard the motor rumble slightly and then stop as Ashley tried to start the boat. She turned the key again only for the engine to stall.

"Ash, hurry!" I shouted.

"I'm trying!" she snapped back before turning

the key again.

I swung my sword again. Ulysseus fired a few more shots. With the last blast, the engine roared to life. We had only a moment to grab onto the railing before we took off down the river. Had my reflexes been any slower I would have been someone's dinner. For a mere second, some twisted part of me wondered if I would have tasted fatty or gamy.

I hobbled to the wheel, taking in the appearance of the rust bucket. The deck was covered with the disgusting brown mess that only tiny specks of the steel managed to peek through. Sections of the railing were coated with algae and bird droppings. Behind the captain's chair rested what seemed to be a sofa that had been made with plastic seats rather than cloth, and could seat several passengers. Between the captain's chair and the sofa rested a small, rusty table that was bolted to the deck of the ship.

Ashley tightly grasped the dingy wheel as she steered us away from the shore. I wobbled a little and grabbed the back of the captain's chair. She turned to me, then looked forward again.

"Sit down Logan," she said.

"I'm fine," I replied.

I stepped forward and wrapped an arm around her.

"Close call, huh?" I asked.

"Way too close."

I rubbed her arm.

"I hope everyone else is okay," she murmured.

"I'm sure they're fine."

Ulysseus looked around the boat.

I let her go before continuing, "I'm going to help him look around. Maybe there's a hatch or something with supplies."

She nodded, refocusing on the water.

I took another sweeping glance across the boat and noticed an ice chest a few feet away. I stepped forward to crouch beside it. As my hand rested on the latch, I froze. There was something inside, scratching and squealing in a sort of pint-sized rage.

Cautiously, I just barely opened the top, only to quickly close it as a horde of rats tried to escape. The box shook and writhed beneath my hands. I sat on top of the chest to keep the vermin inside.

"What is it?" Ashley asked.

"Rats. Big, angry rats."

"Can we just throw them overboard?"

I thought for a moment, then shook my head, "We should keep them."

"Why?" she asked, sharing a disgusted look with Ulysseus.

"Never know when we might need them. I need something to weigh this down though."

Ulysseus searched around the boat until he found the anchor, a huge chunk of metal attached to iron chains.

He grabbed it and started dragging it toward me, his muscles slightly straining to get it across the deck. Once he was close enough, he lifted the anchor. I reached out to help him carefully place it on the lid of the ice chest without breaking the plastic.

He stepped back to continue searching for supplies. I rose slowly as my eyes scanned the deck once again. They landed on a small trapdoor, its outline barely noticeable since most of it hid under a tarp.

I limped closer and lifted the sheet of plastic, which seemed to be in decent condition. The hatch was held shut by a chain link wrapped around the handle at one end and tightly knotted around a steel peg at the other. The chain had been hastily wrapped around and put through a ring at the top, with the mess holding the door shut with a rusted padlock.

"Hey Ulysseus, is there anything in that bag that can break this?" I asked.

He looked over my shoulder, then removed his bag to look through it. He stopped after a moment to hand me a small pocket knife.

"It can't break it, but maybe you can pick it," he said.

I took the knife from him and picked at some of the rust. Once I had removed enough, I placed the end of the blade inside the lock.

Ashley stopped the boat while I fiddled with the lock. She zipped the jacket she wore.

"What all is in that bag?" Ashley asked.

"Uh, mostly food. Some water bottles. I tried to grab some of the essentials. Plus, that knife and the box of ammo for the rifle."

"How did you have time to pack that?"

"I saw them comin' from the road straight ahead of the van. I didn't want us to be trapped or overwhelmed by them, but goin' hungry's not much better."

Ashley and I shared a brief look.

Ulysseus shivered slightly before adding, "If I had thought about it, I would have grabbed a blanket too. It's going to be a cold night."

"Especially on a boat," Ashley groaned.

"I got it!" I exclaimed as the lock finally gave a satisfying click.

"What's in there?" Ashley asked.

"Hopefully not any more disgusting rats," Ulysseus added.

I lifted the hatch, knife raised for defense. Inside was a small, empty crawl space. I raised an eyebrow, looking at the others over my shoulder.

"Probably supposed to be some form of shelter," Ulysseus said.

I closed the trapdoor while Ashley turned back to the wheel.

I stood and looked over the edge of the deck. My nose wrinkled at the smell of the decayed flesh that melted off of the zombies that had wandered into the water.

"Glad you brought water," I said as I turned to Ulysseus, "You couldn't pay me to drink this."

He peeked over the side and winced at the thought.

I looked back at the water. Despite it being midmorning, the river had the color and consistency of oil. Fragments of bones and chunks of pale, gnarled flesh floated along the surface.

The boat chugged along through the day. Ulysseus laid on the sofa and slept most of the afternoon, preparing to steer and guard the boat through the night.

I grabbed a bottle of water from his backpack and took a sip. When I finished, I held it out to Ashley. She took it and drank a few sips before giving it back.

I looked up at the sky after dropping the bottle back into the bag. The bright beacon seemed to slowly but surely come closer.

Ashley cut the engine and sat back in the chair.

"Something wrong?" I asked.

She shook her head, "No, I just don't want to use all of our gas at once. The water is pushing us this way already. I think it's better for us to save the fuel in case we need a quick escape."

I nodded, then turned my head to look toward the front of the ship.

"Are you tired?" she asked.

I shook my head, still looking forward.

"I think I'm going to get some sleep then. I can barely keep my eyes open," she mumbled.

"Go ahead. I'll keep watch."

She stood and took a seat at the empty spot on the sofa. As she sat back, she propped her feet up on the table to get more comfortable. Moments later, she was asleep.

I woke Ulysseus as the sun started to set. He grumbled under his breath for a moment before opening his eyes.

"You sleepin'?" he asked as he sat up.

I shook my head, "I don't think I could if I tried."

"Why?"

"I don't know. Something just feels...off."

He raised an eyebrow.

"It's just too quiet," I continued, "I find it hard to believe that we're actually getting a moment to breathe."

"Worryin' won't do anythin' for you," he said, "I'll keep watch, just go to sleep."

He stood so I could take his spot on the sofa. I sat next to Ashley and propped my feet up next to her's. It wasn't until then that I realized she was quaking with fear as she slept. Probably from a nightmare of some sort.

I wrapped my arm around her and slowly pulled her against me. She mumbled something inaudible before snuggling with my shoulder.

In my peripherals I could see Ulysseus watching us for a moment. He then sat back in the Captain's Chair with his rifle nearby to guard the boat.

"Logan," Ashley mumbled.

I looked down and shushed her, "It's alright. Go back to sleep."

She shifted to get more comfortable. I watched the water for any threats, but once the sun was gone, it was a useless effort.

As my eyelids started to droop, something scraped against the side of the boat. The sound was almost like nails on a chalkboard, but more deafening.

Ashley flinched next to me. Ulysseus was already up and looking for the source of the sound. My eyes widened when I heard a familiar groan in the same direction as the screeching steel.

I jumped up and raised the pocket knife. Ulysseus lifted his gun and aimed it at a ghoulish creature in the water, barely visible in the dim moonlight.

It looked much like the zombies we saw on the shore, but its skin was gone, likely among the other human remains residing in the river. The only thing keeping the corpse in one piece seemed to be the ligaments holding the bones together.

"Wait," I murmured.

I could barely make out Ulysseus's confused glance in the moonlight.

"We don't know how many more there are," I whispered, "We need to keep it quiet."

He kept his rifle up a moment longer before nodding. He then lowered the weapon.

Meanwhile, I leaned over the boat to quickly push the monster's head against the side of the boat. I pierced its skull with the knife and let the body slowly drift away in the water.

"Looks like we're almost there," Ashley said.

I looked up to see the beacon was much closer. Maybe a mile or two away.

"Do you think we can reach it by boat?" Ulysseus asked.

The two of us then fell to the deck as the boat hit something.

He just had to ask, I thought.

"I guess not," he growled.

We stood slowly, checking the shoreline for the dead, but none were in sight.

Something touched my empty hand. I turned to find Ashley had taken it, careful not to hurt my wrist.

"If we go now, maybe we can make it by the mornin'," Ulysseus suggested.

"Should we go out there in the dark?" Ashley asked.

I looked at the trees beyond the shore. The beacon was so bright that it wasn't difficult to see through them.

"It looks like there's plenty of light," I said, "We'll just have to be careful and stay quiet."

They both nodded. Ulysseus pulled on his backpack and slung the rifle over his shoulder.

"Want your knife back?" I asked.

He shook his head, "Nah, I've got enough to carry. Thanks."

I rolled my eyes and put it in his hand, "You need something quieter than that gun. Besides, it's not that heavy you wimp."

He chuckled and bumped his fist against my shoulder. After a moment of hesitation, he opened the gate and hopped down from the boat. I followed close behind, then turned to help Ashley down.

We walked quietly between the trees, careful to avoid the twigs and leaves on the forest floor. Along the way, we saw a few more zombies wandering lazily nearby, but they did not seem to notice us walking by.

The Base

As the sun started to rise again, we reached the final clearing. At the center rested what seemed to be a military bunker with the beacon coming from a device sitting at the top. From the distance, I assumed that it had two floors considering the set of windows near the top of its tall, cylindrical frame. As we drew closer, I could see through the large open door that there was a set of stairs that led to the second floor.

"Hey!" someone shouted.

We looked to see Adrian waving at us from the bunker. Natalie and Diego turned at the sound of his voice and began waving at us too.

The three of us checked the field once more before jogging to them. When we arrived, Natalie and Ashley hugged almost immediately. Ulysseus and Diego started talking to one another about how we had found our way to the base. Adrian clapped me on the shoulder.

"Good to see some more familiar faces," Adrian said.

"Same here," I replied, "What happened to you guys?"

"We've been here the whole time. Our objective was to defend the base until everyone else got here."

I looked them over and realized they were all in tactical gear while carrying military grade equipment.

"We were starting to wonder," Adrian continued.

"So were we."

We looked back toward the tree line.

"Have you seen any of the others?" I asked.

"Not yet. You?"

"We were with Melvin, Brandie, and Vivian for a while, but we got separated."

"Viv alright?"

I nodded.

"Good. Hopefully they aren't too far behind you."

We stood in silence for a moment.

"Have you guys gone in the base yet?"

"A few times. In the middle there's a bunker, but the level ends if we go inside. No one else left outside of the base can continue if anyone goes through the bunker doors before everyone is inside the main building. So we've just been using the main base as shelter and keeping the bunker door locked just in case someone came while we were asleep."

"Hey, I see more over here," Diego said.

"More of the dead or more of us?" Adrian asked. He seemed to take on the leadership role quite well.

"Ours," Diego replied, "Look."

I walked closer to him to see James, Alice, and Bryan walking toward us. They seemed tired, but no one was hurt. The trio smiled and waved when they saw us.

I made note of their weapons when they arrived, just in case we needed to defend the base. Alice had a small revolver at her waist, presumably full of ammo. James had a machete in his hand as they approached. Meanwhile Bryan held a Bowie similar to Ashley's and had a large, black rifle that I could not identify strapped across his back. It was a bit surreal to see nerdy Bryan with such a heavy duty weapon.

Others slowly trickled in throughout the day until nearly everyone had arrived. Everyone but Peyton.

As the sun set again, Ulysseus became nervous. His foot tapped rapidly and sporadically as his patience wore thin. His hand absently scratched the small scruff of a beard he had been trying to grow out. As his nervous energy grew, he switched from sitting on the ground to pacing.

Ashley and I sat together next to the door of the base. The others were inside talking or sleeping while we kept an eye out for zombies.

Ashley turned to me, "Do you think she's okay?"

"I'm sure she's fine," I replied.

I turned to look at our friend as he began gnawing at his fingernails.

"It's him I'm worried about."

She waited a moment before replying, "Maybe you should talk to him."

I raised an eyebrow, "Me?"

She nodded, "Yeah you."

"I don't know if that's a good idea."

"Why not? You guys get along well."

"I know that. I just don't think this is something he's really going to be interested in talking to me about since he doesn't know me that well."

"I heard you guys talking in the van. You opened up to him, why wouldn't he open up to you?"

I turned to her, "Were you being nosy?"

"No. You were just moving your arm too much for me to fall back asleep. Believe me, I tried."

"Right," I said, "Sure that's what it was."

I grinned, letting her know I was joking. She rolled her eyes and gently bumped my arm with her fist, smiling back.

I thought for a moment before saying, "I guess he did open up to me once already."

Her brow furrowed, "When?"

"When we were in the sewer level. He told me about his grandpa and how they stayed with you guys a lot growing up."

She seemed surprised, "Wow, it's hard for Melvin to get him to talk about that some days."

I turned back to Ulysseus as he stopped pacing. His eyes carefully traced the tree line, searching for signs of his sister.

Ashley nudged my shoulder, "Will you please go talk to him?"

I nodded, holding her hand for a moment before standing. She sat back against the steel wall as I walked to our friend.

I lightly rested my hand on his shoulder. He flinched slightly and turned.

"How are you holding up?" I asked.

"I'm fine," he replied halfheartedly, "I just wish she'd hurry."

"You know I'm here if you need to talk, right?"

He eyed me for a moment, then nodded. I let my hand fall.

"I'm sure she'll be here any minute," I said, now standing next to him, "I'll even help you look."

"What's the point?" he huffed.

He sat down, continuing to watch the trees despite his statement. I sat beside him.

"Do you think she's hurt?" he asked nervously.

I rubbed his shoulder, "Like I keep saying, she's probably fine. Think about it, she's on her own, so she has to be more careful getting here. Especially with so many undead freaks right around us."

"I guess so."

He did not feel like talking anymore, so I just sat quietly next to him. We listened to the crickets and frogs sing all around us as the sky turned black with the new moon. The only light emitted from the beacon above us.

After a while, someone tapped my shoulder. I turned to see Ashley crouched down behind me.

"Hey," I said.

"Hey, our shift's over," she replied.

We both turned to Ulysseus, who either did not hear her or chose to ignore what she had said.

"Let's go inside bud," I said.

He shook his head.

Ashley sat on the other side of him, "Ulysseus–"

"I'm not goin'," he declared.

She hugged him tightly, "Ulysseus, there's no point in wearing yourself out. You know Peyton wouldn't want that."

"I don't care."

Melvin and Bryan stepped out of the base, ready for their shift.

"Everything okay?" Melvin asked cautiously.

I turned to Melvin and nodded, then looked back at Ulysseus. His brow furrowed. He squinted as if looking for something.

When Ashley let him go, he stood and took a few steps forward.

"Ulysseus," I started, but he shushed me before

I could finish my sentence.

I looked in the same direction as him. A bright light peeked through the oak curtain, waving wildly between the tree trunks.

Ulysseus grinned slightly as he turned to look at us.

"Do you think it's her?" he asked.

"Probably," Melvin said, walking closer.

"Looks like she's running," Bryan chimed in.

Ulysseus's smile fell. I could almost read his mind as the same question popped into my head.

Running from what?

Peyton suddenly emerged from the trees, sprinting even faster as she reached the clearing. Her bright red hair was pulled back in a messy braid. She wore a black tank top, ragged jeans, black tennis shoes, and had a small backpack strapped to her shoulders. At her belt rested a small handgun on her right side and a dagger on her left. In her right hand, she was waving a dimming flashlight as she ran.

She seemed fine at first, but we all froze when we heard the rattled groans and rasps of racing corpses.

"Peyton!" Ulysseus shouted.

Melvin jumped forward and clapped a hand over Ulysseus's mouth.

"Are you crazy?!" he said quietly, "You'll just attract more!"

"I'll get the others," Bryan said, running back into the base.

As the dead began emerging from the trees, I drew my sword, prepared to fight them off until everyone could get inside. Melvin raised a rifle that had rested on his back. Ashley hurried back in the base, looking for a gun while helping Bryan wake everyone up.

Peyton strained to reach us. Melvin put a hand on Ulysseus's shoulder and pulled him back.

"What are you doin'?" Ulysseus growled.

"We need to move back. The closer we are to the base, the quicker we can close the door when she gets inside," Melvin said firmly.

Ulysseus hesitated, his jaw set for a moment, before nodding. The three of us walked back until we were only a couple of paces from the door. Melvin aimed the rifle and began to fire at the dead that he deemed too close to our friend.

At first Peyton ducked as she ran, afraid of being shot. When she realized who was firing, she seemed more comfortable. At least as comfortable as you can be while running for your life and also running toward a guy who's shooting at the monsters that are chasing you.

Ashley and Bryan returned moments later. Bryan raised his own rifle and began firing. Ashley raised a handgun she had grabbed from the base and did the same.

My muscles tensed as I heard another groan, this one much closer than the others.

"They're coming from behind the base!" Vivian shouted from inside, looking through one of the battlement windows.

Ulysseus drew his knife, glancing at me. I nodded, understanding what he meant. He stepped next to Melvin while I stood next to Bryan, my sword raised and waiting for the zombies to draw too close from behind us.

I did not hesitate to strike as the first one dashed around the corner. Then came two more. I swiped my sword and managed to decapitate both in one move. After a few more swipes, I could feel the muscles in my arm getting tired.

I looked over my shoulder to check on the others. Ashley was reloading her gun with some of the bullets just inside of the base. Ulysseus drove his knife into the skull of a zombie he held by the shoulder, letting the body drop as another rushed forward. Diego and Natalie emerged with their own melee weapons to help him. Brandie hurried out to help me, still using the hatchet I had given her days before. Those that chose to remain inside stood at the windows on the second floor and fired at the zombies now coming from all sides, although many of the shots missed their marks. I assumed that the best shooters among our group were already standing next to me.

Melvin and Bryan continued shooting the zombies while Peyton struggled to reach the base. As she drew closer, I could tell she was wounded. Her left leg had a slight limp and her left arm was covered in crudely applied bandages.

"Come on," I mumbled.

I turned back to the zombies coming from the side. Brandie had become much more skilled at using the axe and removing it from the skulls of the dead, having almost no issues between attacks.

"We're going to be overrun if we don't make a new plan," Bryan said.

Ashley's gun suddenly gave a small click rather than a boom. She checked her ammo.

"I'm out," she said.

"Me too," Melvin said.

"I'll try to find more bullets," Ashley said.

She hurried back into the base. The sound of gunshots grew quieter while the growls grew louder as others inside ran out of bullets as well. By then, Peyton was only a couple of yards away.

"Come on Peyton!" Ulysseus shouted, driving his blade through another brain.

Peyton drew her pistol and fired behind her, trying to keep the dead back. When she ran out of bullets too, she threw her gun at one of the zombies, causing it to stumble back while also lightening her load.

Then Bryan emptied his last magazine.

"Get inside," Natalie said.

He hesitated, but then nodded and hurried in.

"Get the door ready to close!" Adrian shouted from inside.

Fatigue was quickly setting in. All I could hope for was my adrenaline rush to push me through the battle.

When Peyton's shoes finally hit the steel stairs, Natalie and Diego hurried inside. Brandie followed close behind.

"Ulysseus!" Ashley shouted.

I turned to see her holding two more guns, probably holding the last of our ammo. She tossed one to him and started shooting with the other. I struck a few more monsters with my sword.

"Logan get inside!" Ashley growled.

"Yes ma'am!" I shouted back.

I made one more swipe, then hurried in the doors as they started to close. The herd behind Peyton seemed to be thinning slightly, and nowhere near as many came from behind the base. Ulysseus and Ashley shot a few more that were nearby as Peyton slowed, exhausted from her wounds and exertion. As she walked inside, Ashley and Ulysseus followed her through the door as it creeped down.

Ulysseus dropped the empty gun and wrapped Peyton in a tight hug.

"Don't ever scare me like that again!" he said.

She hugged him back and said, "It's okay bubba. I'm okay."

Ashley and I tried to keep an eye on the herd as the door took its sweet time closing.

"Can we go into the bunker yet?" Vivian asked.

Adrian shook his head, "Not until the main door closes completely."

The siblings let each other go and Ulysseus sat down to rest. Peyton stepped closer to the door to watch the dead as well.

"Could this thing go any slower?" Ashley growled.

I walked up to her to wrap her in a hug. As I did, I gently rubbed her back to ease her tense muscles.

The others began talking and laughing amongst themselves, celebrating another victory. Ulysseus chugged a bottle of water as he looked over his sister, worried about her injuries. Ashley and I took a few steps away from the door to get water as well.

Ulysseus laughed at something Melvin said, then turned back to Peyton. By then the door was less than half a foot from the floor.

Then his eyes widened in terror, "Peyton get back!"

But it was too late. One of the zombies had managed to reach through the opening and grabbed her ankle. It jerked her to the floor to drag her back outside.

On instinct, I dove for her, clutching her hand in both of mine despite the sharp, stabbing pain in my wrist. Ulysseus followed suit with the other hand. Other zombies tried to crawl under the opening as the door stopped.

"It has a motion sensor!" Diego shouted, "It's like the garage doors at home!"

Meaning it would stop if it sensed something underneath.

Ulysseus and I fought against the zombie, trying to pull Peyton back inside. She screamed in agony. I glanced under the door to see that the monster had bit down on her foot.

Others in the group grabbed melee weapons and stepped forward, stabbing the zombies and kicking them away from the door, trying to buy us time. We heaved, trying to drag her further inside as tears streamed down her face from the pain.

"Just hold on!" Ulysseus said, desperate to save his sister. I could tell that another corpse had grabbed her as we were slowly being pulled closer to the door.

Peyton started to loosen her grip on our hands, but I soon realized it was not from her being too weak to hold on.

"Peyton, don't," I said, "We can get you back in."

Ulysseus seemed to realize what she was doing and pulled even harder, his muscles straining from the effort.

Others around us seemed to want to help, but there were too many monsters trying to get inside. If any of them stepped away it would have quickly become a disaster.

"Bubba," Peyton said.

Ulysseus propped his foot against the door, trying to get more leverage.

"Bubba, it's okay."

"No, it isn't. Even in a virtual world, I ain't lettin' ya die," he snapped, his accent getting thicker.

"Ulysseus William Byrne, you listen to me," Peyton growled.

He froze at the sound of his full name. I was taken aback for a moment. Peyton had always seemed fairly timid when I was around her. Then again, she had essentially raised Ulysseus while growing up herself. She had probably figured out how to keep him in line a long time ago.

"It's just a game. I'll catch up to you. But if you don't let me go then we all have to start over. That will just ruin the game for everyone."

He seemed torn. I knew why. Everything just felt too real in this to set emotions aside like he could while playing other video games.

"Maybe I'll even get a menu saying I can quit the game. We'll have to go home soon anyway. I'll be waiting for you."

He nodded slightly but squeezed her hand a moment longer.

"I love you bubba. I'll see you soon," she said, giving him a slight smile.

"I love you too, Peyton. I'll quit soon so we can go home."

She nodded. He hesitated a moment longer, then looked up at me. We let her go. Ulysseus's muscles tensed as he watched Peyton disappear out from under the door. Adrian stabbed the last zombie that was under the door at that moment and shoved it back out so the door could finally close.

Ulysseus's body began shaking as he heard Peyton's horrific screams. He held back tears, unable to keep his emotions in check. Ashley hurried forward and hugged him.

"I know," she murmured, "I know."

A few tears fell from her own eyes as she held him. Real or not, the sound was just as heartbreaking. We waited a long while for the screams to stop. But they never did.

"I hate to say it, but can we get out of here?" Alice asked after a long pause, "I don't know how much longer any of us will be able to handle this."

Adrian looked at Ulysseus, who begrudgingly nodded in return. Adrian turned to the door of the bunker. I looked over to see a keypad next to a block of steel with a handle. He pressed a few numbers on the keypad and the buttons flashed red. The keypad made a loud buzzing sound, rejecting the code. Adrian raised an eyebrow and tried again. The keypad reacted the same way.

He tried one more time, thinking he may have just entered the code incorrectly. But after the third time, a mechanical, but masculine, voice came from the keypad.

"We're sorry, we are unable to grant your request at this time. Please bring all remaining players into the main base to continue."

Adrian turned to us slowly.

"Is there a way to open the door back up?" Vivian asked.

He shook his head, "Once it's closed, it's closed."

Peyton cried out again. Ulysseus pulled away from Ashley to cover his ears.

"We can't wait this out," Brandie said, "It'll kill him."

"Well, we can't leave unless she's in here! So, I don't know what you expect me to do," Adrian growled.

There was a long silence among those within the base. That is until Ulysseus spoke up.

"That's not necessarily true," he said, his voice somber.

Everyone turned to him. He bit his lip.

"It said all remaining players," he continued.

Everyone stood in silence for a moment.

"So, we have to wait it out," Melvin said sadly.

"That's just cruel!" Brandie snapped.

"It's a game! Besides, we don't have any ammo, so what else are we supposed to do?!" Bryan growled.

Some of the others started arguing, everyone still on edge between the battle and Peyton being ripped away from us. Ashley looked at me, seeming unsure of what to do. I returned the same look, my stomach turning at the sound of Peyton's cries.

And then I remembered something.

I felt along my waistband until I found it. The handgun I had grabbed in the van. I removed the weapon from my jeans and checked the chamber. Still one bullet left.

I looked back up at Ashley. She seemed to understand. She took Ulysseus's hand and pointed at me. He turned. His jaw set as he looked at the gun. After a moment of contemplation, he nodded solemnly.

As I turned to walk up the stairs, I saw Ashley hug him again. She told him that it would be fine and we could leave when this level was over if that was what he wanted. He was shaking as she held him, still fighting back tears.

I walked up the steel stairs, my boots emitting a slight thump with every step. Peyton's cries seemed weaker with every minute, but still wouldn't stop.

I could not help but hesitate as I reached the window. My eyes searched until I found the window with the best angle, especially for an awful shot like me. A lucky hit would be the best I could hope for.

I looked down at her, now surrounded by a few zombies as she laid weakly on the metal porch. My stomach wretched as I saw a group of three tearing into her, while others seemed to aimlessly wander.

Tears poured from her eyes from the pain. She was slowly bleeding out while the dead ripped her apart in a slow, cruel fashion.

When I managed to get enough control over my stomach, I raised my gun. As I tried to aim, her eyes caught mine. We looked at each other for a long moment.

"Please," she cried weakly.

I paused a moment longer, my hand shaking slightly. There was a moment where I did not know if I could go through with it, but by then it was too late to turn around.

When I was finally satisfied with my shot, I said, "I'm sorry," just before pulling the trigger.

Error

Somehow, I hit my mark. Peyton had managed to close her eyes before the bullet hit her. When it was over, she slowly dissolved into ash and smoke, reminding me that it was not real.

I slowly walked back to the stairwell, bracing myself to see the others. I heard the thumping sound from the stairs and found Ashley standing near the top when I arrived. She looked me over before tightly wrapping her arms around me.

"Are you okay?" she whispered.

I nodded, "Yeah. Yeah, I'm okay."

After a moment, I added, "She disappeared."

She looked up at me, "What do you mean?"

"When she died. She just disappeared."

She raised an eyebrow.

"Go look if you don't believe me."

"No, I believe you. It's just weird."

"Are you really surprised by now?"

"Not really, no."

I pulled her back against me and swayed slightly.

"How is he?" I asked.

"He's okay. Mel's with him right now."

We stood there a moment longer, then I said,

"We should get out of here. I'm sure Ulysseus is going to want to see Peyton again as soon as possible."

She pulled away, taking my hand as we started down the stairs. When we reached the bottom, the others watched us for a moment. Ulysseus walked up to me slowly, then placed a hand on my shoulder.

I looked up to see the keypad beeping and flashing green.

"Congratulations," the mechanical voice said, "You will now be able to move forward."

Adrian's jaw set as he looked at the keypad a moment longer, then waved to us to follow him inside the bunker. He was followed by Vivian, Diego, and Natalie, then slowly by the others one at a time until Ashley, Ulysseus, and I were all that was left.

I turned back to Ulysseus. He let go of my shoulder and held a hand up before I could speak.

"Don't," he said, "I'll see her soon. When we get to the next level I'm going to mess with these darn watches and see how we can save and quit."

I nodded. He stepped away and walked through the bunker door, with Ashley and I following soon after.

The bunker door disappeared behind us as we entered a dark room. A dizziness set in and I stumbled slightly. Ashley tripped, but I caught her as she started to fall.

"I've got ya," I said, helping her lay down on the floor.

"Is this going to happen every time we get through a level?" she growled.

"I guess so."

I laid down next to her and closed my eyes as the nightmare finally seemed to end.

I woke up abruptly, my body shooting straight up and my arms swinging as if in terror. My chest heaved for a moment as I took deep breaths to calm myself down.

When I came to my senses, I realized I was inside a small tent. I looked myself over, finding that I was bundled in a sleeping bag while wearing a dark t-shirt, jeans, and fleece socks. Next to me on the floor of the tent sat a pair of brown hiking boots and a brown fleece jacket.

I rolled out of the sleeping bag and slipped the shoes on.

When I left the tent, I saw others around mine, all in a circle around a fire pit in the middle. I saw my friends slowly peek out of their own tents to see the new level outside.

Ulysseus was the first to fully leave his tent, tapping away at the settings on his watch.

"Where's the quit button on this stupid thing!" he growled.

I heard a familiar whirring sound coming from the sky. As I looked up, I saw the familiar GuideBot floating from above.

"Hey!" Ulysseus shouted, "How do you shut this stupid thing off?!"

"Greetings players!" the GuideBot exclaimed, "You have made it through Level Five!"

As it spoke, the rest of us stepped closer to listen.

"Are you even listenin' to me?" Ulysseus asked.

The GuideBot turned, "Yes player, I am. But I am confused by your question."

"What is there to be confused about? I want to quit! I want to go home and see my sister!"

"Well player, as you can see there is no way to quit this game. You will have to remain until it ends, one way or another."

My brow furrowed, "What does that mean?"

The orb turned to me, "It means that there is no option to leave. There are only two ways to leave this game. You can either win the game by making it through all seventy five lives or-"

"Or we die," I said.

"Yes! Very astute player!" the robot said happily.

"So, what? There's a menu when you die so you can quit or start over?" Melvin asked.

"Incorrect. Which is why I am here. Because the new function you have found is what happens after a player dies."

From the eye of the robot, a holographic screen appeared in front of us.

"You see, in development there was a bug that showed up early on in testing that the developers seemed unable to remove. This is likely due to errors in the programming, but nevertheless, the head developer decided to implement it as a main function of the game rather than deem it a defect."

The screen showed a silhouette of the human mind as it continued.

"As you can see here, when the game is suddenly ended by the player losing their life in the game, the hardware and software react in a very dramatic way. In fact, it reacts in such a way that the human mind cannot properly process. This reaction also causes electric shocks to fill the human body from the earpieces, contacts, and microchip which is inserted under the skin once the player starts the game."

"Whoa, whoa, wait. What microchip?" James growled.

"Your watches implant these microscopic chips once you enter level one. It is a safeguard to ensure that you remain within the game until either one of the endgame options occur, even if someone in the real world removes your watch."

"Why would anyone add something as stupid as that to a video game?" Adrian asked.

The robot waited a moment, then said, "Hmm, it seems that it is not within my programming to grant you such information at this time."

Ulysseus grew angry, "You're not even real! None of this is real! You're just lying to progress the game!"

The robot turned back to him, "No player, you are incorrect. While I am just a program of ones and zeroes, the Endgame Error is very real."

Then the screen changed. It showed a black screen, then seemed to be the first person point of view of someone's eyes opening. As their vision cleared, we could see Peyton's reflection on the computer screen at the desk.

"It seems your friend will be learning about the Endgame Error very soon."

We all watched helplessly as Peyton stretched, then froze. She clutched her chest and cried out in pain. With her other hand, she grappled onto the desk. She started taking deep, forced breaths. Sweat beaded from her forehead. Then, after struggling to breathe for a long set of minutes, she collapsed on the floor, her body jerking sporadically due to a seizure. When she finally stopped, her vision dimmed, and then finally went dark.

Ulysseus seemed drained. He fell to his knees as his legs gave out from under him. Everything in the room on the screen was too accurate to be fake. Every detail from the words on the whiteboards to the random controller that had been left on the floor, which was shown as Peyton fell to the floor. It was all too real to be fabricated.

Ashley burst into tears, because not only had our fears been proven, but the girl who had become her sister had died in the process. I reached for her and she quickly hid against me, unable to stop the sobbing. Ulysseus could no longer hold onto his tears, nor did he care who saw anymore. Small rivers ran along his cheeks as he realized the last person in his family that he loved had died. And he had been the one that let her go.

Adrian hugged Vivian tightly, who was the last person I thought I would ever see cry. Many others in the group looked on in disbelief and shed a few tears themselves.

I looked at Melvin, whose face was a mix of emotions. He had lost his second sister. And as family oriented as the Evans's were, I was not sure what he would do. Suddenly, he charged the robot in a fit of rage, but it just flew higher out of his reach as the screen disappeared. He shouted in anger, a side of him I had never truly seen. His hands tore at his scalp, as if he were going to tear his hair out of his head. A wave of grief and guilt swept over me.

If only I held on longer. If I were stronger. If we had more help.

More thoughts like that flashed through my mind. I hid my face in Ashley's hair as I felt tears trying to break free.

I shot her. I killed her. If anything, I killed her twice.

I squeezed Ashley tighter as my emotions grew stronger. She did not fight it, trying to hide just as much as I was.

"Players, you have found the last of the game functions you are able to access at this time," Guide-Bot said, "Please enjoy the remainder of your game, and we hope you have had a wonderful experience thus far."

Epilogue

The man on the television stepped out of his car, finally home after a trip to Tennessee. He had been asked to make a guest appearance on a web show and happily obliged, leaving his two children home alone. Considering they had just graduated and were nearly adults, he had not worried about leaving for a few days.

He had noticed that his driveway was filled with a few extra cars, recognizing the vehicles as those of frequent visitors. Of old friends his son and daughter had had since childhood.

He grabbed his suitcase and closed the door of his silver Sedan. The car beeped as he locked the doors. His fingers ran along his chin as he thought about how his beard needed a trim.

Harold opened the door to his home. The home he and his late wife had worked so hard for so their children could have a good life. Better than either of them had known when they were young.

"Hello?" he said, seeming confused. Normally when guests were over, at least a few would be in the dining or living room. Both were empty. Even the kitchen was free of hungry football players or teenagers hyped up on caffeine.

He set his suitcase in the dining room and removed his jacket.

"Melvin? Ashley? I'm home," he called.

Still no response.

"Probably playing games," he mumbled to himself.

In no hurry, he walked to the kitchen to make a small cup of green tea for himself, something he enjoyed most afternoons as he conducted research and wrote scripts for his show or other projects. Normally he would drink it at the small wooden table on his back porch with his laptop and notebooks spread across it, but today was his day off. As was the next. He smiled a little at the thought, hoping to take his children to one more relaxed family dinner before they left for whatever came next. And while his daughter would likely remain nearby, his son still seemed uncertain of what to do with his life. All Harold hoped for was that his children would do what made them happy in life, and for Melvin, more school likely would only do the opposite.

With a mug of hot tea in hand, Harold walked around the house, looking for some sort of mess his children may have left. They were normally good about cleaning up after themselves, but they would forget at times when friends were over.

He saw the many dirty mugs and plates in the sink, with a pan that once held eggs and a flat pan covered in biscuit crumbs on a nearby counter.

That's odd, he thought.

Ashley and Melvin had been switching between making dinner and doing dishes when they were home alone for years. They had never missed cleaning up, even if it was a day later before it was done. And while he thought the mess could have been made that morning, one look at the egg remains told him that the mess was several days old.

He sipped his tea and continued looking around the house. The living room was fairly neat. Harold stepped through it and returned to the entryway in order to reach the stairs.

"Ashley? Melvin?" he hollered, a bit louder this time.

He peeked into Melvin's room at the top of the stairs, which was neat and empty as well.

As I thought, playing games. They probably have that volume too loud again.

But as he walked toward the game room, he heard no sounds. No virtual guns blasting or fictional characters speaking. Not even the sounds of teenagers shouting in both frustration and excitement as they played together.

His brow furrowed. He reached for the handle and pushed the door open.

He set his mug down on a coaster that rested on the entertainment center. He stepped closer to the computer desks at which his children and their friends were sitting.

"Melvin? Ashley?"

They all seemed to be asleep at the desks. All except for a red-headed girl who had fallen out of her chair but was still unconscious.

"Peyton?" he said.

He crouched down beside her and gently rubbed her shoulder. For a moment, he glanced up to see that her little brother Ulysseus seemed to be asleep too but was still in his chair. He fondly remembered when the two were much younger. When his wife had brought them home for dinner after work one day. They had been like his own children since.

Harold turned back to Peyton and shook her

shoulder a little more.

"Peyton, sweetie. Wake up."

He stood and slowly observed the others. He found Ashley and Melvin toward the middle of the group of tables. He tried to wake them to no avail. He even tried to wake Logan, Ashley's new boyfriend.

Something kept pulling him back to Peyton. Maybe a sort of parent's instinct. He returned to her and tried to wake her once more.

Now worried, he touched her hand. He flinched away as he touched her icy skin. He felt her neck and wrist for a pulse.

Terror seized his chest as he felt nothing. He quickly but carefully rolled her over and put his head over her heart but heard nothing.

He reached for his cellphone and quickly dialed 911. He fumbled for his earpiece as he began checking others in the group for a heartbeat. When he checked the pulses of the others, they still had normal heart rates.

"911. What is your emergency?" the operator said.

"My name is Harold Evans and I need paramedics at my house immediately. I just returned home and found my children and their friends in my home. They are nonresponsive and one's not breathing."

He gave the operator his address and the number of people who required medical attention as he crouched beside Peyton to perform CPR. After the paramedics arrived, he gave her hand a final squeeze before she was taken away. A hole seemed to form in his heart that only served as a space for guilt to fill, which seemed to indulge in the cavity.

He watched helplessly as his remaining children and their friends were taken away, loaded onto the ambulances. He followed the paramedics outside.

The children were loaded in pairs. All but Peyton, who was loaded into one of the vehicles alone with a white cloth over her body. Harold, a usually stoic man, fought back tears as he watched one of his daughters being taken away from him. One that would never come back home again.

As the ambulances began to pull away, he stopped one and asked to ride in the back. When he explained he had three children in the vehicles, the woman agreed, giving him a pained look.

She led him to the back of the ambulance she would be driving. Inside lay Logan on the bench seat of the ambulance, with Ulysseus strapped to the nearby stretcher.

Harold slowly sat down in the small, remaining seat in the back of the ambulance. He sat silently for a long while as the ambulance was driven to the hospital in town. He soon rubbed his hands over his face.

What am I going to tell him? he thought, *He's going to be devastated.*

He reached for Ulysseus's hand. His foot tapped softly on the floor as thoughts of Melvin and Ashley raced through his mind.

Harold sat impatiently in the waiting room of the hospital, awaiting word from a doctor. He called the parents of the other children, unsure of what else to do.

Slowly, the other parents started to pour in. The Lees were the first to arrive. They hurried to the reception desk only to be told to wait as well. When they spotted Harold, they walked toward him. Harold stood to greet the couple. Ryū Lee, Vivian's father, shook Harold's hand. Isabelle Lee, his wife, gave him a brief hug before the three sat to talk about their children. Others filed in soon after. All but Stan Penner, the guardian and biological grandfather of Peyton and Ulysseus. Harold had not even bothered to call him. If the man already did not care if the two ate, he would not care about them being in the hospital. The Evans family had been feeding and taking the two to their family doctor for years to make sure they stayed healthy.

The parents slowly gathered around Harold, asking him for details he was unable to provide. While they spoke, a man cleared his throat. The group turned to him. He was dressed in a white coat with a clipboard in hand.

"Mr. Harrison?" he said.

Jared Harrison stood slowly to follow the doctor down the hall. The doctor spoke to Jared in a hushed tone as they walked. Other doctors soon called for the other parents, eventually leaving Harold alone once more.

Finally, Dr. Felisa Baker, the Evans' family doctor, emerged from the double doors. Harold stood quickly to meet her.

"How are they?" he asked urgently.

She motioned for him to follow her back through the doors as she spoke, "Their vitals are stable for all three of them."

"And Peyton?"

She gave him a pained look, "We did our best, but I'm sorry. She's gone."

Harold's emotions attempted to take over, but he once again managed to keep them under control, despite the despair that threatened to escape.

Dr. Baker stopped walking and put a hand on his shoulder as she said, "I'm so sorry."

He took a deep breath, then asked, "Will the others be okay?"

She bit her lip, hesitating to answer the question.

"We're not sure," she said finally.

His brow furrowed, "What do you mean you're not sure?"

"It's not common to see all of their symptoms for one type of illness. Their heart rates keep changing sporadically. Their breathing gets heavy and then normalizes. Other than that, they don't move. They can't hear anything. None of them are injured in any way."

"What about Peyton? Why did I come home to find her dead?" he snapped, his patience wearing thin.

"We think she may have had a heart attack, but we can't find what caused it."

He rubbed his forehead in frustration, "So, what? Do they have some kind of disease?"

"Not any that's been previously discovered," she leaned closer to him and added, "But these aren't the first cases of this."

His brow furrowed further as he awaited elaboration.

"There are reports of children, teens, and young adults facing similar symptoms. There are also cases of a few patients in their thirties."

"What about older patients?"

"Almost none. And of the few there are, most of them died soon after having symptoms."

"And no one knows what this is?" he growled.

Dr. Baker shook her head, "No. But we're told to keep it quiet for now. If this sparks a panic things could very quickly get out of control."

"And I'm assuming there's no cure?"

"Not now, but we've been working on it. It may even be easier for us to find it now that there are patients here."

"If you think you are experimenting on my kids-"

She raised her hands in surrender, "No, no, no. That's not it at all. You can even stay in the rooms with them if you're that worried about it. But if we monitor them and do more research, we may be able to find what's wrong."

Harold watched her for a moment, then dropped his defensive posture, reminding himself that Dr. Baker had been taking care of his children since Melvin was born.

"Can I see them?"

She nodded, "The boys are in a shared room. We put Ashley in a private room."

"Is her leg okay?"

"Yes, her leg is fine. We'll keep an eye on it in case any additional symptoms show up."

"Such as?"

"It's been rare, but there have been reports of patients who have had seizures or have started thrashing while unconscious."

Dr. Baker led him to the shared room where Melvin and Ulysseus were sleeping. They were both given oxygen masks and hooked up to heart monitors.

He walked to Melvin's cot to look at his son. The one thing Harold had wanted for his son was to be happy. Growing up, Harold had been through many hard days in a poor household. Maybe it had made him more driven to be successful, if not for himself than for his family. But sometimes he wondered if it had hardened him. While he didn't have a temper, Harold had worked hard at a young age to keep his emotions in check and focus on work. And while he had taught Melvin to work hard and practice prudence, Melvin had managed to take Harold's best qualities and mix them with his own light-hearted nature.

Harold felt a sense of pride in his son, but despair seemed to cover him evermore as he tried to remember the last time he had told Melvin that. He had been so focused on work that there were times he would not see his children for more than a few moments out of the day, if even that.

Harold took Melvin's hand and gave it a light squeeze, missing his son's silly jokes and hectic personality more with every moment.

He then turned to Ulysseus, whom he loved as if he were his son. Harold remembered growing up with the boy's mother. He remembered when Helen and Sean Byrne had asked him and Tonya if they would be Peyton's godparents, and then Ulysseus's about a year later. He remembered them honoring that promise to take care of the children, even though much of the legal paperwork had been lost long ago, barring them from adoption until the lawyers sorted it out.

He took the boy's hand and squeezed it tightly. *I'm so sorry,* he thought.

Unsure if he could bear more, he turned to Dr. Baker.

"What room is Ashley in?" he asked.

She quietly led him to a room only a few doors down. He opened the door to find Ashley in a cot with a similar setup as Melvin and Ulysseus.

"I have to go," Dr. Baker said, "I'll be back in a

while to check on them."

Harold nodded. Dr. Baker hurried off to another private room.

Harold turned back to his remaining daughter. His heart ached at the sight of her.

He closed the door before sitting in a chair next to her bed. He was almost unable to take his eyes off of the heart monitor. The only image flashing in his mind was that of Peyton in a stretcher with a white sheet over her body. And the image soon evolved into others of his three remaining children under similar sheets.

He kissed Ashley's forehead and took a hand in both of his.

"I'm sorry," he whispered, "I'm so, so sorry. I don't know how to fix this."

In anguish, his jaw clenched. Despite the pain in his chest, his mind worked to find a solution that did not exist. A few silent tears rolled down his cheeks as his anger grew.

"If only your mother was here," he whispered, "At least I wouldn't be alone in this."

He sat in his grief for a moment, only to wipe his tears away. He then ran a hand through his daughter's hair.

"I'm going to fix this, or I'll find someone who can," he murmured, "I don't even know if you can hear me, but I promise. I will figure something out."

He kissed her forehead again softly as he finished speaking with, "I just need the three of you to hold on."

End of Book One

To learn more about Lauren and her work, follow her on social media.

Facebook:
LCMotley Media

Instagram:
@lcmotleymedia

Youtube:
Lauren Motley;
Guardian Falcon Gaming

Lauren Motley began creating characters and writing short stories at a young age, and made her first attempts at writing a book at the age of twelve. She was born and raised in the state of Arkansas, and at an early age had a fascination with video games and the written word. This, along with a wild imagination and games with wonderful friends in the cul-de-sac where she grew up, eventually led to the creation and development of Player 767.

Early drafts of Player 767 were created while Lauren attended high school and the final manuscript was completed in June 2021, the summer before her graduation at the University of Arkansas Fort Smith. When she's not writing, you can find Lauren spending time with her family, her friends, or her pug. You may also catch her fighting dragons, arguing with video editing software, driving tractors, and hitting trees with sticks to prepare for her next martial arts class.

Enjoy the book? Feel free to leave a review!

Your feedback makes it easier for other wonderful readers, such as yourself, to find books they enjoy. Why not help them out?

You can leave an honest review on Amazon, Barnes & Noble, and wherever else this book is available for purchase.